THE *P*RINCESS

A Novel

LORI WICK

Harvest House Publishers
Eugene, Oregon 97402

Cover by Terry Dugan Design, Minneapolis, Minnesota

THE PRINCESS
Copyright © 1999 by Lori Wick
Published by Harvest House Publishers
Eugene, Oregon 97402

ISBN 0-7394-0189-0

Printed in the United States of America.

I wish to dedicate this book to a young woman
who resides deep within my heart,
Holly Short.
Thank you for your love,
tender heart, sweet temperament,
and your love for the Lord.
I can't tell you what an
encouragement you are to me.
I hope this small word gives you some idea.

ACKNOWLEDGMENTS

This might be the first book I've written that did not sit in my mind for years before I wrote it. For this reason, my first word of thanks goes to Harvest House for supporting me in this project. Thank you for always being in my corner.

I would also like to thank all my Hand and Foot compatriots from DuBay and elsewhere: Jess, Jules, Kate, Jo, Barb, Matt, Tim, Abby, Derek, Jane, and Margaret, just to name a few. I love you all.

Thank you, Mary Vesperman, for always being there. You're with me on every book, through thick and thin. Thank you for your skill, understanding, and insight. It's a joy to work with you.

Thank you, Steve and Becky Miller. Your enthusiasm and technical support were so valuable to me. Dearest Becky, I love to watch you sign.

Thank you to my mother, Pearl Hayes, who loves this book. I think you must cheer the loudest. It's so good having you as my biggest fan.

And always last—because he remains in my heart the longest—thank you, Bob, for being my very own prince.

PROLOGUE

Henley, Wainwright
Pendaran

Pen in hand, Daria Parker bent over her personal journal, her eyes and mind intent. Unless she was very sleepy, she wrote in the leatherbound book every Saturday night. The entry for this day began:

> OCTOBER 11, 1988
>
> *Is there any way to describe my joy, Father? I am thankful beyond words for what You have done. Long have we prayed for Shelby, and in Your great mercy, You have now reached down and made her Yours.*

Daria sat back in her chair, her eyes on a distant spot out the window. The moon hung in the sky like a huge white ball, making it seem earlier than 10:15. Her husband, Josiah, was already asleep in the bed they had shared for 19 years, but the soft sound of his breathing was a comfort to her.

> *I knew that someday she would see the truth; I just didn't know when. Who would have thought You would use a poor test grade to make her see her need of You.*

Daria set her pen down for a moment as she thought back to her own salvation seven years earlier. And not just hers, but

Josiah's as well. Shelby had been ten at the time, and their son, Brice, six. Her marriage to Josiah had been a bit rocky in those days. Then one of Josiah's customers had invited them to his church. Daria balked, so Josiah began to attend on his own, and it wasn't long until she noticed a difference in him. They began going as a family, a life-changing experience for both them and their son—but not for their daughter. Now, seven years later, Shelby had seen the truth for herself. Daria picked up her pen.

We plan to go on a trip this summer, Lord, and I look forward to our time together as I never have before. I know Shelby will see things through new eyes and with a new heart. Thank You for the promises of Your Word and Your faithfulness to us. She's been such a wonderful daughter, Lord, and this step of faith in her life will only enhance that.

With a soft sigh, Daria sat back again. For a moment her mind ran to fanciful thoughts and suppositions about her 17-year-old, redheaded daughter. She knew it was normal for every mother to think that her children were the most talented and wonderful in the world, and she was no different, but a sudden thought occurred to her that was almost frightening, a moment of unsettledness that she couldn't define.

She's so special already, Lord, Daria prayed. *She's obedient, warm, talented, intelligent, and so caring of others. Now she has You, and I can't help but wonder if You might have something very remarkable and unfamiliar for our Shelby.*

Daria shook her head. Clearly she was growing tired, and her imagination was playing tricks on her. She closed the book, set the pen aside, and turned off the desk lamp while telling herself not to let her mind run away. As she slipped beneath the covers and cuddled the pillow against her cheek, a slight smile managed to turn up the corners of her mouth, a smile she couldn't wipe away. It lingered until the moment she fell asleep.

The
Princess

One

Toby Newbury walked into the palace with comfortable familiarity, knowing he would be welcome but not certain he would find the monarch available. He wasn't against talking to the queen alone, but the purpose of his visit made him hope he would find Pendaran's king and queen together.

"Mr. Newbury," a voice greeted with utmost respect. Toby turned to find Wallace headed his way. Wallace was the king and queen's house minister, a man of indistinguishable years who kept the east quadrant of the palace moving on well-oiled wheels.

"Hello, Wallace. May I go up?"

"Certainly, sir. I'll just ring through and let the queen know you're coming."

Now knowing the king was not available, Toby crossed the black-and-white-tiled foyer and started up the wide staircase that led to the second floor and the palace's private chambers. The queen, he knew, would be in one of the salons, and because there was always someone hovering in the hallway nearby, finding her would be no effort. "Someone" turned out to be the queen herself. Having received the call, she was waiting just outside the double doors of her favorite salon. Dressed in a beautiful blue pantsuit that matched her eyes, she looked delighted to see him.

"Hello, Toby," she greeted, smiling as they embraced.

"Good morning, Erica." His own smile was warm as he kissed her cheek. "Alone this morning, are you?" he wasted no time in asking.

"For another 15 minutes," she said as she led the way to the plush yellow davenports that sat in a half circle and allowed a lovely view of the inner courtyard.

"Good."

"Why is that good?" her eyes twinkled as she asked.

"I have something to tell both of you. Do you think Rafe will have time?"

"Yes. Unless something has come up, he's free until this afternoon."

"Good," Toby repeated, but Erica fell silent, watching as her guest's gaze went to the windows. She had learned from childhood when to ask questions and when to keep silent. Toby clearly had something on his mind, but it wouldn't have been fair to ask him to explain it twice.

"Did you have a speaking engagement last night?" the queen, remembering suddenly, asked.

"As a matter of fact, I was at a banquet, but I didn't address the group."

"I'm surprised you're here so early."

"It wasn't a late night. The dinner was right here in Faraday." His voice had grown rather soft while speaking, his eyes moving back to the windows, and for this reason Erica fell silent again.

Without invitation the years fell away in her mind, back to the time she had met both Rafael Markham and Toby Newbury. Having grown up together, the two had been best friends for years. Not for a moment had Rafe seen a future as Pendaran's king, but that was before meeting King Anton's daughter, Erica. His view of a place in the palace had changed a great deal after that introduction, and with Toby's encouragement, Rafe had courted Erica with an interest that turned her head. Very impressed with the young man who seemed ready to lay his life down on her behalf, King Anton and Queen Ketra, now King Regent and Queen Regent, had given the couple their blessing. In a month Rafe and Erica would celebrate their thirty-second wedding anniversary.

"Wallace told me you were here," the king said as he entered the room. "Hello, Toby."

"Good morning, Rafe."

Although he greeted his friend, the king made a beeline for his wife and bent to kiss her. "Hello, love," he said softly before turning back to Toby. The men shook hands but didn't exchange words. Rafe sat down and stared at Toby for a long moment. The other man looked back.

"I think you have something on your mind, Toby."

"You're right, I do, and since I hate beating about the bush, I'll come right to it. It's about our conversation two weeks ago concerning Nick."

Both men noticed the way Erica tensed, and Rafe, who had taken a seat on the davenport beside her, reached for her hand.

"I've been praying about the situation, as I told you I would," Toby explained, "but then last night I met a young woman whom you need to know about."

Rafe sat forward. Knowing how he and Erica felt about the marriage of their son, his friend would not have come on a whim.

"What is her name?"

"Shelby Parker. I met her at a banquet honoring her father, who has been deaf since he was ten. Shelby interpreted his speech."

"So he doesn't speak?"

"Actually he does."

"Why did she interpret?"

"Protocol. Most of the room's occupants were also deaf, so

Mr. Parker signed his speech, and Shelby voiced for him. I met Shelby and her parents after we dismissed. I've never been so impressed with a family in my life."

"How old is she, Toby?" This came from Erica.

"I didn't ask. She looks young, but she's out of school, so she must be in her early twenties."

"What was it about her that so impressed you?" Rafe asked his friend.

"The first thing that catches your eye is her gracefulness. When she's talking, signing, or even walking, she moves like a dancer. She's tall and slim and extremely poised. Then after I met her, I noticed her relationship with her parents. The three of them adore each other. They laughed and shared secret smiles like the two of you. You can't be with them and miss it."

"And she's a believer?" Erica tried to keep the tenseness from her voice, but even she could hear the slight wobble.

"Yes. Her father gave a brief testimony last night, and it included the salvation of his wife, son, and daughter."

"Do you know for a fact that she's not spoken for?" Rafe asked now.

"Positively? No. But I would be very surprised if there was any man in her life outside of her father."

The king and queen looked at each other.

"I was just praying about it again this morning, Rafe," Erica said in her soft, gentle manner. "I told God I knew He would show us, even if I didn't know what that would look like."

Rafe smiled, his hand still holding his wife's. "The Council dismissed early this morning, so Nicky and I had a few minutes to talk. I felt a burden to tell him again how proud we are of his decision to go through with this and to trust us. He told me that he knew it wouldn't be easy but that God had been working on his heart. He has been asking for even greater trust, and he knows he'll never need it more than when he marries again."

For some minutes the three fell silent, their thoughts going to Prince Nikolai, Rafe and Erica's only child. Nikolai's first wife had been a shy French woman. Her name was Yvette DuBois, and the prince had adored her. Still quite young, the two had met while Yvette's family was visiting Pendaran. They corresponded for more than a year before Nikolai, accompanied by his parents, went to France to ask for her hand in marriage. She was two years older than he was, but that never mattered to the enamored couple. With the blessing of both families, they married in 1989, when Nikolai was 20 and Yvette was 22. Then without warning, Yvette died of a heart attack two years later, leaving Nikolai a widower.

For Nikolai the loss was huge. Pendaran's traditions were not worshiped, but they were honored and held in high regard. With a view to the beloved royal-family line, the heir to the throne was expected to be married by the time he or she was 26. Nikolai more than met this requirement until his wife was taken from him. Had the death been closer to his twenty-sixth birthday, the time would have been extended in accordance to his grief, but the Council, comprised of men who shared equal power and were required to come to unanimous agreement on every decision, decided that for Nikolai the tradition would be upheld. If effort was made and no wife could be found, the time would be extended, but as it stood, Pendaran's prince now had just over 18 months to marry again.

For a time courtship and remarriage were unthinkable to the still-grieving prince, but recently he'd come to his parents with a surprising request. It was for this reason they had asked Toby to pray, never dreaming that he would meet someone he found suitable to be the prince's next wife.

"Is there anything more I can do?" Toby asked.

"Did your meeting with them go well? Were you well received?" Rafe questioned right back.

"Very much so. Mrs. Parker heard me speak about two years ago, and Mr. Parker has read one of my books. He said he enjoyed it. They were very gracious and kind."

Rafe looked at Erica, whose brow was furrowed in thought. "Do you have any suggestions, Rica?"

"Only that we find out a little more before anything is said. I certainly have no desire to invade the privacy of this family, but neither do I want us to approach Shelby, upset her world, and then say, 'I'm sorry, we've just found out you're unsuitable for our son.' "

Rafe nodded. "A point well taken. Is there any way to do this subtly, Toby?"

"Yes, I believe there is. I think they would welcome a visit from me, and I can do so without deceit, because I genuinely liked them and would enjoy seeing them again. Beyond that, I can ask my man, Tyke, to make a few gentle inquiries. He'll be very discreet. As Erica said, we need to respect the family's privacy. It wouldn't be fair to either Nick or Shelby to rush in and make a mess of things."

"Nick or Shelby," Erica said softly. "It has a nice ring to it, but I'm afraid to hope."

"Not afraid to trust, however," her husband said firmly, his eyes on his spouse.

"No," Erica agreed. "Not that." Her eyes swung to her husband's childhood friend. "Do go and see them, Toby, would you? And then come back and tell us if you think we should pursue this."

"I'll do it. Just as soon as I can, I'll visit their home."

Nothing more was said on the subject, but each one had it in mind. Erica went to freshen up for lunch as the men walked to the dining room, but before joining them downstairs, she took a pen and marked her calendar, using specific wording about Toby's visit. She almost immediately regretted the action, knowing it might make her anxious until he had news. She made herself turn away from the page.

Who of you by worrying can add a single hour to his life? Erica's mind was suddenly on Jesus' words from a verse in Matthew 6. *A question you would do well to remember, Erica,* she said to herself. With a prayer to carry out the thought, she went downstairs to join the men.

～

The king only glanced at the small photo provided for him before reading down through the school transcripts of Shelby Leigh Parker, his brows rising at the excellent grades. Toby's man, Tyke, had certainly been thorough and fast. It had been just 11 days since Toby had come to see him. A part of Rafe's mind rebelled at the whole idea of checking up on her, but his son's face came to mind and he pressed on.

The next page he turned to listed school activities. He was again impressed with her diligence and hard work. A copy of an article from her church newsletter, followed by a brief testimony about a Bible study that Shelby was involved in with several other women, was very informative. Clearly she was learning, and while the king was struck with the content of what she wrote, he was also struck with the way she expressed herself. The two other pages were miscellaneous facts, all of which he found quite interesting.

In time, Rafe put the papers aside and glanced down to where Erica slept beside him in their bed. This young woman, Shelby Parker, was impressive—there was no question about that—but how did they proceed?

Rafe found himself staring across the dark room for some time before finally reaching to turn off the light and settle down on his own pillow. He hoped Toby's visit to see the Parker family would provide some answers.

～

Henley

"This cake is delicious," Toby told Daria Parker just a month after he'd first called on Rafe and Erica. He had called them to ask if he could visit as soon as Tyke had gathered the information. As he'd expected, they were as gracious and warm as he had remembered.

"It's Josiah's favorite," Daria informed him, signing with courtesy for her husband as she spoke to their guest.

"He has good taste."

Toby watched Josiah smile before Shelby's father asked in his quiet way,

"Do you live far from here, Mr. Newbury?"

"About 40 minutes. I was looking for an excuse to come and visit all of you again, and then I realized I had to deliver something just a few miles up the road."

"Why did you want to see us again?" Daria asked, a smile lighting her face.

"I was very impressed last month," Toby said honestly.

The family surrounding him smiled at the compliment but didn't comment further. Suddenly Toby wondered if this might not be a bit awkward.

"Are you working on a book right now, Mr. Newbury?"

This question came from the one person he wanted most to speak with, and Toby not only felt rescued but was glad of an excuse to talk directly to her.

"I am, actually. It's an in-depth study guide to the book of Genesis. I'm almost finished with it."

Shelby questioned him more about the process, his publisher, and how swiftly he would start another book when the current one was complete.

Toby was more than happy to tell her everything she wanted to know, and by the time he left an hour later, he was more convinced than ever that this was the woman for Nikolai.

"Why exactly, Toby?" Rafe questioned him when they spoke on the phone that evening.

"At the risk of your thinking *I'm* falling for her, Rafe, I can't say it any other way than to tell you she's perfect. Her parents have certainly done their homework. I still didn't meet their son—he's at school right now—but the four of us never ran out of things to talk about and Shelby was as gracious and intelligent as I remembered. If I had wished to marry and God had blessed me with children, I would desire my own son to meet such a girl."

"All right, Toby. Thank you for everything you've done. I believe I'll write a letter to Mr. Parker. Do you think it will be well received?"

"Absolutely. I can't say he won't be surprised, but from what I know of him, he's a very levelheaded man."

"Can you supply me with an address?"

"Yes, I have it right here."

Rafe hung up the phone just minutes later. He sat at the massive desk in his study and stared across at the book-filled shelves that surrounded him. The fading daylight was at his back, and for long moments he simply prayed. He thanked God for the wonderful son He had seen fit to give them. It had not been easy, but Nikolai had been worth every moment of heartache. He asked God to give him the words he needed and picked up his pen.

~

Henley

Daria studied her husband's surprised face as he stood with the letter in his hand.

"Are you all right?" she felt a need to ask.

"I think so," he answered, immediately handing her a piece of fine stationery. The envelope had dropped to the floor. He had been home from work only a few minutes—he had a barbershop downtown—and had not had a chance until that moment to look at the post. The letter from King Rafe was not exactly shocking, but it was a surprise.

"Josiah, why would the king want to meet with you?"

"I haven't any idea, but did you notice? He would prefer our meeting be kept between the two of us."

"Should you have told me?" Daria asked.

"You must not have finished the letter," he said. "He says at the end that he'll understand my need to discuss it with my wife, but to please keep the letter confined to the two of us."

For a moment they sat without moving. Daria read the letter completely before handing it back to Josiah.

"So you're going to meet him." Daria's reply was a statement, not a question.

"Certainly. I'm going to reply right now."

Josiah did just that, a bit rattled by it all. He forgot he hadn't told the king he would have his wife along until after he walked back to town to mail the note.

No matter, he thought as he went up the stone steps and into his house. *I have to have her with me, and that's all there is to it.*

~

Faraday

The restaurant where Josiah had been invited to meet the king was small but not what anyone would call crowded. The dining facilities included private rooms. Josiah was ushered into one of them, where he met Pendaran's king. He immediately explained his hearing loss and his need to have Daria interpret for him. That woman was in the car, sick with nerves and feeling like an interloper.

She need not have worried. The queen was along, and both Rafe and Erica were delighted that Josiah had brought his wife. She was summoned from the car and in short order met the queen and king herself.

"It's so gracious of you to come," Erica wasted no time in saying.

"We feel quite honored," Daria said sincerely as the two shook hands.

"Please sit down," the king bade them and waited for everyone to get comfortable at the small, square table.

"Erica has asked a huge favor of me," he began almost as soon as they were seated. "She's asked that I not keep you in suspense, so even before we eat, I'd like to tell you why I wanted to meet with you."

Both Josiah and Daria nodded, relaxing in the warmth of the king's manner and words.

"Toby Newbury is a close friend of mine," Rafe continued. "I would never want you to think he was spying on your family, but he was very impressed with all of you, and most especially with your daughter, Shelby. She's the reason I wanted to meet with you."

Rafe took a breath and plunged on. "If you have no objections, I would like to speak with Shelby about marrying our son, Nikolai."

Daria felt the blood drain from her face but was incapable of speech or movement. Josiah was in much the same shape. Daria had signed the words for him, but had it not been for the shock on her face, he would have been certain he'd misunderstood.

"It sounds so crude and unfeeling," Erica inserted softly. "We hope and pray that you're not offended. We're quite eager to do right by everyone, but we know it's all so unusual."

"May I ask you a question?" Daria said, finally finding her voice.

"Please do." Rafe's low answer and sincere gaze told her of his own eagerness to please.

"Why Shelby? Of course, we think she's wonderful, but she's never talked of meeting either of you."

"I'm sorry I didn't explain from the beginning," Rafe began. "Recently Nikolai has come to us for help in finding a second wife. We asked Toby to be praying with us about it, and then he met your family at a dinner some weeks ago. He came to us the next morning and said he was very impressed with Shelby.

"I will admit that we have made some discreet inquiries, and although we haven't had the privilege of meeting Shelby in person, we are also very impressed with your daughter."

"So much so that you wish her to become the princess?" Josiah questioned.

"Not against your wishes, or hers," Rafe swiftly assured him. "We had no desire to upset your family or Shelby's world by rushing in and making a mess of this, and if we've done so already, we are deeply sorry. But both Erica and I feel a great peace about this. If you have no objections and believe she will hear us out, we would like to go to her with the question. If you feel she won't be the slightest bit interested, then we won't bother her with this at all."

"I assume we're speaking of a marriage of convenience?" Daria asked.

"I'm sure it will start out that way. I hope and pray it will become more."

There was no reason to ask why they couldn't hold off on the marriage until they had "more." You couldn't live in Pendaran and not be aware of the tradition.

Looking at their surprised faces, Erica rushed to reassure them. "We'll certainly understand if you don't have an answer for us right now."

Josiah and Daria looked at one another. Shelby's father took a moment to read his wife's face before saying, "As a matter of fact, I don't have any objections to your speaking with Shelby. I can promise you that she'll have dozens of questions, and Daria and I would like to be there when you meet with her, but I feel honored that you would consider our daughter suitable for the prince."

It was now Rafe and Erica's turn to be at a loss.

"Please don't misunderstand us," Daria went on. "We're not saying Shelby will agree, and as you might expect, we

would never pressure her to do so, but our daughter is a very
clearheaded young woman. If she believes she can serve God
and her country in this way, she'll agree."

"And you would support her?" the king asked of Josiah.

"Yes. As long as we were certain that she had given the matter enough thought and that she would be safe and cared for at
the palace."

They eventually ate lunch, but both the Parkers and the
king and queen parted with a feeling of unreality. Erica thought
how she would have reacted if someone had come to her with
such an offer. She had feared the Parkers might run for the
hills; the fact that they hadn't was the most amazing thing to
the queen.

The Parkers were just as overwhelmed. Driving home they
tried to decide if they had dreamed the entire episode.

Two

Henley

Shelby looked around the reception area at the hospital and wondered what the other women would say if she suddenly announced that the king and queen would be at her house tonight. She had no intention of following through with the thought, but even if she had, they would only think her joking. It wasn't that Shelby was known as a prankster; it was just so unlikely that the lovely redhead, who wouldn't even date the interns who gawked at her, could possibly draw the interest of the palace.

A moment later she dug a piece of gum from her purse and spotted her list. She had been working on her questions for the king and queen for the last ten days. Tonight she would have a chance to voice them. She was certain that within an hour they would know how unsuitable she was, but at least she might be able to understand why they were asking her. For the dozenth time she wished her parents had asked more questions, but she understood why they had not. This was a decision they would leave up to her, unless they sensed that something was amiss.

"You're off, Shelby," one of the women broke into her thoughts. "Or are you on until six?"

"No, I'm off at five. Thanks, Alice. I'll see you tomorrow."

"She certainly looked preoccupied," another woman commented as they watched her move away.

"Yes, she did. If it were anyone else, I would say she had a date."

The women liked Shelby, so they only smiled at each other without malice and went back to work.

~

"Are you all right, Shelby?" her father asked during dinner.

"Yes. I'm just a bit stunned. I mean, I've had more than a week to think about this, but it's all too fantastic to be real." She cocked her head to one side and stared at her parents. "You don't seem surprised at all."

"We were at first," her mother said with a wry tone, "but when all was said and done, you're right, we weren't that surprised."

"How can you say *that?*"

"Because it's true, honey. You make a wonderful first impression, which was obviously the case with Toby Newbury, and when people really get to know you, they love you all the more."

Shelby didn't answer, but it wasn't hard to see what she was thinking. Her father voiced the thought.

"We are biased about you, Shelby, but not blind fools. You would do the prince proud, and we all know it."

Shelby smiled at him and tried to eat a little more. The queasy feeling in the pit of her stomach didn't help. *Was this really happening?* There were moments when she just wasn't sure. She was still dawdling in the kitchen when the doorbell rang; reality was coming in for a fast landing.

~

"We want you to feel free to ask us anything, Shelby," the king assured her later. "Anything at all."

"All right. Thank you." She smiled at the queen for a moment and then looked down at the paper in her lap.

Erica was glad that Shelby's attention was diverted. She needed a few minutes to compose herself. Ever since Shelby had walked into the room and met them, Erica had wanted to dance and sing. She was the sweetest girl she'd ever encountered.

"I feel a little funny about this first question," Shelby began hesitantly, "but it's rather important to me."

"Don't worry about anything," Rafe said, smiling warmly. "Just ask."

Shelby looked uncomfortable but still managed to say, "Why isn't the prince taking care of this himself?"

"My wife answers that best," Rafe said gently. "Will you tell her, Erica?"

"Certainly I will, and I'm going to be very honest with you, Shelby. Nicky is still very much in love with his first wife. He never grew angry or distant after her death, but he misses her terribly. He came to us some weeks ago now and simply asked us to handle things for his future nuptials. He's very willing to marry again and uphold the tradition, but he does not feel up to courtship or a large, fancy wedding ceremony."

Shelby nodded. She thought it might be something like that, but the answer brought up another question.

"Is he really willing to marry someone else if he's still so in love with Princess Yvette?"

"He is, Shelby," the king told her. "I can't promise that he'll love you with all his heart, but Nikolai will be a faithful husband and committed to your marriage."

"Would I live at the palace?"

"Yes, with Nicky in the north quadrant."

"What would I do?"

"Probably much of what you do now with the exception of working at the hospital."

Shelby thought about this. She had many more questions but thought it might be time for them to inquire of her.

"Do you have questions for me?" she asked softly, her feelings of unreality showing through.

"We do, several in fact, but we thought we would answer yours first," the king, feeling much like his wife, told her warmly.

This gave her pause.

"I have a huge wardrobe. I'm always buying new things to wear," she admitted, and the queen did not miss the smile her parents shared. For herself, Erica wanted to laugh with delight at this lovely young woman with the soft brown eyes who was such a mixture of confidence and questions.

"I also have a car and a bicycle."

"There is plenty of room in the car barn for your car and bike."

"So I could bring things with me?"

"Anything you wish."

"The prince won't mind?"

"Not at all. The palace would be your home."

"But I could come back here to visit?"

"Of course."

"But why me?" Shelby couldn't help asking. "Why doesn't the prince marry a woman he already knows?"

"We have thought of that, Shelby, and at first it would seem to make sense, but in truth the prince isn't particularly drawn to any of the women he knows. He told us he felt that would be very awkward, especially if he began seeing someone and it didn't work out. This way, you would both come from the same place."

"But what if it doesn't work out for us?"

"If that's a huge worry in your mind, then we wouldn't

want you to come at all," the king said softly. Shelby looked completely at sea.

"Listen to me, Shelby," he said kindly, working to clearly express his thoughts. "Our expectation before God and man is that this is going to be a real marriage, not some trial period or time of testing, but a marriage in every sense. That the two of you may choose to wait for physical intimacy is only to be expected, but we would want you to marry our son with the mindset that this is forever. Nikolai has that mindset because he trusts our judgment. If you don't have the same feelings about this marriage, unusual though it may be, we need to thank you for your time and be on our way."

Shelby nodded. She had understood that marriage was forever and explained that the question had come off the top of her head. She didn't ask much more of them—at the moment her thoughts were too muddled for that. The questions the king and queen put to her in the next minutes were not very deep. Shelby understood why: Until she was a little more certain, there was no need for them to intrude into her private life.

The conversation ended some two hours after it started, as everyone seemed fatigued and Shelby admitted needing some time to think. Rafe was more than happy to grant it to her. She didn't linger downstairs long after the king and queen left but went to her room to think and read her Bible. She ended up doing nothing but praying.

Is it normal that the idea of this does not horrify me, Lord? I'm actually considering the possibility of marrying a stranger. I have questions certainly, but I feel very reasonable about the answers. I've never even seen the prince in person, but I remember when his wife died. I remember the picture of his grieving face in the newspaper. It sounds like he needs someone to take care of him. Is caring enough of a reason to be married?

Shelby suddenly stopped praying. She had more questions for the royal family, but the ones in her mind right now needed to be asked of her parents. That they were not in the living room didn't stop her; she knocked on their bedroom door.

"Come in," her mother called.

"Were you and Fa sleeping?" Shelby asked, even though their light was on.

"No. Come in, honey."

Shelby sat at the end of the bed and stared at her parents for a moment. At last she said, "I want to know why you're so comfortable with this. I want to know why you seem to be sitting back as spectators."

"Because until just now you haven't seemed to want to speak of it. When we first talked to you, you asked us a lot of questions we couldn't answer, but then you wanted to be alone."

Shelby nodded. She had done just that.

"What do you think of all of this, Fa?" she signed to her father.

"We think it's a great honor, but all the honor in the world wouldn't make me agree to this if Nikolai didn't share our faith in Christ. On top of that, I would never have mentioned it to you if I felt you would be miserable or harmed. I'm not saying I think it will be easy, but I've kept track of the prince's activities off and on over the years—he's a fascinating and impressive young man. As the king said, I can't be certain he'll fall head-over-heels in love with you, but I do trust that he'll honor you as his wife and take care of you for the rest of your life."

"Do you agree, Mother?"

"Yes, Shelby, I do, but please understand that your father and I are not bound and determined in this. If you have any doubts—I don't mean now . . . you're bound to have questions right now—but if you can't eventually gain a peace about this, you must not do it."

Shelby nodded. "I was thinking about the reasons someone might have for getting married. I know the two of you married for love. Is it wrong of me to want to get married so I can take care of the prince?"

"I don't believe it is," her father spoke again. "Arranged marriages used to be common. Now, if you're still not living as husband and wife two years after you're married, I'll be wondering why. When two people spend time together, they become attracted to each other. As husband and wife, it needs to be your choice to love each other."

"But if I want to drop the whole thing right now, you won't be upset with me?"

"Not at all. You'll be 23 at the end of the month, Shelby. You're no child. We trust you to be wise and discerning in this, and in case you need it, you have our permission to take all the time you need. I know the prince doesn't have forever, but that's not what you're to be thinking about. You do what you feel is right and best before God."

Shelby warmly hugged both her parents and was able to retire to bed and sleep. She didn't honestly know what she should do, but as her father said, she mustn't rush into this. She fell asleep believing that in time she would know the way to go.

～

"A letter came for you today, Shelby," her mother said just two days later. Getting mail was nothing unusual, but Shelby approached the table slowly after hearing her mother's tone. Understanding dawned when she saw the prince's name, Nikolai Markham, in the corner of the envelope. Shelby opened it slowly, sat down at the table, and read in amazement.

Dear Miss Parker,

I hope you won't find me presumptuous in writing, but my father told me about meeting you, and I wanted to take a few minutes to thank you for your gracious manner in receiving my parents. I can well imagine the surprise it must have been to hear their request, but my father assured me that you could not have been more hospitable or kind.

Above all else, I would not wish for you to feel pressured, so this letter is simply to advise you that whatever your decision concerning the future, I appreciate your willingness to consider my father's proposal. Should you ever desire assistance, the palace would be happy to help you in any way.

> *God bless you in the weeks to come,*
> *Nikolai Markham*

The moment Shelby finished the letter, she went to the kitchen desk for paper and a pen. After sitting back at the kitchen table, she began to write.

Dear Prince Nikolai,

After your kind letter, I hope you won't find me bold in writing back, but in truth it never occurred to me that I could communicate with you in this way. The reason for my letter is to learn from you if I may ask some questions. I have no wish to pry into your private life or seem impertinent in any way, but I would wish to know a little more about you.

If I have been at all offensive, please disregard this letter. I will understand if you do not return my note.

> *Sincerely,*
> *Shelby Parker*

As soon as she was through, Shelby read both letters to her mother, who had deserted her dinner preparations to sit down at the table and listen.

"What do you think, Mother? Did I do the right thing in writing back?"

"I think you did. You didn't pepper him with questions, but now the ball is in his court as to whether or not he's willing to open up to you. I just have two questions for you: If he does get back to you, what will you ask, and what do you hope to learn?"

"I'll ask him a little about his life and interests, but right now I want to hear his testimony. As to what I hope to learn, I've already learned quite a bit."

"Meaning?"

Shelby picked up the prince's letter. "This is very impressive, Mother; you must admit that. He's still in love with his first wife, yet he thanks me, in so many words, for considering a position as his future wife. I can't believe it was easy for him."

Had Shelby been able to see into the palace just two days later, she'd have known how closely she hit the mark. Prince Nikolai sat at his desk and stared down at a photo of his wife. He didn't regret that he'd written to Shelby Parker—he was just sorry that there had been a need to contact her at all.

"Oh, Yvette," he said softly, "will I ever not miss you?"

Nikolai made himself set the photo aside. He was supposed to be putting together the finishing touches on a report that was to be presented to the Council. He had just researched the alarming number of dropouts in the local district's school system and was ready to tell the members what he had learned.

If he was going to think of any woman right now, it needed to be his future wife, whoever she might be. His parents had been very impressed with Shelby Parker, and he could tell they were excited. It had taken everything within Nikolai not to let on how much he hurt inside. It wasn't that his parents were insensitive—they loved him very much—but they had moved past Yvette's death. In many ways he had not.

The phone on his desk rang, and he reached for it. It was his house minister.

"Prince Nikolai, Mr. Cumberland is here to see you. Are you available?"

"Yes, Murdock. Please tell him I'll be right out."

Nikolai knew he would have to put in some overtime to have the report ready by Monday morning, but not for anything would he miss a visit with his closest friend, Ryan Cumberland III.

"Nick!" Ryan came to his feet the moment Nikolai stepped into the small antechamber outside his office.

"Ryan." Nikolai's greeting was just as warm as the two men embraced. "Do you want to sit in the office or walk in the courtyard?"

"I'm here on business, so it'll have to be the office."

"This sounds serious."

"It is," Ryan stated as he dropped into a comfortable chair. "*You* are in big trouble."

"Me?" Nikolai questioned. He had sat down but not leaned back. "What have I done?"

"It's what you haven't done."

Nikolai didn't need to hear more. Moving rather deliberately, he let his back rest against the chair before asking, "How's Beth?"

Ryan allowed the change in subject. "She's starting to waddle."

"How many weeks to go?"

"About seven if she's on time, but the doctor won't make any promises about that."

"Be certain to give her my love."

"You could come by and do that in person," Ryan said softly, coming right back to the first subject.

"I'm sorry I haven't been out much, Ryan."

"Why haven't you, Nick?" his friend asked gently. "It's been at least two months since you visited."

For a moment Nikolai didn't answer. He glanced at Yvette's picture before looking back at his friend. "Mother and Father are looking for a wife for me. I'm all right with it, but I haven't felt very social since we started talking about it."

Ryan sat forward in his chair. "They've actually found a particular woman, or they're just making some inquiries?"

"They have found a woman, and although it's highly unlikely, I fear running into her and having the whole thing be an awkward mess."

"Who is it?"

"Her name is Shelby Parker."

Ryan blinked. "Does she work at the hospital in Henley?"

"I'm not certain. Why?"

"When my mother was in for those tests a few months back, a woman named Shelby Parker came to see her. I think she's a receptionist. Does she have red hair?"

"I think my mother said she did."

Ryan's brows rose. "She's a lovely young woman and extremely kind. You haven't met her?"

"No. My parents are handling it."

The men fell quiet. Right after the princess died, many people had thought to be helpful. *"You'll go on, Nick,"* they said. *"Think of the way you would have wanted Yvette to go on if you had been the one to die."* Ryan had been the only person with whom Nikolai had been completely honest. *"No one can picture themselves dead, Ryan, and I'm no different. Selfish as I am, I wouldn't want Yvette to marry again. The thought of another man holding her drives me insane."* Remembering this, Ryan was not surprised that Nikolai did not question him about the woman from the hospital.

In his own heart, however, Nikolai knew the time had come. His parents were finding him a wife, and he must be married by the end of the following year. If he was going to do the right thing by the woman his parents chose, he would learn to care for her and, at least in time, make her his wife in every way. Where the strength to do that would come from, he did not know.

"Your situation is not going to be helped by your becoming a recluse," Ryan said, choosing not to comment on anything else. "I won't pretend to know how much you hurt, but it's time you start circulating again. If you were already remarried, no one would expect to see you for months or even the first year, but you're still single, and Beth and I feel as though you've dropped off the face of the earth. We have only a few more weeks before our time will be taken up with the baby. Come see us while we're still just two adults."

"I will," Nikolai promised. "By the way, how is business? Will you have some time off once the baby is born?"

"Yes. I'll be home for the first month. I can't tell you how I'm looking forward to it."

"And what happens to your clients in the practice?"

"I've handed off a few things and wrapped up some others. I've sent word to all my regulars, and I'm hoping they won't forget my fine skills in the courtroom before I get back."

The men talked for the next hour before saying their good-byes, and when Ryan left, Nikolai determined to go and see him and Beth right after church the next morning. His friend was right. He was dropping out of existence. Knowing that Ryan was praying for him, and with his own prayer for strength to do as he knew he should, Nikolai went back to his report. He worked steadily for the next hour, his concentration breaking only when Murdock delivered the late post. Nikolai looked through it absently until he happened on a particular letter. The name in the upper corner caused him to set everything aside.

∼

Henley

"He wrote back to you, Shelby," her father said to her about two weeks later. She had just arrived home from work. "Your mother had to run next door and wanted me to tell you as soon as you got in."

"Thank you," Shelby replied softly as she sat down to read the missive. It wasn't overly long but just as gracious and kind as his first. She could ask him anything she wished, and he wanted to know if she would welcome questions from him. Shelby had to sit for a moment to take it in. She didn't know how it would all transpire, but somehow in her heart she knew she would be marrying the prince.

Three

Nikolai stood alone in his bedroom and told himself to breathe deeply. He had the window wide open, cool as it was, but still felt as if he were going to suffocate. This was his wedding day. Resplendent in his black tux, he looked taller than ever and very self-assured, but in truth, he was sick inside. Had he just been sitting in church that morning with his grandparents? The whole day was beginning to feel like a dream. The last months were taking on the same sensation.

Letters had not poured out of him in the months following his first correspondence with Shelby. Indeed, they had exchanged only about one letter a month, and those had been full of facts, not feelings. Those few letters, however, were enough to tell him that the woman he was marrying was a warm, caring woman who loved the Lord with all her heart. Still, one fact was glaringly clear—she was not Yvette. For that reason his heart felt broken inside.

Nikolai gave himself a little shake. He had much to be thankful for, and it was time to remember that. Shelby had been beyond gracious when it came to his requests not to have a large wedding or a reception. She had not expected to meet him, telling his parents that she was comfortable with their handling of things. But what about after the wedding? Would she understand that he would need some time to adjust? He only hoped she would, as he had little of himself to give her at the moment.

A moment of stubborn anger rose in him that he was being forced into this. After all, it was only April. They could postpone the wedding until fall and still be well within the allotted time. A huge sigh lifted his chest. It was no use putting it off.

I told my father one time that when I married again, I would need to learn to trust You in a new way. I don't think I really understood just how hard that would be. Please help me, Lord, and Shelby too. Help her to understand my need for time. Help her to be patient with me.

Nikolai's prayer was interrupted by his father's knock. He came in uninvited, but Nikolai didn't mind. There wasn't anyone else he wanted to see right now.

"How are you?" Rafe asked when he was close enough to see his son's eyes.

"Not so good, but ready to go ahead."

Rafe's eyes were tender as they rested on his only child. "Have I told you lately that I love you?"

Nikolai gave his father a hug that was hugely returned. Both knew that God had been leading all of them in the last months and that eventually all would be well. So alike in height, the men shared a long look before heading for the door.

～

Daria glanced around the spacious bedroom and sitting room and then looked to Shelby with a raised brow.

"Did you know it was black?"

"Not until I visited at the beginning of the week. They told me I could change things."

"Will you?"

"I don't know." She sounded as uncertain as she felt.

"But you hate black."

"True, but if this was Yvette's favorite room, I think I need to live with it for a time."

Daria moved forward and hugged her. "I think you're wonderful." She stepped back and looked her daughter in the eye. "If the prince doesn't figure out how precious you are, I might come back and tell him myself."

"You might too."

Daria smiled. In truth, she felt no such anxiety. Of this Daria was certain: At some point, the prince would fall for his new princess.

"Well, not much time now. Are you ready?"

"I think I am. I'm feeling a little nervous, but I think that will disappear when I put on my veil."

Daria smiled. "You look beautiful. I'm so glad we chose this dress."

Shelby was glad too. It was a simple gown of classic lines, high-necked and long-sleeved—not overly done with lace. It suited Shelby and made her feel special. The veil had lace to match the gown, but its most important feature was the dense lace that would cover Shelby's face. She knew herself to be a woman who blushed easily, and the thought of standing with the prince, lit up like a beacon during the entire ceremony, was horrific to her.

"I've been thinking a lot about arranged marriages," Daria said softly. "They're so unusual, but one in particular keeps coming to mind."

"Which one is that?"

"Isaac and Rebekah."

Shelby nodded.

"I read that passage over several times this morning," Daria continued, "and I guess because I'm a woman, and women tend to be emotional, I can't get over the way she goes into his tent as soon as they're married."

"I've read that too. Do you suppose their intimacy began immediately after they were married?"

"It reads as if it did."

"Are we wrong to wait, Mother?"

"Are you sure you will be waiting?" Daria asked. This possibility had never occurred to her until now.

"I wouldn't swear to it," Shelby said calmly, "but if you could have read his letters, Mother, you would see why I think we'll wait. This man has not opened his heart to me. I know a good deal about him, but unless everyone has completely misrepresented to me how much he misses his first wife, our intimacy will wait."

"Have I upset you, Shelby?" Daria asked, her face pale. "I never thought you would do anything but wait, and then suddenly I wasn't certain."

"I'm not upset at all, Mother. Please don't worry about it. If I'm wrong," she said pragmatically, giving a small shrug, "I hope we can talk about it and he'll listen to me."

Daria smiled at her. *She's so special, Father. I know it's more than my bias. She's a precious girl, and I ache with love for her. Let her and the prince find that same love.*

"Did Fa say he was coming here?"

"Yes. He should be along any minute."

"I'm starting to feel nervous." Shelby glanced around the room; the dark decor did little to cheer her. "I think if we could just get going, I'd be all right."

Daria did not respond. She walked to the door, opened it, and peeked out, only to turn and shrug at her daughter.

Shelby nodded and went to the window. In a way she didn't want to rush this. It was to be her only wedding day, and although not conventional in any sense of the word, she wanted to remember it.

At the window, she gazed out with a smile. She was sure to be homesick for the house in Henley, not to mention her parents, but the view of the park from her bedroom window would certainly take her mind from it.

A moment later her father knocked. They were ready for

her. Daria kissed her cheek and then helped her adjust her veil. A moment later she was alone with her father.

"Ready?"

Looking up at him, Shelby nodded. "I think I am. Are you ready?"

"To lose my girl? Never."

It was said with a smile before he kissed her brow, waited for her to lower the blusher, and then offered his arm. They moved toward the door, both with a mix of emotions. The moment had arrived. Where would God take them from here?

~

Nikolai watched his bride come into the king's ballroom on her father's arm, almost sagging with relief when he saw her veil. He knew she could see him, but he wasn't up to meeting her eyes. He wasn't certain why he thought it would be easier to wait, but at the moment he knew he was the biggest coward alive.

Shelby, on the other hand, was anything but relieved. She knew the prince was tall—very tall—just like the king, but the man her father handed her over to towered above her. He glanced down at her, his look serious, as she suspected it would be, but just the sight of that tall frame and handsome face caused Shelby to blush alarmingly. She suddenly asked herself how she could have thought he needed someone to take care of him. He looked as self-possessed as any man could. She thought she might need a chair.

"Dearly beloved," Pastor Allen began suddenly, and Shelby forced her mind back to why she was there. The mental effort didn't work for very long. She ended up having a ridiculous conversation with herself.

So he's tall, Shelby. What do you care? At 5'8" you're not exactly short. Okay, so I'm above average, but he's even taller than my father and the king. He must be 6'3" at least.

"Marriage is not something to be taken lightly," Pastor

Allen said, and Shelby came back to the moment, her face still flaming. "It is to be entered into reverently, with a heart of commitment."

Shelby heard the word commitment and felt herself grow calm. She was not unusual. She wanted love and romance as much as the next person, but from the time she gained a peace about marrying the prince, she knew she would be committed to this marriage. It was unconventional and a bit scary, but she had seen something in the king and queen, as well as in the prince's letters, that told her she could honor God in this way. Would the prince be pleased to know she was doing it for that reason? At this point it was hard to say, but Shelby knew her own heart, and that heart was filled with commitment and peace.

"Do you, Shelby Leigh Parker, take Nikolai Rafael Markham to be your lawfully wedded husband?" Pastor Allen was saying to her.

"I do," she said softly, listening as the pastor addressed the man beside her, and then as Nikolai's deep voice said his own vow without a hint of hesitation. Not many minutes later, they were husband and wife. Shelby watched as the prince shook Pastor Allen's hand, turned, briefly met her family, and then offered her his arm. The moment Shelby took it they began to walk from the room. Vaguely aware of her parents and her brother, Brice, she barely caught sight of the king, queen, king regent, queen regent, and even the slightly bent queen mother, all of whom stood on the prince's side of the aisle.

Shelby was not completely familiar with the palace. She'd had only one tour. But she knew they were headed back toward the north quadrant. In seemingly no time at all they stood in the spacious sitting room, the green sitting room as Murdock had called it, that was accessible from both of their bedrooms. Once there, the prince stopped and faced Shelby.

"Are you all right?" he asked.

"I am, yes. Are you all right?"

She watched him hesitate; clearly he hadn't expected her to return the question. He stood looking down at her, making no move to lift her veil.

"I believe I am," he said at last. "I wanted to thank you for coming to the palace this way. If there's anything you need, just ask. The staff is most helpful and will delight to serve you in any way."

Shelby watched as he paused but made herself keep silent.

"I wish," he began softly but stopped. "I'm sorry I can't—" Again she watched him hesitate, his eyes looking like those of a wounded animal. Abruptly he turned and walked away. Shelby followed his progress, even going so far as to lift her veil to watch him. He did not turn back, but when he reached the door, he slipped quietly into the wide hallway.

The moment of doubt she'd had in the king's ballroom was long gone. Confident air or not, it was again utterly clear to her that the prince needed great care.

~

Shelby's first night in the palace was not restful, but she didn't feel too bad in the morning. Rising a little before six, she showered and dressed casually, mentally going over the layout of her new home. After a moment's thought she was sure she could find the kitchen. She made her way downstairs and to the rear of the quadrant, through a large dining area and into the spacious, spotlessly tiled kitchen. The room was empty, but someone had put coffee on. Shelby found a mug, poured the aromatic brew, and took a chair at the table. The flavored coffee was delicious. She was joined inside of two minutes.

"Good morning, Princess Shelby," Arlanda said with a smile. She was the housekeeper for the north quadrant. "Did you sleep well?"

"I think I did all right for the first night."

Arlanda, looking wise beyond her years, smiled at her. "I think that was your way of saying it was a bit rough."

Shelby smiled at being caught. She had met this woman just a few days before and liked her in an instant; indeed, she had liked all the staff.

"How about some breakfast in the small dining room?" Arlanda offered.

"Will I be in the way if I stay here?"

"Not at all. What are you hungry for?"

"Were you going to eat now?"

"I've eaten, but I'd be happy to fix whatever you'd like."

"I think I'll just have cereal."

"I'll bring you some."

Shelby didn't try to stop her; she simply noted where everything was located so she could help herself in the future.

"More coffee?" Arlanda offered as she set things down on the table.

"Are you having some?" Shelby questioned, and Arlanda had to hide a smile. So far, the princess had answered half of the questions directed to her with a question of her own.

"I am," Arlanda said, deciding swiftly. "I'll just bring the pot."

After Shelby helped herself to the cereal and fruit that appeared, she bowed her head and thanked God for the food. Her mind thoughtful, she then spooned sugar onto her cereal, adding milk and strawberries.

"May I ask you a question, Arlanda?" Shelby asked between bites.

"Certainly. Anything at all."

"Does the staff live here at the palace? I can't remember if Murdock said."

"Most of us do, yes. Murdock is married to Fran—I think you met her. She does the cooking. They have quarters right off the kitchen. Gilbert and Hank, who take care of the cars and do some of the grounds work, live above the car barn. So does Kris. Gilbert is my father and Hank is my brother, by the way."

"Oh, I didn't realize."

Arlanda was in the midst of explaining where her room was when they were joined by Murdock and Fran.

"Good morning," Shelby greeted them. They looked as delighted to see her as they had when they first met her.

"Good morning, Princess Shelby," Murdock returned. His very manner begged to serve. "Is there anything I can get for you? Would you be more comfortable in the dining room?"

"I'm fine here, thank you."

"How was your room? Did you lack for anything?"

"No. It's all very nice."

"Whenever you're ready," Murdock said as he opened a thick leather book he'd set on the table, "I'm free to go over your daily and weekly schedule with you. You don't have anything scheduled today until noon, when the king and queen regent are expecting you to join them for lunch."

Shelby nodded, thankful that the queen had warned her of the schedule she would have. Most activities would be arranged through Shelby, but some would come through Murdock who, knowing her schedule as well as the prince's, might accept for her. Shelby was always free to cancel.

"Does that work for you, Princess Shelby?"

Shelby suddenly realized that Murdock was waiting for an answer.

"Yes. That's fine. I'm not sure, however, if I can find the door to the south quadrant."

"Arlanda or I will see you there."

Shelby smiled, but inside she had questions. Would the prince be there? Was the prince even in the palace right now? With the way their rooms were set up, it was fairly easy not to see each other, but she had the vague impression that if he was around, she would know it. There was a door in her bedroom that led directly into the prince's bedroom, but Shelby wouldn't have gone near it even if there had been a fire.

The princess finished eating, thanked everyone in the kitchen, and made her way back to her room, her mind still on the meal at noon. She wouldn't have risked any wagers on the matter, but something told Shelby that the prince would not be in attendance.

~

"The queen was hoping to have breakfast with you this week. She said Wednesday or Friday would work for her," Murdock said later that morning as he looked over the appointment book on the table in front of him and then to Shelby's. They were working in Shelby's sitting room.

"Either day is fine for me."

"All right. Let's go with Wednesday, and if we have to change, I'll tell you."

Shelby made a note even as Murdock went on to say he would confirm the time with her later. They worked over the entire week's schedule and even went into the next week before finishing. Shelby was closing her book when the phone rang. Murdock made his way to the door as Shelby picked it up. It was the king.

"Good morning, Shelby."

"Good morning."

"I'm sorry to disturb you, but I have something I need to ask you. Is now a good time?"

"Yes. I'm quite free."

"Good. Have you heard of the Royal Care Center for the Elderly? It's right here in Faraday."

"I'm familiar with it. Some years ago my grandmother lived there for a brief time."

"She did? That's very interesting, and I'll tell you why. The care center likes to have a representative from the royal family on their board of directors. The queen mother served for many years, but she curtailed most of her duties about four years ago. Since then no one has replaced her. The center contacts me every so often about getting involved again, and now in the early post I've had another letter. I will admit that I immediately thought of you."

"What is involved?"

"The directors meet and go over business about once every two months. Beyond that, the duties are light. You're welcome to visit or join the residents for a meal any time you like."

"Would it be possible to see the letter you just received?"

"Certainly. I'll send all my correspondence with the center to you. Wallace will bring it over within the hour."

"All right."

"Shelby?"

"Yes?"

"You don't have to do this. I did think of you, and your being familiar with the center helps, but if you don't want to get involved right now, I'll simply thank them for their letter and we'll drop it."

"I'll remember that."

"Call me if you have any questions."

"Thank you, sir."

"You're welcome, my dear. I'll check with you later."

Shelby was off the phone for some minutes before it hit her. *I'm the princess. I'm the princess of Pendaran. I'm living at the palace and talking to the king as though it were an everyday occurrence.*

For a time Shelby had to sit very still. Pendaran was not a country whose citizens had little to do but follow their royalty around and snoop into their private lives, but everyone was aware of the royal family, and for the most part, the family was respected. The newspapers covered stories that the king and queen released; in fact, someone from one of the papers was coming on Friday to take her picture, but as a rule, Shelby had not followed the media very closely. She knew about the big events, but lately there hadn't been many of those.

Will my marriage to the prince be considered big? I hope not. I find I just want to be on my own, left to myself to do my job.

Shelby had a sudden need to read and study her Bible. The only thing in her life that never changed was God's love for her. She spent the next hour studying in the book of 3 John and praying. By the time she left to eat lunch with King Regent Anton and Queen Regent Ketra, her head was out of the clouds and her feet were firmly planted on the ground.

~

"We won't keep you very long," Ketra said as soon as the three were seated. "Nikolai was not available for lunch, and we know you must be busy too. It's hard to settle into a new place, and I am well aware of how strange it can all be."

Shelby felt herself relaxing. If memory served her correctly, Anton had been the royal in this marriage, not Ketra. Shelby thought they might have much in common.

"I am wondering when I'll know my way around," Shelby admitted.

"There's always someone to ask," King Anton put in, "but a map would probably help."

"Yes, it would," Ketra inserted, "and I have just the one. Anton drew a map for me after we were married, and I know I still have it. It's probably yellowed and bent, but I'll find it after you leave and send it over."

"Thank you," Shelby said sincerely.

"We enjoyed your parents and brother, Shelby," the king offered. "Brice told me he's studying physics. He's an impressive young man."

"I think so," Shelby agreed, "but then I'm biased. I've really missed him since he went to school."

"And how about now?" the queen asked. "Do you miss your parents?"

"I haven't had time yet, but I know it will come. It's nice to know I can see them whenever I want to."

"I'm glad for you that they're close," the king stated. "Ketra's family was from the north, and she pined for them, didn't you, my dear?"

"I thought I would die that first year. I was so much in love with Anton but so lonely for my family. Finally the girls started to come, and I didn't have as much time to miss them." Ketra suddenly stopped and studied Shelby. "I can't remember the last time we had a redheaded king or queen. This should be fun."

Shelby's face reddened in an instant.

"Now, Ketra," the king chided compassionately, "see what you've done."

The queen looked apologetic, and Shelby was thrilled when lunch was served and she could bow her head, first for the prayer and then over her food. She had an enjoyable time with the couple and even made a swift visit to meet Anton's mother, but Shelby walked back to her room with her head in a muddle. Right now she felt as though she were swimming in mud, with no clue as to the direction of the surface.

Four

Within a week of living at the palace, Shelby was finding her feet. She liked to rise early and even fixed her own breakfast most mornings. Someone always had coffee on to brew but wasn't always present when she arrived. The staff, however, was swiftly growing accustomed to seeing her at the kitchen table for breakfast. Invariably she had her Bible, the newspaper, her date book, or all three. On this morning, just eight days after she'd been married, she ate without looking at any of them. The staff moved around quietly, seeing that she was in great thought.

And indeed she was. Shelby's mind was still on the church services the day before. One of the first questions Shelby had asked the king and queen was about the church they attended. She had been glad to hear it was a church she was familiar with, one that shared her biblical beliefs, but her next question had been almost as important to her: Did the church have a ministry to the deaf? Shelby had been involved in that ministry in her own church for a long time and had no desire to give it up.

Yesterday she had come into church on her own, gaining stares that told her many people had seen her picture in the paper. She deliberately sat far over on the right-hand side so she could see the man signing at the front. Having grown up with a deaf father, she had been able to follow every word but soon chose to look at the pastor and concentrate on her notes. She had enjoyed it very much and been convicted several times. While she knew dozens of people who went to church because it made them feel good, Shelby didn't want that. Her desire was to be convicted of sin and to change to be more like Jesus Christ, even if it hurt.

She was still in the midst of all these thoughts about the day before when the prince walked into the kitchen. She was glad that she'd just swallowed the toast in her mouth, or she might have choked.

"Murdock," he began genially, "I have to make a change on the schedule. Do you have your book?"

"Of course, sir. What day?"

"This Friday."

Shelby stopped attending at this point and simply watched him. He was in slacks, white shirt, and tie; clearly his jacket had been discarded elsewhere. And she had been right—he was very tall. Handsome too. His hair was jet black, and although she couldn't see his face clearly, she had seen through her veil that his eyes were a startling sapphire blue. Shelby was still just watching him when he turned and noticed her.

"Hello," he spoke kindly, smiling a little in her direction.

"Good morning," Shelby said softly, keeping her seat.

The prince finished his business with Murdock and finally turned to look at her again.

"I don't believe we've met," he said conversationally, shocking Shelby into silence. The redhead stared at him until he laughed a little and glanced at Murdock and Arlanda.

"I take it I have met our guest and forgotten."

But the two servants were staring at him in equal shock, and a cold feeling swept down his spine. The face he turned back to Shelby was not at all friendly. That lady stood to her feet before speaking.

"I'm Shelby," she said breathlessly. "I'm sorry I didn't tell you sooner."

The red in Nikolai's face could only be matched by Shelby's, which was nearly purple with mortification.

"The apology should come from me," Nikolai said stiffly. "I'm sorry I didn't recognize you." He said not another word, gave a slight nod in her direction, and strode from the room.

Shelby watched him leave but couldn't bring herself to look at the housekeeper or minister. She gathered her papers, her eyes downcast.

"Thank you for breakfast," she said just before she walked out, still not looking at either of them.

On her exit, Arlanda and Murdock shared a long look, both feeling as miserable and confused as the princess had looked.

~

The prince felt a headache coming on as the day limo took him to his first appointment. He had told himself that if he just had a little time it would be easier, so he had stayed away for a week. Now he'd made a complete fool of himself.

He was not accustomed to seeing anyone but the staff in the kitchen. Having the princess sitting there was the last thing he had expected. *You have no one to blame but yourself, Nick, and you know it. You could have stayed and talked to her a little, but no, you ran like a fool.*

"And that's just what I am," he said softy. "A fool."

"Did you need something, sir?" Ivan, his driver and companion, asked from behind the wheel.

"No. Thank you, Ivan."

Nikolai gave himself a little shake. He had to meet with a Council member in a few minutes, and his head must be clear. Much as he needed to think of a way to handle this marriage that he found himself a part of, he welcomed the excuse to put it from his mind for a little longer.

~

"The king said he had a picture," Shelby said in the quiet of her room. "I assumed he'd shown it to his son."

Shelby sat down on the sofa in the small sitting area in one corner of her bedroom, her gaze on the window. As had become her routine, she was scheduled to meet with Kris, a man the palace referred to as her companion, just before lunch, but right now she wondered if she had time to go home for a little while. She didn't want to talk about the scene in the kitchen, but she thought it might do her some good to see her mother.

She bit her lip as she tried to remember if she was to call ahead to the garage or not. She was on the verge of going to the phone when someone knocked on her door. Shelby opened the door to find Murdock waiting in the hall.

"Oh, Murdock, I was just wondering whether I should call ahead to get my car or just walk down to the garage?"

"It's up to you. If you do call, they can have it started and waiting for you or even delivered to the door. Or if you like, one of the limos can take you wherever you wish."

Shelby nodded.

"Are you ready to go over your schedule, Princess Shelby, or should I come back?"

In truth, Shelby had forgotten all about reviewing her schedule, but she covered nicely and told the house minister to come in. By the time the two of them had gone over everything, it was too late to go to Henley. She went down to the garage before lunch to meet with Kris, telling herself the worst was over and hoping it was true.

~

The prince was glad to be done with his meeting and headed back to the palace. He had a good deal of paperwork staring at him and some phone calls to make. He still hadn't decided how to handle his encounter with Shelby.

Ivan sat competently behind the wheel while they were at a stoplight, and although Nikolai's mind was busy, his gaze began to roam. What he saw at the corner caused his brows to rise.

"Is that Kris sitting on a bicycle, Ivan?"

"I believe it is, sir."

"What is he doing?"

Ivan had summed up the situation in a heartbeat. "He's watching over the princess, sir."

Nikolai's eyes began to scan the street before he realized he was staring right at her. Clad in long bike shorts, a baggy T-shirt, helmet, knee guards, elbow guards, wrist protection, sunglasses, and in-line skates, stood his wife. While he watched, the light changed and she took off in a smooth glide, Kris just ten feet behind her on a bike. Nikolai knew his mouth was open but was too amazed to care. Gawking until they were out of sight, he tried to find her when the car pulled forward into traffic. He caught a glimpse of her as she maneuvered down the street, but she was clearly not headed back to the palace. Nikolai was only glad that he was. He still had paperwork and phone calls, but they were going to have to wait. He needed to see Murdock first.

~

"Not only does she enjoy skating, sir, she has a bike. She's been out a few days on that."

"And Kris goes with her?" Nikolai asked for the second time, needing to make sure.

"Always, sir."

"Does he keep a close watch on her? Faraday is much busier than Henley."

"I believe they are both very careful, sir."

Nikolai leaned back in his desk chair, his eyes on the ceiling, his brow lowered in thought.

"Does she always eat breakfast in the kitchen?"

"Yes. I can tell she's quite comfortable there."

"What about lunch and dinner?"

"When she's here, we serve those in the dining room and she eats there."

Nikolai didn't need to ask if she ate alone; he'd eaten plenty of meals alone in the dining room. It wasn't at all unusual for him to ask for a meal in his sitting room just to avoid the loneliness of the spacious room.

"Is she home tonight?"

"No, sir. She's been invited to dine with some of the Council members and their wives."

"I was asked to that, wasn't I?"

"Yes, but you declined. Councilman Royden was already expecting you."

Nikolai was torn between relief and disappointment. He had to find a way to see his wife and get to know her on some level, but the thought alone left him at a complete loss. What would he say to her? How did one talk to a wife who was nearly a stranger?

"Is there anything I can do, sir?"

"Just this, Murdock. I would like Hank or Kris to call as soon as they leave the Lindells'. If I'm still at the Roydens', call Ivan."

"I'll take care of it, sir."

Murdock took himself back to his duties then, his heart very light. He had lost a bit of hope in the kitchen that morning, but the concern on the prince's face was very encouraging. It might take some time, but it looked as if there might be a happy marriage after all.

~

"She is the sweetest girl I've ever met," Moyra Lindell, Shelby's host, told her husband, Tyler, as soon as she had a chance. "I'm so sorry Nikolai couldn't be here. He must hate to be separated from her."

"We'll have to have them again," Tyler decided, thinking of how lonely the prince had seemed at times and how much he would enjoy seeing him with his new wife.

Across the room with a woman she knew from her Bible study, Shelby was blissfully unaware of the Lindells' plans. She was very pleased to see her friend—she hadn't known anyone else—but the evening as a whole had been something of a trial. She hadn't had over five bites of food. Every time an hors d'oeuvre or her fork had headed toward her mouth, someone had asked her a question. For the most part, the people were very kind, but she was quickly seeing that she was something of a fascination. Shelby could have told them that she was no such thing, but until they all grew used to seeing her, it looked as though she was going to be invited out to dinner but not allowed to eat.

The evening ended on a friendly note, but Shelby couldn't stop the growling of her stomach as Hank let her into the car. She had no more than taken a seat in the formal limousine when the phone next to her rang.

"Hello," Shelby answered uncertainly.

"Princess Shelby, could you lower the window for a moment?"

"Oh, certainly."

Shelby cast about for a switch, and when she couldn't find one, listened as Hank told her where to look. The moment the window between them was lowered, he turned to speak with her. Shelby finally remembered to hang up the phone.

"Princess Shelby?" her chauffeur began.

"Yes, Hank?"

"Is there anything I can get for you?"

For a moment Shelby sat in embarrassed silence, knowing that he had heard her stomach growl. Thinking he must be tired, she was tempted to say no, but he'd put the light on over his head, and she caught his look, a look of compassion and an eagerness to serve.

"Did I see a Burger Haven on the way, Hank?"

"Yes. Does that sound good?"

"Yes, please," she said very softly, sitting back with relief. Food was on the way.

~

Hank, who knew every foot of the drive into the palace, how things looked when all was calm, and every inch if there was a change, saw in an instant that the prince was waiting for his cargo. He also suspected that the princess hadn't seen him at all. "Oh," he heard her say softly as the door was opened and a figure loomed above her.

Indeed, it took Shelby a moment to even see who was giving her a hand out. Catching herself, she snatched her greasy hand back very quickly and explained without even looking up, "My hands are a bit messy. I don't want to get you dirty. Oh," she said again, this time looking up and recognizing her husband.

"Did you have a purse or a coat?" Nikolai asked softly.

"No. I don't, I just—I don't," she finished lamely, glad for the cover of darkness on her red face.

The prince gestured to the door, and Shelby preceded him, asking herself the whole way if something was wrong. She didn't think he had been around the first week they were married, but neither did she think it was normal for him to meet her when he was home.

"Did you have a good time?" Nikolai wasted no time in asking.

"I did, yes. I hadn't met the Lindells before. They were very kind."

"Who else was there? Do you remember?"

Shelby named a few couples and Lenore from her Bible study. As they talked, the prince moved them into one of the upstairs salons and directed Shelby to a chair. She found herself under his scrutiny for a moment and thought she was expected to fill in the silence.

"Did you have a good evening?"

"Yes," Nikolai said politely. "I was invited to the Lindells' as well, but I had a meeting I could not miss. Thank you for attending for both of us."

Shelby nodded. There were questions on her mind, but she didn't want him to think she was prying.

"The streets in Faraday are busier I think than those in Henley," he said suddenly. "Are you careful on your skates?"

Shelby blinked in surprise but then nodded yes. "I try to be. It's hard to find quiet streets, so I do try to watch out."

The prince nodded. He didn't even know this woman, but right now the thought of having her harmed was unbearable to him.

"I could drive to another area to ride," Shelby offered suddenly, "if you would rather I didn't ride in town."

This gave the prince pause. Had she really just volunteered to adjust her plans on his say-so? This seemed unreal to him.

"Where would you go?" he asked out of pure curiosity.

"Right now I don't know, but I could look around and find a place or ask Kris or Murdock. If it bothers you, I will."

A moment later the prince frowned. She almost sounded as if she had rehearsed that line. Or did she hope to gain his approval by saying only what he wanted to hear? He worked to push thoughts of comparing Shelby to Yvette away, but it didn't completely work.

"I don't think that's necessary," he said at last, his voice a bit cool. "Just be careful."

Seeing that he hadn't cared for the idea, Shelby only nodded. His face had been so polite, but now he looked a bit testy. She watched him in uncertainty, just wishing she could go to bed.

"I'd best let you retire now," the prince said formally. "Unless there was something you needed."

"No, thank you. I'll say goodnight."

Like a perfect gentleman, the prince stood, but Shelby was

only slightly relieved. Something had gone wrong; she just didn't know what. She readied for bed, praying for wisdom all the while and wondering when she would know where she stood, or if she ever would. The idea was so depressing to Shelby that she forced herself to concentrate on sleep before the thought could blossom.

Had she known that for the next month she would see the prince only from time to time and find him little more than a polite stranger, she might not have been able to push the thought away. Indeed, the prince and princess went in different directions most of the time. Shelby had no reason to believe that this was not normal and carried on as best she could.

To the outside world all seemed well, but Nikolai Markham knew better. What he didn't know was the high price he would have to pay, and that the day of reckoning was much closer than he would ever have imagined.

~

"Okay," Shelby studied Fran's bangs and bent to make another cut. "Check the mirror now."

"Oh, Princess Shelby, you're a dream. They've been driving me crazy."

"Do they look even?"

"They look perfect. Where did you learn to cut hair?" the older woman demanded.

Shelby smiled. "My father's a barber. I've always had the knack."

"Well, I can't thank you enough. The shop said they couldn't fit me in until next week. The back I can live with, but not these bangs."

"Do you want me to do the back? I'd be happy to."

"No, this will be fine. Arlanda said you cut her hair yesterday and Gilbert's last week. I think you've put in enough time for now."

Shelby only smiled. She honestly didn't mind. Some days

she was so busy she couldn't find herself, and other days, like this one, she found she had time on her hands. She left the kitchen porch just moments later. Her schedule was so clear that she was headed home to see her mother. They were going shopping and to lunch. She could hardly wait. Not 30 minutes later she made her way to the car barn, feeling as though she had the entire day at her disposal, climbed into her small green sports car, and headed toward Henley.

The king, watching her leave from an upstairs window, knew it was time to speak with Nikolai about the relationship. He had been hesitant to probe too deeply before now, but it had been more than a month, and the loving father in him had to know how his son was doing.

However, the time to speak with him didn't come for another 24 hours. Nikolai came to see his parents, and when Erica was called away to the telephone, Rafe suddenly felt the time was perfect.

"How is Shelby?"

"She's fine," Nikolai spoke quietly.

"Do you know that personally or from Murdock?"

Nikolai looked at his father a moment before answering.

"I keep track of her. She seems content with her schedule and such."

"Any chance she's expecting?"

Nikolai blinked. Did his father really think . . . He then caught the older man's eye.

"I don't care to joke about it, Father."

"No, I don't suppose you do. I'm sorry. I do wonder, though, how long you're going to wait to get to know her."

"It's only been a month."

Rafe nodded. He knew only too well how one month could turn into six, and then six months into a year, but he kept silent on this.

"You said you knew it would be hard, Nick. Has it been better or worse?"

This really was the last subject Nikolai wanted to discuss, and the short answers he gave his father told the older man as much. The king did not grow angry, but he knew very well what his son was about. He debated just how direct his next words should be, but before he could speak, Erica returned. While remembering the patience of Jesus when it came to working with the disciples, Rafe reminded himself that not everything needed to be covered in one day. He continued to pray, not content to wait on God for a better time to discuss the princess.

Rafe would never have let his son go had he realized how much he had upset Nikolai or how dark the storm was that brewed inside.

~

With a schedule change that would be easier to discuss with both the prince and the princess, Murdock had asked Shelby to wait in Nikolai's office. Shelby had never been in this room before and wasn't even comfortable sitting down, but she liked the colors and the way the prince had things arranged. She stood just five feet inside the door and let her eyes do the walking. Some of the bookshelves were full of leatherbound volumes, and there were tall oak file cabinets too. It all looked so neat and important that for a moment, Shelby felt a bit insignificant.

"What are you doing in here?"

The prince's voice startled Shelby so much that she jumped and spun, her face looking guilty for no reason. She watched the prince come into the room, his face showing his disapproval. Her thoughts scattered, Shelby began to back toward the door.

"I'm sorry," she said softly, bumping into the doorjamb before she found the actual doorway to the anteroom. Once outside, the office door was shut, and Shelby looked around in dismay. She knew she'd handled it badly, but he had so taken her by surprise. Debating what to do next, Shelby decided to take a seat in the anteroom and wait for Murdock. She had been waiting only a few minutes when the office door opened.

"You could have told me Murdock asked you to wait here," the prince began without preamble, his voice still agitated. "He just called to explain he would be late."

"I'm sorry," Shelby said again, and without thinking the prince took his anger out on his wife.

"Are you always such a little doormat?" he asked suddenly. Shelby blinked. "No."

"You could have fooled me," Nikolai muttered as he turned away, shooting an angry glare in her direction.

At a loss, Shelby moved against the wall and stood still.

What in the world have I done? What am I doing here? I don't even know this man.

Working hard not to overreact, Shelby wished she could stop shaking. She heard a phone ringing and started to move but realized she was headed back toward the office door. She had just begun to head in the right direction, toward the door to the hallway, when the prince spoke her name again. Shelby turned swiftly to see him coming toward her. She froze, not knowing if he was still upset, but he didn't even notice her stricken face.

"Murdock has been tied up and needs to meet us in the kitchen." Nikolai said these words without even looking at his wife. He simply led the way, and Shelby, not knowing what else to do, followed in his long-legged wake.

"Thank you for coming," Murdock began the moment he saw them. "Let's see . . . Friday night—" the house minister began but stopped suddenly. "Princess Shelby, are you all right?"

"Yes," she said, her voice unnaturally pitched.

"Are you certain?" he asked, bending a little to look into her face.

Shelby could only nod, and although she didn't look at Nikolai, he noticed her face for the first time. Her lipstick stood out like a child's crayon mark, so pale were her features. She kept her eyes glued to Murdock or the floor as the minister told of the weekend plans, but the prince could barely take his eyes from his wife's face. What he saw alarmed him. He had done this. He had frightened her. He knew he had to make it right. He determined to do so the moment Murdock was finished, but that man had a few more details for him. By the time he was finished, the princess had slipped away. Nikolai went to her room to speak to her, but Arlanda was there alone and told him the princess had remembered an appointment and left immediately.

Nikolai could have kicked himself. He had appointments of his own and knew he would be tied up for the rest of the day. The next day was no better. Nikolai was determined to see Shelby in person but was told she had gone out of town.

Shelby, who had been dreading the trip she had been scheduled to make to Yelverton, now found herself comfortably away from the prince and more at peace with every mile. She knew she couldn't run forever, but right now she was feeling too fragile to face him. All too soon she would be going back, and by then, she hoped she would have her emotions under control.

What Shelby failed to remember was that she wasn't due back until late afternoon on Friday, just a few hours before the King's Ball, the first official event where she was expected to make an appearance as the princess of Pendaran.

Five

Prince Nikolai, you have married the sweetest woman in the world. If the prince had heard this once, he'd heard it a dozen times since he walked into his father's ballroom. The King's Ball had been in full swing for more than 45 minutes, but he had yet to see his wife. Indeed, one of the staff told him she hadn't made an appearance yet. He'd stopped at her bedroom door before he'd come down, hoping to clear the air between them, but there had been no answer to his knock.

"You're taking me into dinner," Erica said, suddenly appearing at her son's side and slipping an arm through his.

"That works for me," he replied, smiling as he leaned to kiss her cheek. "Who is seeing to Shelby?" he asked, his voice a study in nonchalance.

"Your father gets that honor tonight." This said, Erica studied him for a moment. "You look very nice tonight, Nicky. Has Shelby seen you in this tux?"

"As a matter of fact, no. I haven't seen her at all today."

"Oh, that's right. Your Aunt Paige was having trouble with her hair. Shelby is giving her a quick trim."

"Shelby cuts hair?"

"Yes. Fran and Arlanda say she's a marvel. Oh, there's Toby. I must speak to him. Find me for dinner."

"I will."

Nikolai was delighted that an older couple claimed his attention, or he might have begun searching the palace like a madman. He listened, his head bent with proper courtesy, but whenever he had a chance to glance around the king's ballroom, he took it. The couple was just moving off when he spotted her. Shelby was with her parents, both she and her mother talking and signing with ease. Nikolai had never seen her do this, and for long moments he watched in fascination. He was still staring when they spotted him. Without discussion, Mr. Parker headed his way, his wife just behind him. Nikolai felt relief flood him until he watched Shelby catch her mother's arm, say something, and then move in the opposite direction. She didn't even look at him. He managed to keep the discouragement from his face as his in-laws neared.

"Good evening, Prince Nikolai," Josiah began. "I'm sorry we haven't had a chance to speak to you before now; our meeting at the wedding was so brief."

"It's a pleasure to see you both. Your dress is very beautiful, Mrs. Parker. You look wonderful."

"Oh, thank you, Prince Nikolai. Shelby helped me pick it out."

"You both have good taste then, and please call me Nick."

"You must call us by our given names as well," Josiah spoke up. He was so eager to get to know this young man. Shelby had said things were going well, but there was a strain in her face that he hadn't seen before. He knew she was busy and wanted to believe it was only that. He thought getting to know this man might put his mind at rest.

"I want to extend an invitation to you, Nick," Josiah continued, trying the name for the first time. "You're welcome to visit us in Henley anytime. We plan to have you and

Shelby to dinner very soon, but we want you to know you're welcome."

"Thank you. I'll plan on stopping. As a matter of fact, I have a friend who works in Henley at the post office."

"That would be right across the street from my shop."

Nikolai nodded. "I've seen your barbershop many times. If I recall, you've been in business there for years."

"More than 20."

"And I understand Shelby has inherited your skill with scissors."

Both Parkers laughed and Daria answered, "She told us she's been called into service here at the palace. She loves doing it."

"May I interrupt?" a female voice broke in at Nikolai's side. He looked down to see his aunts, Paige and Marla. "Erica said you were talking to Shelby's parents, and we wanted to meet them."

"Of course," Nikolai replied as he graciously turned. "Josiah and Daria Parker, please meet two of my mother's sisters, Paige Marshall and Marla Simms."

Nikolai stayed quiet for a time and listened to the four of them talk about his wife. Both his aunts had been delighted to meet her and, yes, her parents thought she was very sweet too; she always had been. They were still in deep discussion when he spotted the object of their exchange and slipped away. He would have caught up with her too, but another group caught her attention first. Nikolai stopped and watched her.

At one point Shelby glanced up and noticed Nikolai watching her. It was all such a mess. She had not had time to even see him, and if he approached her, she knew she wouldn't be able to keep the tension from her face. This was her first official public appearance. The thought of doing something to bring shame to the crown was abhorrent to her. If her husband approached, she might show her uncertainty, and in her estimation that would be unforgivable.

She was still mulling it over when the gong sounded for dinner. The king found her just a minute later, and she smiled up into his kind eyes.

"Are you hungry?" he asked.

"A little," Shelby said honestly, "but mostly nervous. It's all a bit new."

The king placed his free hand on hers. "You're doing beautifully, and you look lovely. That blue is wonderful on you."

"I've never had a reason to wear a formal gown before. It's quite fun."

The king's smile was huge. There was something so likeable and guileless about this woman that his heart turned over in his chest. For a moment he begged God to let Shelby and Nikolai find love. He thought of the relationship he shared with his own precious wife and wanted nothing less for these two dear young people.

"Your parents seem to be having a good time," the king said as they found their seats in the huge dining room at the long table.

"It was so kind of you to include them," Shelby said, her look a bit anxious. "I was so glad when Mother called to say she'd received the card."

For a moment Rafe was struck dumb. Had she really thought that they would be excluded? Again he was reminded about how new this was for her, and also how little she expected from all of them. He glanced down at her to see that she'd spotted Nikolai and Erica at another long table. He was still observing the scene when Nikolai's gaze rested on her. Shelby's eyes dropped in an instant, and Rafe's heart knew a moment of heaviness.

He still believed that God had a hand in this marriage and that Shelby was a gift from Him, but how long it would be before things were as they should be, only He knew.

Shelby told herself not to panic. Her husband was just 30 feet away on the rim of the dance floor and had finally caught her eyes with his own. Not taking any chances, he lifted his hand and beckoned to her with one finger, even as he worked to close the distance between them. Shelby felt rather than saw someone coming up from the other side. She glanced and saw that it was Toby.

"Hello, Mr. Newbury," she said too loudly, stopping him in his tracks.

"Well, Shelby, you're not dancing."

"I was waiting for you," she improvised.

"Well, by all means then, let's dance."

Shelby allowed herself to be led onto the dance floor. The waltz was half over, but Shelby forced herself to relax and, even though she was tired, accepted the next dance with Toby as well. They were talking on the subject of the Royal Care Center when Nikolai cut in. It was done so smoothly, Toby bowing away with a huge smile on his face, that before Shelby knew what was happening, she was dancing with her husband. She couldn't bring herself to look higher than his tie, but Nikolai did not hesitate.

"You've been avoiding me, Shelby."

"I suppose I have," she admitted, her voice soft and breathless. "I find I'm not up to pretending everything is fine, and I didn't want to ruin the king's party."

"No one has ever expected you to pretend anything, least of all me. I owe you such a great apology."

This brought Shelby's eyes to his for a moment, so Nikolai felt emboldened to continue.

"I'm not sure how I'll convey to you how deeply I regret my words and actions to you, but I'm going to try. I am deeply ashamed, Shelby, that you are now frightened of me."

Again Shelby looked up, this time for a bit longer.

"I suppose I shouldn't be so quick to try to please everyone," she said in a small voice.

"You're talking as though you've done something wrong. I was angry with my father and took it out on you. I can only hope you will forgive me."

"Of course I will," Shelby said in an instant. It never occurred to her to do otherwise, but that didn't change the unsettledness inside. She knew all about bad moods and anger and what they could do to a person's disposition, but that didn't alter the fact that his response to her had given her second thoughts. Every time Shelby saw his face, she remembered his angry gaze.

The dance ended, but Nikolai still wasn't certain where he stood. Choosing for the moment to proceed as if nothing had happened, he said, "Thank you for the dance."

"Thank you," she replied in return.

"Did you enjoy dinner?" he asked, hesitant to leave things alone.

"I did. The staff did such a good job with everything."

"I see someone I need to speak to, Shelby," the prince told her honestly. "Would you excuse me for a moment?"

"Of course."

Nikolai started away but came right back. "I'll find you for the last dance," he said, bending low to speak into her ear.

"All right."

Shelby stood for a moment, trying to dispel the feeling of unreality. She had just danced with the prince, who was also her husband and who scared her in no small measure.

Fear is a sin, Shelby. He apologized. You're going to have to get over it.

She knew it would be easier to acknowledge than accomplish, but that didn't excuse her from trying. She was still thinking about it and asking God for help when her father asked her to dance. For the moment she would enjoy this time with Josiah Parker and do as she was asked—keep herself free for the last dance.

~

Nikolai and Shelby walked together back to the north quadrant. The ball was over, hailed as a success by all, and the royal family could finally seek their rest. The newly married couple did not speak as they walked, but Shelby had no more said goodnight and shut her door when the phone rang.

"It's Nick," her husband said into her ear. "Can you work me into your schedule in the morning?"

"I think so. Shall I check my book?"

"If you would, please."

Shelby left the phone long enough to find the book on her desk. She came back and sat on the edge of the bed before picking up the phone.

"My day is clear."

"Can I meet with you about nine?"

"Yes. Where should I find you?"

"I think in our parlor. I'll knock on your door about then."

"All right."

"Thank you, Shelby."

"You're welcome. Goodnight."

"Goodnight."

And it was a good night for both of them, but for very different reasons. Shelby fell sound asleep and stayed asleep the whole night, something she needed very much. Nikolai spent many hours lying in his bed and praying, confessing to God the poor choices he'd made and sins he'd committed against his wife in the last six weeks and then discussing with Him all the things he needed to tell her in the morning and asking for strength to do just that.

~

Did you have a good time? Shelby typed on the teletype machine she used for phone calls to her father.

We had a wonderful time, he replied. *We spoke with Nikolai for a while and told him we wanted to have the two of you to dinner. We'll have to do that soon. You looked a little tired at times last night. Did you enjoy yourself?*

Yes. I had something on my mind that I found stressful, so I imagine this was what you saw in my expression.

It was hard not to ask you last night.

I'm all right, Fa, thank you. By the way, tell Brice he missed a great party.

We already did, but I could tell he was glad he'd kept to his original plans. He did say he wants to come see you soon. I think he said something about skating or biking.

Tell him to come. I would love it. Do you have my extension?

Yes. I'll pass the word along.

Someone knocked on Shelby's door just then, so she told her father she had to go. They said goodbye with some regret. It seemed like their time together these days consisted of brief snatches on the run.

"Good morning," Nikolai said as soon as Shelby opened the door. "Are you ready?"

"Yes." Shelby took in the prince's jeans and T-shirt and was glad she hadn't dressed up.

Nikolai noticed her attire as well. He had yet to see her looking anything but nice, but like this, in white jeans and a pale peach blouse, she looked so at home she might have been living in the palace for years. Telling himself to keep his mind on the task ahead of him, he led the way to the comfortable sofas in the private, forest green parlor they shared and waited for her to sit down.

"I won't keep insulting you by apologizing, Shelby, but I feel we need to talk a little more about what happened." It did not escape his notice that although Shelby had sat down, she was not at all relaxed.

"All right," Shelby said, thinking she'd been right about why he wanted to see her.

"I frightened you quite badly, didn't I?"

Shelby nodded a bit reluctantly, not certain she was going to enjoy this.

"Can you tell me why exactly?"

Shelby played with her watch for a moment, her gaze diverted. She had to be honest but feared it would make him angry again. She tensed and tried to smile, but it didn't work.

"It sounds so silly now, but for just a moment I thought you might be tempted to hit me."

She said this and leaned a little away from him. Nikolai had all he could do not to react. He didn't know when he'd been so surprised. He forced himself to nod in seeming calmness, but inside he was miserable. *All this time, Lord, You've been prompting me to get to know her, to talk to her, but I ran from my job. Then I thought my parents had been duped. I thought she was a complete phony, but she really is extremely sweet and accommodating.*

"Were you tempted to hit me?" Shelby asked in a small voice.

"No, Shelby," Nikolai said, finding it no problem to keep his voice gentle; she was looking frightened all over again, and his heart wrung with compassion.

Shelby shrugged uncomfortably. "I told myself it was silly, but sometimes I don't listen very well."

Nikolai stared at her for a moment, the full import of what she had done coming home to him for the first time. Would he have left his home, all that was familiar and dear, to marry a stranger who had complete control over him? He didn't think he would.

"I'm glad you told me, Shelby—very glad. I was angry with my father and took it out on you. It's probably impossible for you to believe that right now because you don't know me, but I hope in time you'll come to see that I mean it."

"Thank you."

"Tell me something, Shelby. Did you have an appointment

after Murdock spoke with us, or did you just feel you had to get away?"

"A little of both. I had an open appointment, one that I could take care of anytime, and I decided to go then."

"Did it go well?"

Shelby blushed. "I can't say as I remember very much about it. I'll have to go back."

"Murdock said you were also out of town this week."

"Yes. I went to Yelverton. That's been on my calendar for a few weeks. One of the Council member's wives asked me to lunch, and when the queen learned of it, she asked me to stop in on an old friend for her."

"It's pretty up there in the north. My grandmother's family is from there."

"She told me about that."

"That's right. They said you had lunch with them."

Shelby nodded again, feeling terribly insecure inside. This man was larger than life to her. He was tall, yes, but it was more than that. Even before the incident, she'd been slightly in awe of him. In a move to appear calmer than she felt, Shelby tucked her hair behind her ears and crossed her legs.

"Am I going to offend you if I ask you about your hair?" Nikolai asked suddenly. He'd been watching her quite closely.

"No," Shelby told him sincerely.

"Is the color yours?"

Not expecting this, she laughed a little. "Yes. For better or for worse, it's mine."

"What would make you say for worse?"

Shelby could have given him several reasons, but Murdock came to the door.

"I hate to interrupt, sir, but a call has come in, and I thought you should take it."

"All right. Thank you, Murdock."

Shelby stood so the prince would feel she understood.

"I'm sorry to cut this short," Nikolai said sincerely.

"That's fine. I understand."

Feeling a bit thwarted as Shelby seemed on the verge of relaxing, Nikolai saw that he had no choice. He wished her a good day and went to take his call. By the time he finished, she was gone. The temptation to let her live her life so he could continue to cherish his memories of Yvette was very strong, but he'd already made that mistake and wasn't going to do it again. He didn't see Shelby again that day but prayed off and on until bedtime about the next opportunity to speak with her.

~

"Do you still drive yourself?" Lenore asked.

"Yes. I drove myself today."

"But you don't have to?" Deb checked with her.

"No. I can ask to be taken in the day limo."

"You make it sound like the limousines are different at night," commented Grace.

"They are," Shelby answered, not minding the questions from the five women in her Bible study group. She was closer to these women than just about any others she could name and had not the slightest qualm in answering their naturally curious questions. Other than Lenore, she was seeing them for the first time since she was married.

"If I have to go out in the evening," Shelby explained, "I'm taken in a regular limo—big, black, and very formal. The day limo is actually a nice car, no dark windows or glass divider."

"And how does it feel?"

"A little funny at times, but the staff is so kind."

"And the prince?" Natty asked in her quiet way. "Is he kind too?"

"I think so," Shelby answered, being very honest with them. "I know it isn't easy for him, but just this morning we talked for a while. We haven't really had that much time together. You can pray for me about the relationship."

"Like we've done anything else for the past six weeks," Deb said with her classic sarcasm. She could always make Shelby laugh.

"Okay, okay." Shelby's hands went in the air. "Enough about me. How's chemo, Natty?"

"It was better this week. I know the Lord is always with me—I never doubt that—but there are times when *I'm* more mindful of Him. This week was like that. I was even able to tell the chemo tech a little about my faith."

"That's great," Connie spoke up. "I was at the hospital on Thursday about ten, and they told me I'd just missed you."

Shelby listened to the women talk, amazed at the friends they had become. She hadn't seen it coming, but the woman who had originally led the study had become pregnant and very sick. She'd met Shelby at the hospital and instantly thought of her. That had been more than two years earlier. Shelby had been meeting with the women weekly ever since. They had studied Romans, 1 and 2 Peter, and Hebrews. They were now tackling 1, 2, and 3 John.

The women studied for the next 40 minutes and took some time for prayer requests before Shelby headed on her way. Both Deb and Lenore had had a few more questions for her, and Shelby left with a small shake of her head and a huge smile on her face. She was in her car and halfway back to the palace before she wondered if she would ever know Nikolai well enough to invite him to meet the ladies. If their questions were any indication, they would thoroughly enjoy it. Right now the thought of asking him caused Shelby's face to heat. Without a bit of hesitation, she pushed the thought far to the back of her mind.

Six

In town for the first weekend in much too long, the prince stood at the back of the church on Sunday morning, determined not to sit down until he found his wife. Murdock told him that the car had brought her here, and he was going to find her. He had checked with his parents but was told that she never sat with them. Nikolai began to grow anxious. He was not a small man, and to wander around when most people were sitting was starting to draw stares.

A moment later he noticed a man signing to someone near the front of the sanctuary on the right-hand side and suddenly knew where to look. He moved to the far right, still staying at the back until he spotted that bright copper head. He was immensely relieved to see she was not in a crowded pew. In fact, he was able to sit beside her on the end of the pew with room to spare. She was so *un*crowded, in fact, that for several seconds she didn't look up from her church bulletin to see who had joined her.

"Oh, Nikolai," Shelby said softly, looking shocked and immediately feeling her face go red.

"Good morning. May I sit with you?"

"Yes, certainly."

Nikolai looked at his own bulletin and sermon notes in an effort not to stare at her, but he'd seen her red face and could tell by the movements he caught out of the corner of his eye that she was unsettled by his presence.

A few minutes remained before the service began, so he leaned slightly and said, "Do you always sit on this side?"

"Yes. Is that all right?"

"Of course. Did you know that my parents sit on the other side?"

"Yes. I talk to them when I come in. If you want me to sit with them, I can."

"No, it doesn't matter," Nikolai told her quickly as the service was starting. He listened with great attention, but not before reminding himself that he would need to find a way to let Shelby know she could relax. He suspected that she thought he had rules and regulations for everything, and in a desperate attempt to do the right thing, she was terribly nervous and contrite in his presence. That he had frightened her was not lost from his memory either. That matter was his last prayer as the announcements were completed and they sang the first song.

~

"And where did you go after that?" Shelby asked the little girl in the kitchen.

"We ate dinner at Samba's. I had pie."

"That sounds wonderful. What type of pie was it?"

The child, Emma Greene, looked to her Aunt Arlanda.

"I think you had the berry," Arlanda filled in.

"Berry," Emma told Shelby, her hand still touching Shelby's hair. The housekeeper had tried to tell her not to touch, but Shelby had waved her away. "I like red," Emma went on. "I wish I had red hair."

"Do you want mine?" Shelby checked with her.

"Your hair?"

"Sure!" Shelby rounded her eyes and said, "We'll just trade."

Emma laughed. "I don't think we can. My daddy likes my hair too much."

"I like it too. Black hair is beautiful."

Emma smiled with pleasure and then heard the timer. She stood with reluctance but didn't complain. Her Aunt Arlanda had told her they could stay until the kitchen timer buzzed.

"It was nice to meet you, Emma."

"Thank you," the little girl said as she smiled up at her.

Shelby walked them to the door and even outside, waving as the car pulled away. She had been on her way to the park and passed through the kitchen to find Emma and Arlanda. They had been on their way out, but Arlanda held back when Shelby had begun to speak with Emma. Now Shelby stood and waved one more time before moving toward the dense growth of trees and the path she knew she would find. She had been tempted to get her skates but hadn't found out yet if the park allowed skates and bicycles on the paths. She was vaguely aware of Kris following some paces behind her. He had become a part of her world, and most of the time she took his presence for granted.

"Well, Shelby, hello," the queen said from down the path, her own companion trailing her at some distance.

"Hi." Shelby smiled when she spotted her, gladly moving forward to accept her embrace. "How are you?"

"I'm fine and loving this weather. How about you?"

"I'm fine."

"Are you really, Shelby? I mean *really*?"

Her tone was so suddenly serious that Shelby stared at her.

"I think so," she answered uncertainly. "Why do you ask?"

The queen searched the younger woman's face before saying, "Shelby, come sit on this bench with me, will you?"

The two women got comfortable before the queen went on quietly.

"I want you to know, Shelby, that Nikolai came to us about the way he treated you."

"Oh," Shelby said uncomfortably, still sorry she had been so foolish and run. "I didn't handle that very well."

"Shelby, what are you talking about? I've seen Nikolai angry. It's not a pretty thing. The only difference is that I know he wouldn't do anything. You had no such guarantee because you're still too unfamiliar with him. Now, I want you to tell me if you're all right."

Shelby's gaze went to the trees overhead. "I haven't been able to talk to anyone, not even my parents. I can't stand the thought they'll think badly of Nikolai. I know he was upset, but at the moment I didn't stop to analyze it. I just had to get away."

The queen picked up Shelby's hand. She held it gently and continued.

"You're still speaking as though you did the wrong thing, dear. Nikolai was completely at fault, and his father and I know that. We're so pleased with the way you let him apologize and that you forgave him. He knows he was wrong."

For the first time since the incident, Shelby began to listen. She had been wrapped up in her own little world of hurt and not thinking clearly. She stared at the queen as understanding dawned and then admitted quietly, "I thought you might be sorry you chose me to marry Nikolai."

For a moment, the queen's eyes closed in pain. "Nothing could be further from the truth, Shelby." She bent close now to be sure she was being heard. "If Rafe and I could do it all over again, you would still be the one."

As if her heart was a bird that had been set free of its cage, Shelby felt as though she could fly. For the first time in days, she felt she could take a deep breath. So completely out of her depth in this place, terrified of making a mistake and disappointing the king and queen—not to mention being of no use to the prince—Shelby suddenly knew the worst was over. The prince might never love her. She might never have an intimate marriage or children with him, but she could be herself, she could be the woman God had created her to be, and that was worth almost any cost to Shelby.

"Thank you," Shelby said at last. "I can't tell you what a help you've been."

"I'm glad, Shelby. I can't stand to see you hurting."

"Well, I'm sure I'll hurt again, but the Lord never promised a walk in the park, and in the future I know I'll be able to handle it."

Erica couldn't resist hugging her again, an embrace Shelby gladly returned. Shelby was just starting her walk, and Erica was on her way home, so after a few more minutes the women parted company. Shelby's long legs ate up the path as she kept herself just short of a run, her heart prayerful and light as a child's. She decided she would have to drop a note to the queen, thanking her again.

"But how would I word it?" Shelby asked the air in front of her. "Never mind, Shelby. You already thanked her. Let it go at that."

Kris, still trailing her and keeping his eyes open, had the impression that something was different. As was his job, he would just have to wait and see.

～

"And where is the princess?" the prince asked of Murdock. It had been his standard question for the last ten weeks. It had started after the King's Ball. Princess Shelby was constantly in demand, and unless she was with the prince, the rather shy, quiet young woman was gone.

The staff had had a small taste of Shelby in the first several weeks she lived in the palace, but the real woman, the woman who liked to bake cookies at ten o'clock at night or slide in stocking feet along the polished floors of the hallway, was now out in full force. They also found her kinder than ever—taking hot soup to one of the staff members when she was down with a cold and cookies to the queen mother when she learned her favorite type.

Nikolai had foolishly packed his schedule when they had first married and now found himself always moving in the opposite direction from his wife. That he had originally wanted this and was still tempted to do it was beside the point. He knew it was wrong, but in some ways the damage was done, at least for a time. Other than Sunday mornings and evenings when they were both in church, he would never have known where she was if it hadn't been for Murdock. There were times when things were too set to be rearranged, but the prince was making a genuine effort to get to know his shy wife. In the process he was finding out that she was one popular lady.

"Let me rephrase that," the prince said. "Is there any place I might catch up with her today?" He watched his minister check his ever-present calendar book.

"She's at the care center this morning, but at noon she's scheduled at the Faraday Garden Club for a luncheon with your grandparents. The ladies and gentlemen of the club have asked her to be a member. They will present her with a dozen trees to plant here at the palace and a dozen more to plant where she chooses. They have asked her to address the group after the presentation."

The prince looked thoughtful. "Have you heard her speak, Murdock?"

"Not personally, sir, but both Kris and Hank tell me that she holds an audience in the palm of her hand."

Nikolai nodded slowly. "I'll head there as soon as I finish my Bible study assignment from Grandfather."

"Will you make it for the luncheon, sir?"

"I should."

"I'll call ahead and warn them," Murdock said as he made a note in the daybook.

"Is she happy?" the prince asked suddenly, his voice low.

The faithful house minister looked up at him. "I would say she's very happy, Prince Nikolai."

"Does she ever ask about me or where I am?"

Murdock shook his head no. "If I may be so bold, sir, I think she would say that it's none of her business."

Nikolai nodded. "It's an unconventional situation; there's no doubt about that."

Murdock opened his mouth to speak but closed it again. The prince caught the action and commanded him to "spit it out."

"I was going to say that given time I think that will change, but I remembered, sir, you may not wish for that change, and then my words would be of little comfort to you."

Nikolai stared at his old friend and servant. "You're right. At this moment I wouldn't care for that, but I have a responsibility. Shelby's parents gave her hand to me, believing she would be well. I want to know that she's happy and cared for."

Now it was Murdock's turn to nod. Shelby was happy, he had just told the prince that, but as to the future—a future with a man who kept her at arm's length—that would remain to be seen.

~

"We're so glad to have you again, Princess Shelby," the matron, a Mrs. Radford, at the care center said. "Will you be staying until lunch?"

"Not today," Shelby said calmly, but her mind was racing. She had seen some things in this place that made her uncomfortable. As one of the directors, she had been allowed to question and inspect to her heart's desire. She hadn't seen anything too noticeable, but the matron was always so swift to point out the ways she was saving money. Shelby hadn't seen anything in the books that would indicate the center was in financial trouble, so this made no sense to her.

Then she began to notice where the cutbacks were taking place—they were all in the dining room. Shelby had eaten with the residents twice and both times was very uncomfortable with what she'd seen and eaten. She was not a person who usually made snap judgments, willing to give others the benefit of the doubt, and she was not going to be hasty now, but after visiting with a few of the residents as well as the staff, Shelby made a mental note to visit at mealtime the next chance she had.

~

"I was at the care center this morning," Shelby told Nikolai's grandparents as they walked toward the August Botanical Gardens. The day was sunny, not a cloud anywhere, but the temperature was only in the mid-seventies.

"You're a director now, aren't you?" King Anton asked.

"Yes. I took over for your mother. She was delighted when I told her."

"We plan to take her a flower, Shelby," Ketra told her. "We'll be sure and tell her you were back at the center today."

"Or I could take the flower for you," Shelby offered with a smile, "and tell her myself."

The three were still talking as they entered the gardens and were almost immediately joined by some of the members. Shelby met several dozen people before having a chance to excuse herself, wishing she'd used the ladies' room at the care center; the bathroom at the gardens was quite a long walk away. She was still in one of the stalls when at least two other ladies came in.

"Is my slip showing?"

"No, it's fine."

"Did you see him?"

"Yes. I'm telling you, Liz, he's the best looking man I've ever seen."

"You're not kidding."

"The princess is here today too."

"Really? I didn't know that."

"That's what my mother told me. I've heard she's beautiful."

The other woman sniffed, her voice playful. "I don't care what she looks like; he should have married me."

Both women left in laughter, but Shelby didn't join in. She didn't know what happened to her when her husband was near, but she definitely wasn't herself. She didn't really think it could be called fear—no, it was more like awe. Yes, that was the word. Awe was when something made you a bit tongue-tied and put you at a loss. He had been nothing but a gentleman for weeks now. Indeed, Shelby had never known such a gentleman, but she still felt awkward and shy in his presence.

She exited the bathroom with a small measure of panic rising in her breast, all the while telling herself to calm down and be respectful. She wasn't ten feet outside the door when she stopped to look to where they would eat lunch and have the program, the fronds of a large plant making it almost impossible. She was in the midst of taking a deep breath to subdue her nerves when he spoke from behind her.

"Shelby."

"Oh, Nikolai!" she exclaimed, a hand going to her heart. "I didn't see you." Her eyes huge with fright, she looked up at him and saw him smile. Did he think it was funny? For the first time since she'd met him, she found herself feeling grumpy toward him.

"I didn't know you were going to be here," she said, her voice a bit formal.

"My plans were of the last minute variety, or I would have informed you."

Looking unconsciously regal, Shelby nodded and began walking down the path, not caring if he followed or not. He stayed right at her side, matching his longer legs to her steps. Still a bit miffed, she didn't speak to him again but smiled at a few people who passed.

"This is quite an honor," Nikolai spoke up. "I think the average age of the members here is about 50."

"If I didn't know better, I'd say you just told me I looked old."

Nikolai looked down at her profile to see if she had been joking and couldn't tell. He opted not to smile again, even though he wanted to, but he suspected she might be upset with him about something.

"How old are you, Shelby? I can't remember."

"I'm 23," she told him, not bothering to mention that she would only be that age for a few more days.

Hearing the note in her voice, Nikolai decided to stay quiet again. He honestly didn't know her well enough to gauge whether she was upset with him or not, but he wasn't willing to chance it. Both the prince and princess were relieved to look up and see Anton and Ketra ahead of them.

"You found her, Nicky," Ketra said with a smile. "I think they want us to take our seats."

The president of the garden club, Mr. Potts, came forward then to show them to their seats and give them a rundown on the next few hours. Shelby found herself quietly taking it all in and smiling only when Mr. Potts looked in her direction. The three people with her were old pros at this sort of thing, and she thought she would do best just to watch and listen. She was so quiet in fact, that when lunch was over and she excused herself before it was time to make her address, the queen regent mentioned it to her grandson.

"She's so shy around you, Nicky. I've noticed it before."

"You don't find her shy with you?"

"Not in the least. She was those first few weeks, but no longer. She even calls at times to ask me questions or say hi, and she visits with Anton's mother at least once a week."

Nikolai was silently amazed. He knew he had a long way to go, but not until that moment did he realize how far. If he could have looked into his date book right then, he might have started to adjust his schedule on the spot. The Lord had been speaking to his heart and leaving no doubt as to what he should do: He needed to get to know his wife. He often felt the Lord prompting him to talk with her, to share his life and ask her about her own. He was asking the Lord to give him strength to do just that when he saw Shelby heading up to the temporary speaking platform.

"King Regent Anton, Queen Regent Ketra, Prince Nikolai, President Potts, members of the August Garden Club, gardeners, and guests," Shelby began, "thank you for presenting me with this honor. I have long loved flowers, although I've been accused of having a black thumb, and I find myself delighted with the chance to visit here and feel at home.

"For as long as I can remember, my mother has had a summer garden. Some years it flourished and some years it didn't. She was never very interested in houseplants, but come the spring, you could find her amid her flowers in the backyard of our home. The only drawback for her was the honey bees. My mother hated the thought of getting stung, and just the buzz would cause her to flee to whatever she deemed a safe distance.

"My father had no such problem. He enjoyed the garden on weekends, and you could always find him out with my mother. The bees didn't bother him. The reason for this might be that my father has been deaf from childhood. My brother and I watched all of this as we were growing up, and somewhere along the line I made a connection in my mind. You see, my mother was never stung, and neither was my father, but my mother's hearing put her in a position to fear.

"I found myself asking, 'What do I listen to that causes me to fear?' It might seem like a small thing to you, but over the years the sight of flowers or trees has often helped me remember to whom I should listen when it comes to the subject of fear. It is for this reason that I will plant my 12 trees at the palace in a place where I will be able to watch them grow. And selfishly enough, I'll plant the 12 other trees where I can see them on occasion. I'll think of them as my 24 reminders to listen to the right voice and be wise about my fears. Thank you for the trees. I know God will use them in my life in a special way."

The applause was thunderous. Nikolai joined in, but he was stunned. She had been wonderful. Toby had come to his parents and said he'd found someone special—this had been what he was talking about. She was coming toward him now, and Nikolai stood, smiling down on her as she neared. On impulse he bent and kissed her cheek.

"That was wonderful," he whispered in her ear just before he helped her with her chair.

"Thank you," Shelby said as she smiled at him, but she couldn't stop the blush that stained her cheeks.

Dessert was served after that, but Shelby wasn't given a chance to enjoy it. Many people came to their table to thank her or share their own stories. Nikolai watched the gracious way she received everyone and had to keep his mind from turning to bitter thoughts. Yvette had not liked public appearances or been good in crowds. The prince had no trouble with this, but in his mind he pictured some of these people comparing the two women. The thought of his Yvette coming up short was intolerable to him.

The prince did not let his feelings show, but neither did they put him in a good humor. He made no attempt to engage the princess in conversation on the way home. She had come to the garden club with the king and queen regent but naturally departed with her husband for the return trip to the palace. His silence unnerved her, and Shelby found herself wishing she had come in her own vehicle. It wasn't surprising that when the car delivered them to the front door, she escaped his presence just as soon as she was able.

Seven

"Is the princess out of town this weekend, Murdock?" Nikolai asked the minister as soon as he arrived home from church Sunday morning.

"She went to Henley for the day, sir. Do I need to contact her for you?"

"No. Thank you, Murdock. I only wondered because I didn't see her this morning."

The house minister exited the room then, seeing that the prince was lost in his own thoughts. Nikolai, working hard to keep his frustration at bay, didn't even hear him leave. He knew very well that he was paying for his own mistakes, but that didn't change the angst he felt broiling inside.

It takes me forever to obey You, and when I'm ready to do the right thing, my wife disappears. She has got to be the busiest woman I've ever known. Nikolai knew he sounded irritated and also knew that he had no right; he had no one to blame but himself. Shelby had been in the car with him on Wednesday after the garden club meeting, and he'd even seen her a few times the rest of the week, but the willingness to try again did not come until Saturday night. On Sunday she was gone for the day. He knew very well that he'd had opportunities and lost them.

Nikolai sat back in his chair. Shelby's face was in his mind the way he'd seen her briefly on Friday, and a plan was also forming.

Murdock needed time off as much as anyone, so Nikolai would let it go for the day, but first thing Monday morning he would meet again with his house minister.

~

"Oh, Mother!" Shelby exclaimed when she tore the wrapping off her last birthday gift. "My favorite."

Daria smiled but then shook her head. From the time she was little, Shelby had loved Fairy Cakes, a white cake and frosting confection that could be found in any market. Daria, knowing she probably hadn't had them in ages, had bought two boxes and wrapped them.

"I think I'll eat one right now," Shelby declared. "Do I have to share?"

"Yes," Brice told her in no uncertain terms.

"All right," she said, her voice playfully grudging. "But only one, Brice. You can buy your own."

"The whole country thinks you're the most wonderfully giving woman in the land," he teased her. "What would they say if they could see you now?"

"They wouldn't say a thing," she said, her smile cheeky. "Everyone but you seems to understand that no woman should be asked to part with her Fairy Cakes."

"Pathetic," her brother pronounced about her but still took the one cake she offered.

"Did you want one, Fa?" Shelby, relenting, asked Josiah.

He shook his head. "I don't know how you stand those things when your mother made that delicious cake."

"I'll eat some of that too," Shelby told him placidly, making her mother laugh.

Daria was delighted to have her daughter home for the day and told her as much, but before Shelby left to return to the palace, she was determined to learn why Nikolai had not accompanied her. Often she had held her tongue, knowing her daughter needed time, but on this occasion, both Daria and Josiah agreed that if Nikolai did not come with her, they would want to know why. When Shelby had not been looking, she had asked Josiah if he'd asked the question. When he said no, Daria planned just how she would get Shelby alone. Now was the time.

"Shelby, will you come help me with the cake and ice cream?"

"Sure."

Shelby rose without hesitation, and just as soon as they were behind the closed kitchen door, Daria spoke.

"We had hoped that Nikolai would come with you, Shelby. Was he busy today?"

"I don't know. I didn't ask him."

"You didn't ask him if he was busy, or you didn't ask him to your twenty-fourth birthday party?"

"I didn't ask him anything," the redhead admitted, looking across the room at her mother, who was taking bonbons from the freezer.

"Can you tell me what's going on?" Daria asked, her face open and showing all the love and caring she felt.

Shelby shrugged as she got out napkins and forks. "I went to the palace with such noble ideas, Mother, but the prince doesn't need me. It's taken a while to see that, but it's true. Most of the time I can tell he doesn't want me anywhere near him, so I don't try to push in."

"What do you try to do?"

"Be helpful to everyone else. I honestly enjoy it, Mother, and I can't imagine leaving there, but I'm not important to the prince. I seem to be important and loved by the staff and even Nick's family, but Nick doesn't want or need me."

"Oh, Shelby," Daria whispered, her heart breaking with this news. "Do you think it will stay that way? Do you think he'll never get over her?"

Shelby tipped her head to one side in thought. She was doing her best to be pragmatic about it. "As you like to remind me, never is a long time, and I have to keep reminding myself that it hasn't been that many months. But for the present, at least, I think the best thing I can do is stay out of the prince's way. He checks with Murdock about me—I've heard him do it—and he does ask me how I'm doing if he sees me, but that's not very often."

"Are you going and doing too much? Should you make yourself more available to him?"

"I wouldn't know how to do that. I do have a pretty busy schedule, but I'm home a lot too. Unless we end up in the same place, and that rarely happens, he just doesn't seek me out. If I were to make myself more available, I think I'd end up sitting around the palace while the prince leads his own life."

Daria nodded but didn't speak. Something wasn't right. Whenever she read of one of the royal couples going out, they were together. It was something of a tradition. Not knowing if this fact had escaped Shelby's notice, Daria opted not to mention it. Clearly the prince was keeping them apart. The thought was enough to cause Daria to weep. Forcing herself to remember that this was her daughter's birthday, she put the thought aside.

"I'm glad I checked with you, dear," she said instead. "Know that your father and I will be praying."

"Thank you, Mother."

Shelby gave Daria a hug and the older woman held on tightly. *Will she ever know a mother's love, Father? Will the prince ever love her? Will she ever hold their child in her arms? You are able to do this, Lord, and I pray that You will—in Your time and in Your way.*

~

"What do you mean he changed my schedule?" Shelby asked softly, staring at Murdock. That man shifted a little in his chair.

"He didn't give his reasons, but he asked me to cancel certain of your appointments."

"Did he say I should see him?"

"No," Murdock regretted to admit. "But—"

"Where is the prince?" Shelby cut him off with this question.

"He was in his office earlier, but I'm not—" Murdock stopped speaking. The princess had already come to her feet and was headed toward the door.

~

Nikolai's head was bent over the papers he was studying when Shelby appeared at his doorway. Thinking it was Murdock, who would know to come in if the door was open, the prince did not immediately look up. Sure she was being ignored, Shelby became all the more upset.

"I would like to speak with you," she finally blurted, and Nikolai looked up in surprise.

"Come in," he said as he stood, his expression open.

"You changed my schedule," Shelby stated without preamble.

"Yes, I did, Shelby. I thought it was for the best."

"What do you mean?"

"You looked tired to me, and we need—"

"*Tired!*" Shelby interrupted, sounding as shocked and angry as she looked. "Most of the time you don't even know I exist, and now you say I'm tired."

The prince looked surprised by this pronouncement, but Shelby, still feeling very upset, gave him no time to speak.

"I may be the princess, Nikolai Markham, but you don't own me. I'm 24 years old, and I'm perfectly—"

"You're 24?" the prince said with a frown. "I thought you were 23."

"I had a birthday, and don't change the subject! The fact is I'm not a child, and you had no right to change my schedule." For several moments the two stood in tense silence.

"As a matter of fact," Nikolai finally began quietly, "as your husband, I have every right."

Knowing how correct he was, Shelby's shoulders slumped in defeat. Looking utterly miserable, she stood in subdued silence, her bruised heart making her feel pain all over.

"I do wish, however," Nikolai went on, "that I had spoken to you. I'm sorry I didn't."

"I'm sorry I spoke to you that way," Shelby said in return, her voice soft. "I'll leave you to get back to your work."

Shelby was at the door before he called her name. She stopped but didn't turn. Nikolai went to her, slipping around her in the doorway in order to see her face, but she still refused to look at him. Even the lowering of her eyes didn't hide the moisture there.

"Oh, Shelby," Nikolai whispered. Without giving himself a chance to reconsider, he took her in his arms. "I'm so sorry."

"I just wish I understood," he heard her say before she tipped her head back to look up at him. Nikolai stepped back until his hands were on her shoulders. She looked so puzzled, but he didn't have the words to explain it right now.

"Tell Murdock I made a mistake about your schedule and to do whatever you think is best, Shelby. All right?"

"Okay."

Nikolai studied her face a moment. "Are you all right?" he finally asked.

"Yes. And I am sorry, Nick."

"As am I. We'll forget it, okay?"

Shelby nodded, and he dropped his hands from her shoulders.

"I'll see you later."

"All right."

Nikolai slipped back into his office, and Shelby went with Murdock, who had come to tell Nikolai that a call had come in. They met over her schedule for the next hour, a little longer than usual, and had things worked out by late morning. Shelby did leave some time open, thinking if she did get tired and the prince wanted to see her, she would need to be fresh.

The rest of the day was a blur of activity that lasted well past dark. That evening Shelby attended a birthday party by herself—the invitation had been for her alone—but her mind was almost constantly on her spouse. Nikolai was in the same boat and had gone to see a friend as soon as he finished his own dinner. He was there for one reason: to talk about his wife.

~

"I make such a mess of things, Ryan. It's not as if I've never been married before, but I'm such a klutz around Shelby."

"It's not the same type of marriage, Nick. Surely you can see that. Stop expecting it to be the same."

Nikolai only shook his head and told about what had happened that morning.

"But she seemed all right when you left her?" Ryan checked with him.

"As much as could be expected. I know she's still somewhat frightened of me."

"Why is she afraid of you?"

Nikolai told that story, and again his good friend listened quietly until the end.

"So what's the plan at this point?" Ryan asked.

"Accountability. I'm here to ask you to check on me."

"And what do you want me to ask?"

"*If* I'm talking to my wife. Not *if* I've asked Murdock about her, but *if* I've talked to her myself. I also want you to check with me about whether we're doing things together. I've got things scheduled in such a way that it's going to take some time to merge our calendars, but it's time to start working on that."

"And are you dreading this?"

"Yes," Nikolai admitted. "She's a very sweet woman, and she makes no demands on me, so it's easy to forget she's even there, but she's not the woman I love. She is my wife, however, and I need to face that responsibility."

Ryan looked at him for a moment before saying, "I'm proud of you, Nick."

Nikolai shook his head. "I don't think there's anything to be proud of."

"You're wrong about that. You're hurting and yet carrying on, and I don't know how many men could do that."

"I am hurting," Nikolai admitted softly. "Some days I'm not even sure I believe Yvette is gone, yet I already have another wife. It's the strangest thing I've ever experienced. I'd be ready to throw in the towel if it wasn't for the woman herself." Nikolai had been staring across the room but now looked at his friend. "It's so easy to see people as less than they are, as less than people. Until our wedding day, Shelby Parker was just a name. It's no longer possible to think that way. I see her, and I see the result of having her live at the palace. There's no ignoring that this woman *is* in my life. Then there are times like this morning when she looks at me in confused vulnerability, and those are the times I no longer *want* to ignore her presence. Those are the times I finally see her as a person with feelings and needs and know that I have a job to do if I'm going to answer to God about the type of leader I've been in my home."

Ryan smiled. "Like I said, Nick, I'm very proud of you."

Nikolai left some time later, his heart encouraged. His parents were out of town, and for a time he'd felt at a complete loss as to whom he should counsel with. Talking to Ryan at this time had been like going to God for strength and encouragement, and Nikolai believed that God had used his friend. When he woke in the morning, the evening was still on his mind. He showered and dressed, hoping he hadn't missed his wife for the day.

~

Her breakfast ignored, Shelby was buried in the newspaper when Nikolai walked into the kitchen. Fran smiled at him but didn't speak, so Shelby had no idea that her husband had sat down across from her until his finger curled over the top of the paper and pulled it down just enough to peek at her.

"Good morning," he said quietly.

"Good morning," she returned, her face going pink when she realized she hadn't even felt his presence. "I didn't see you." She folded the paper and set it aside.

"You must have been reading something interesting."

"The cricket scores."

"You follow cricket?"

Shelby nodded, now playing with the toast and melon slices on her plate. "My brother plays."

"What school is he attending?"

"Milton West."

"What day was your birthday?" Nikolai asked suddenly, not willing to beat around the bush any longer.

"Sunday."

"What day shall we celebrate?"

"Oh, well, um, anytime I guess. Nikolai?"

"Yeah."

"Were you around on Sunday, or were you busy?"

"I was here."

Shelby sighed. "I'm sorry I didn't invite you home with me. My folks had some cake and gifts. I just didn't think you would want to come. I'm sorry I didn't check with you."

"I understand why you didn't, Shelby. We don't see that much of each other."

Shelby smiled at him, relieved that he understood. He had

put his finger on it very well. It would have been like asking a stranger to help her celebrate.

"I think your parents still plan to have us over for dinner."

"Yes, they do. They asked me on Sunday if I knew a good time, and I had to be honest and tell them I wasn't sure."

"Have them call Murdock. He has a finger on both our schedules."

"I'll do that."

"So," Nikolai said, coming back to the celebration. "What day should we go out?"

Shelby shrugged. "I don't know."

"What type of celebration do you like—lunch, dinner, dressy or casual?"

Shelby's head tilted in thought. "I have to dress up most days, so I guess I would go for casual, maybe something outside in the sunshine." The words were no more out of her mouth than she thought she sounded presumptuous and blushed again. "But anything is fine," she hurried to say. "We don't have to do anything if you're busy."

"Leave it to me," Nikolai said calmly, even though he recognized that he'd just seen through a small window into who she was. "I'll get back to you or have Murdock put something on the calendar for both of us."

"Thank you."

Nikolai checked his watch but surprised the princess by not rushing away. He asked Fran for some breakfast and sat across the table from Shelby to eat it.

"May I share some of this paper?"

"Certainly."

The two ended up eating to the rustle of the newspaper and the sound of Fran working on pastry dough. Shelby was the first to leave the kitchen. Nikolai told her to have a good day, but other than standing out of courtesy, he stayed where he was. Shelby was gone before he set the paper aside and ate in thoughtful contemplation.

Nikolai hugged his mother when she met him in the foyer downstairs. She had called to tell him she was coming over with some papers. Nikolai had wanted to stretch his legs, so he left his office and waited for her in the spacious foyer that was the hallmark of each of the quadrants.

"How are you, dear?" Erica asked warmly as she looked up at him.

"I'm doing well. How are you and Father?"

"We had a great time at the lake—so peaceful. Do you have plans to go soon?"

"I don't think so, but it sounds wonderful. You look tan and rested."

Erica was opening her mouth to say that Nikolai did *not* look rested, but she glanced up and saw Shelby coming toward them.

"Oh, Shelby's on her way."

Nikolai turned and froze. Coming toward him was his wife, but unlike he'd ever seen her. She had cut her hair off to well above her shoulders and dyed it black. If a slight breeze had come down the hall, it would have been enough to push Nikolai over.

All this time I've never told her how pretty her hair is, and now she's dyed it.

"Shelby," Erica called and then greeted her with a hug, "you must be off to Bible study."

The rest of their conversation was lost on Nikolai. Now that Shelby was very close, he suspected she was wearing a wig, but all he could do was stare at his wife and then at his mother, who was acting as though everything was normal.

"I'd better go," Shelby's voice cut back through his trance. "Goodbye."

"Goodbye," Erica said warmly. Nikolai managed only a wave.

"What is it, Nicky?" Erica asked when she saw her son's face.

"How did you know she was going to Bible study?"

"The wig."

"She wears a wig to Bible study?"

Erica's look was thoughtful and faintly disapproving.

"Shelby has Bible study with several ladies, all of whom have cancer and are in various stages of treatment. She wears a wig in empathy and camaraderie."

Nikolai nodded, another glimmer of light coming through about his wife.

"Tell me, Nicky," Erica asked softly, "are you working at all to get to know her?"

Nikolai did not immediately answer. He wanted to be completely honest, but things were changing so fast.

"It's coming, Mother, but I won't tell you I'm there. Just in the last week I've realized some things, and I'm working on them, but to date, I don't know her at all."

"Thank you for telling me, Nicky. I'll keep praying, and you keep working at it."

"I will. She's pretty busy right now, and since I was deliberately trying to keep busy and away from her, we're like ships in the night. It may take some weeks to fix that, but Murdock is aware of my desire to schedule more things together, and I'm working on my attitude."

Erica looked at him in frank curiosity. "What has your attitude been, Nick? Can you tell me?"

Again Nikolai thought and said softly, "There is a lot of fear involved, and you'll probably be surprised to find out that it's not over loving again or finding out that Shelby is a wonderful person. It's over the public's reaction to Shelby and how popular she is. I can't stand the thought that my precious Yvette would be found wanting in their eyes."

Erica put her arms around her son and hugged him for all

she was worth. Her eyes had flooded with tears on this report, so it took a moment for her to speak.

"There will always be vicious people, dear—always. But everyone who knew Yvette adored her. Everyone, Nicky. I don't think you have anything to worry about. Satan is just using this line of thought to distract you from building a marriage with a woman who could stand by your side and work with you to glorify God."

"No one has actually said anything, so you're probably right. I'm torturing myself for no reason."

Erica took Nikolai's hand in her own. "I loved Yvette and always will. I have mourned for her as though she were the child of my own body, but I will be honest with you, Nick. Shelby has been like a balm for that pain. My only daughter is your wife. I loved Yvette and I love Shelby. Both women have, and do, make it very easy. Give yourself time, Nick, as much time as you need, but don't underestimate Shelby. I think you will be very surprised by what you find in the woman you've married."

Nikolai bent and kissed his mother's soft cheek. She always smelled sweet, and for a moment he was transported back to childhood and sitting in her lap, safe in the circle of her arms. He could honestly say that she had never misled him. She had held him often, through tears and laughter, and never once had she taken a joke so far that he mistrusted her.

Give yourself time, as much as you need, but don't underestimate Shelby.

As much as he wanted to act on his mother's words, Nikolai found himself asking God to work a miracle in his heart, certain beyond a doubt that this was the only answer.

Eight

"Murdock," his wife said to him as soon as she spotted him in the dining room. "Did the princess get the food I wanted to send with her?"

"Of course," Murdock answered quietly, thinking his wife was losing her senses; he would never forget such a thing.

"Good," she said complacently, setting the dishes down for the prince.

"Where was Shelby taking food?" Nikolai asked from his place at the table.

"To the lake house, sir," Murdock informed him. "She left this morning."

Nikolai didn't reply. He thanked Fran for dessert and went back to his eating. Fran left the dining room, not looking at her husband but knowing his eyes were on her. She exchanged a look with Arlanda as soon as she was behind the closed kitchen door, but neither woman dared to speak.

Another ten minutes passed before Murdock returned to the kitchen, and when he did, it did not escape his notice that his wife was too busy to speak to him or meet his eyes. She looked so adorable that he decided to drag her into the pantry for a scolding and a kiss, but the prince joined them.

"Murdock, I think I want you to ask my grandfather if we can take a week off from our Bible study."

"All right, sir. Is there anything else I can do?"

"Yes. Let Ivan know that I wish to go to the lake house tonight after my meeting. Tell him to get some rest if he needs to."

"I'll take care of it, sir."

Nikolai took himself from the room, and Murdock wasted no time in looking at his wife. The smile on her face was positively wicked.

"Francis Diane," he began but stopped and laughed.

"I told you last night," she said, coming close as she spoke, her eyes still sparkling. "Sometimes love needs a little help." She went on tiptoe to kiss him, and it was some time before he remembered he had to contact the king regent for the prince.

~

Shout for joy to the Lord, all the earth. Worship the Lord with gladness; come before him with joyful songs. Know that the Lord is God. It is he who made us, and we are his; we are his people, the sheep of his pasture. Enter his gates with thanksgiving and his courts with praise; give thanks to him and praise his name. For the Lord is good and his love endures forever; his faithfulness continues through all generations.

Early Saturday morning Shelby sat in a lounge chair on the deck and read the verses from Psalm 100. She had been rushing for more than a week and taking little time with her Bible study. She had learned long ago that strolling through Scripture would not feed her. She must dig and mine for the truths God had for her and take time to find passages to refresh and remind her of the great God who loved her.

The whole point of coming to the lake was to rest and take it easy for a few days, away from appointments and the telephone. This had been easier said than done. So married to her routine had she become that Shelby had woken before six and not been able to sleep again. Hoping not to disturb the staff, she pulled on shorts and a baggy T-shirt from her suitcase and went to the deck that overlooked the lake so she could study her Bible. The plan worked for a time, but the busy week was catching up. Feeling the effects of the early hour, Shelby pulled a light blanket over her shoulder and closed her eyes to pray. She was still sound asleep when the prince found her almost an hour later.

~

Shelby woke slowly and frowned at the waters of Lake Alston before remembering where she was. She stretched like a cat, groaning in pleasure, as she removed the kinks from her back and neck.

Watching her from another padded chaise, Nikolai remained quiet until she spotted him. As he had come to expect, she blushed.

"Good morning," he said, ignoring the blush and trying to dismiss the way she blinked at him and looked so uncertain. "Did you wake early?"

Shelby nodded. "It's such a habit, I guess." Her voice sounded croaky, and she swallowed. "Did you get in last night or this morning?"

"Last night. I didn't wake you?"

"No. I didn't hear a thing. Nikolai, did I take your bedroom?"

"At the lake house, everyone fends for himself."

"But the bed is so large. Maybe you would be more comfortable in my room."

"All the beds are large, and I'm fine, but thank you."

While Shelby watched, his gaze went to the water. He really was remarkably handsome, just like his father, but Shelby gained so little warmth from him. She knew he was trying, but they had a long way to go.

As she watched, a moment of pain seemed to cross his face.

His eyes narrowed, and his chest lifted in a sigh. Shelby wanted to look away—it seemed so private—but she kept on staring.

Where she got the courage to speak she did not know, but when he looked at her she said very quietly, "It looked as though you were thinking of Yvette just then."

Nikolai looked back at her. "I was. How did you know that?"

"I didn't know, not for certain."

Again Nikolai's gaze went back to the clear blue water of the lake. "She enjoyed this lake house. Her family lived on the Mediterranean, and she always loved seeing the water. Then there was a storm when we were staying here one night, and she never wanted to come back here alone."

"I'm not crazy about storms myself," Shelby told him. She glanced up at the house. "The wind would be scary against all those windows."

"A tree came through one of the windows in the living room. That about did her in," the prince said. His voice had dropped as he shared, and Shelby watched as tears came to his eyes. Shelby's own eyes were huge in an attempt not to join him.

"I didn't expect to feel this way," he said softly. "I came without thinking."

"Would you like us to leave?" Shelby offered, and Nikolai looked at her for a moment, working to stem his emotions. Shelby only looked back at him, her eyes full of understanding.

You're just as sweet as everyone says you are. Tell me, Shelby, do you ever put yourself first?

"No," Nikolai said at last, giving a small shake of his head. "I think it will do me good to stay, but thank you for offering."

Nikolai fell quiet then, and Shelby let him. They both still had their eyes on the lake when Colleen, the cook and housekeeper for the lake house, came to offer them coffee. This they enjoyed in silence as well.

Shelby's thoughts began to drift, and for a time she might

have been alone on the deck. When she did think to look over at her husband, she found him as he had found her: sound asleep.

~

"Okay," Shelby said, her eyes and voice intent. "Put a stick in this little tower and one here in this larger one. Now, what do you think?"

"This is the best sand castle in the whole world," the little boy on the beach informed her.

"I think you may be right, Monty. What else do we need?"

"Some water," Monty exclaimed, grabbing the bucket and heading toward the small waves that lapped at the shore. Shelby watched him with a smile on her face. He had told her he was five, and Shelby would have been concerned but took note of the fact that his babysitter never let him out of her sight. She had smiled at Shelby but kept her distance as the little boy asked the redhead on the beach if she wanted to play. What she wanted to do was fall asleep in the sun, but she took one look at his huge gray eyes and said yes.

"I've got the water. Now we can build more."

"All right. Where shall we add?"

The remodeling was just getting started when Monty spotted his sister.

"Oh look! Jenny's coming, and she's bringing the prince. Hi, Prince Nikolai. We're making a sand castle. Come play with us."

Monty threw himself at Nikolai when he was near, and the prince swung him up into his arms for a hug. Clearly the two were familiar.

"Hello," Shelby said to the little girl who had come with the prince. Shelby guessed her to be three or four years older than her brother.

"Hello," she said, smiling when Shelby met her eyes. "Are you the princess?"

"Yes. I'm Shelby. Did I hear Monty call you Jenny?"

The little girl nodded as she dropped to her knees in the sand. "It's short for Jennifer."

"I like that name."

"I like your hat," Jenny said, taking in Shelby's huge straw hat. "I have one, but I didn't wear it."

"I have to or I'll burn."

"My Aunt Lucy has red hair, and she burns whenever she comes to visit."

Nikolai had dropped onto the beach as well, his long legs curled to his side as he rested a palm in the sand. He had woken from his nap and found himself alone. His stomach had rumbled so he went in search of food, which he ate on the deck. That was when he'd spotted the hat on the beach. He had still been watching when Monty Stevenson joined her. Even with as little as he knew, it wasn't any surprise to him that she seemed to welcome the child's presence.

"Are you going to live here all the time now?" Monty asked hopefully as he dropped into Shelby's lap.

"No, just until Monday," she said as she put her arms around him, not seeming to care about the sand and moisture he was getting on her cotton dress. "But I think I'll visit again."

"We live here," Jenny informed her. "Our mother is going to have a baby, so sometimes we have to go to Grandma's, but when Misty babysits us we can stay here."

"Is your mother not feeling well, Jen?" the prince asked. It was the first comment he had made.

"She's real tired, and the doctor said she has to rest or the baby might be hurt."

Nikolai nodded but knew that the situation was probably much more complicated. He had known the Stevensons for many years and made a mental note to check on them.

"We need a king and queen," Monty declared suddenly. "We have to have a king for our castle."

"Go get your men, Monty!" his sister told him. "You know the ones."

"Okay. I can bring the cars too. We'll make a road."

Monty was off before anyone else could speak, and Misty told Jenny to stay put until they returned. Shelby and Jenny began to work the sand and talk. Nikolai helped as well, but what he did the most was watch Shelby. She knew she didn't look her best, but she didn't think he would be rude enough to scrutinize her for that. Not until Jenny scrambled off to get some water did he speak.

"Are your arms going to burn, Shelby?" he asked, noting that the rest of her was shaded with the hat or covered with her dress.

"I put sun block on," Shelby said, looking down at her arms for signs of pinkness and not finding any.

"What protection factor?"

"I think it's 50," she said as she dug into her bag. "Here it is. Maybe I should put some more on."

"That's probably a good idea."

For some reason the conversation and his concern dwelt in her mind for the rest of the day. They ended up eating lunch on the beach with the children and then disappearing inside to lie around with books. Dinner was informal but plentiful, and Shelby turned in early.

I can tell he's trying, Lord. He looks after my well-being, and I think that means he's trying to take this seriously. If I could just assure him that I don't have huge expectations of him—if I could just find a way to show him that he can be himself when he's with me . . .

The thought no more materialized than Shelby realized what she had prayed. Was it fair to ask God to help Nikolai act himself around her when she wasn't sure she was doing that with him?

How does a person stop blushing and get comfortable? was

Shelby's last question before she slept. She hoped by morning she would somehow have an answer.

~

Nikolai didn't bother with his jacket for breakfast, but he did come downstairs early on Sunday morning completely ready to attend church. The stairway was wide open to the living room below, so the prince was only halfway down when he spotted his wife. She was under a blanket, sleeping on the sofa. To give her privacy yet still be available, Kris had positioned himself by the kitchen door. Nikolai went to him.

"Is she not feeling well?"

"I think it was the storm. I heard a noise about 1:30 and came in to find her sitting on the sofa. She said something about the window breaking and not wanting to go back upstairs. She sat up for a good two hours before lying down and falling asleep."

Nikolai looked over at his wife. He approached quietly but reached for her shoulder as soon as he was near.

"Shelby," he whispered. "Are you all right?"

"Yeah," she said with a dry throat as she tried to open her eyes. "Is something wrong?"

"No. You fell asleep on the sofa. Do you want to go up to your bed?"

Shelby blinked at him and tried to focus. "Do you have a meeting?"

"No, I'm just ready for church early."

"Oh, that's right, it's Sunday. May I get ready and go with you?"

"Certainly. Are you up to it?"

"I think so."

She blinked and sat up, tugging her robe a little closer around her. Kris was no longer in the room, but she remembered speaking with him and had the impression that he had just been there. Shelby made a move to rise, and Nikolai moved from her way. She felt awful but thought that a hot shower might clear the webs.

"Take your time, Shelby," she heard Nikolai say as she mounted the stairs. "We don't need to leave for almost two hours." Shelby thought she might have waved but wasn't certain. All she wanted to do was get her eyes open and stay on her feet. She worked on this for the next 90 minutes and finally sat down at the kitchen table across from her husband, who was still reading the paper. He set it down and stared at her. She wore a mint green jacket and skirt; her blouse was white.

Shelby started on the coffee Colleen had set in front of her but was certain she knew what her husband was thinking. Finally she said, "I know, I know. I should go shopping this afternoon and fill these bags under my eyes."

Nikolai laughed. "Actually I was thinking that you don't look as though you've lost any sleep at all."

"Thank you," Shelby said succinctly, not sure she believed him.

"Did I scare you about storms up here?"

She took a thoughtful sip of coffee and said, "I'm not sure. I do know that I'm not at all crazy about storms, and when I woke and heard the rain and wind, I felt rather panicked. Somehow I thought it would be easier to be in the living room."

Again Nikolai watched her.

"You're doing that a lot lately," she gained the courage to say.

"What's that?"

"Staring at me."

"I'm sorry, Shelby, but I guess I'm a little amazed. You've been placed in such an unusual situation, but most of the time you seem so at ease."

Shelby gawked at him for an instant before bending her red face back over her cup.

Nikolai felt he learned a lot in those few seconds. She wasn't the type to rattle on or flap about when nervous. Her movements were totally composed, but she tended to blush. Did that mean she wasn't as calm as she appeared?

"I guess I just meant that you're very poised," Nikolai said, feeling he needed to explain. "I shouldn't have expected less, but somehow I did."

Shelby now understood. "I think any composure you might see comes with interpreting for my father on various occasions and being asked to stand in front of large groups of strangers."

"Was he deaf from birth? I can't remember if you've ever said."

"No. As a child he ran a very high fever, which resulted in his hearing loss."

"Can he hear anything?"

"No."

"How was that for you and your brother?"

"We've never given any thought to it. As you might expect, we learned to sign at an early age, and that's been the norm for as long as I can remember."

"Can you teach me some sign language?"

"Sure."

"All right. Teach me how to say something to your father the next time I see him."

"Okay. This is *how are you?* Do you want to try that?"

Nikolai didn't even hesitate. Shelby found he was a quick study, so much so, in fact, that if Ivan hadn't told them the day limo was ready, they might have been late for church. Once in the car they fell silent, each thinking about the time during breakfast, a time when they had both forgotten their reserve and been themselves. It would have been easy to speculate over the camaraderie they shared during breakfast, but neither was ready for such introspection.

Thankfully, both were able to put the morning behind them in time to concentrate on the service. The pastor of Lake Alston Community Chapel was preaching from the book of

1 John. Shelby's Bible study had been studying that book, so she listened carefully, thankful for the detailed outline he provided. She found it very helpful, and he covered two points that she was excited to share with her class. She was still writing when the service ended.

"You look as though you're afraid you're going to forget something," Nikolai mentioned quietly as he watched her.

"I am," Shelby answered as she finished writing. "We're studying these letters in my Bible class, and I want to tell the women a few things Pastor Bingham said."

"He would welcome any questions you have if something wasn't clear," Nikolai told her. "I've gone to him several times over the years, and he always takes time for me."

"I'll remember that. I think it's so special to come to the lake house and still have a chance for fellowship. Is there a service tonight?"

"Yes. Six o'clock. I usually attend."

"May I come with you?" Shelby asked softly, not wanting to push in or presume.

"Certainly," Nikolai said, thinking he wouldn't have turned her down for the world.

Shelby smiled up at him. Wanting to say thank you but thinking it might be insulting, she remained quiet.

"Ready to head back to the house?"

"Yes, I think I'm ready for lunch."

"You didn't eat breakfast, did you?"

Shelby shook her head no but didn't speak. They were acting so normal that for a moment she wasn't sure how to think. That they might eventually fall for each other had never actually occurred to her. The thought stayed with her all through lunch. She was still thinking about it when she stretched out on a deck lounger, a book in hand, and fell asleep before she could read two pages.

~

"How about we go out for lunch on the way home?" Nikolai asked Shelby the next morning. "There's a great restaurant in Upper Nave about an hour from here. We'll make it your birthday lunch."

"I would like that," Shelby told him with pleasure. "Is it dressy?"

"Not at all. I'll be in jeans."

Shelby followed suit, and just an hour after they left for Faraday, they pulled into the parking lot of The Bayside. The staff had called ahead for a reservation, and five minutes later the prince and princess were shown to a table on the open deck, a view of Princeton Bay and the Capetown Mountains spread out before them.

"Oh, Nikolai," Shelby breathed, "this is lovely."

"Not quite a picnic but still outdoors. We can shift around until you're in the sun or stay under the umbrella."

"I'm fine where I am. Thank you."

Nikolai watched her, waiting to see if she opened her menu, but she seemed in no hurry. Her eyes took in the mountains and then the water for long moments before she noticed him.

"I'm sorry," she said as she hurried to open the menu. "I'm daydreaming, and you must be hungry."

"Tell me something, Shelby. Do you ever take care of yourself, or do you spend all of your time looking after the needs of others?"

"You make me sound like a selfless individual, Nikolai, and I'm not," she said frankly. "Had I looked over and found you studying the water, I wouldn't have mentioned the menu, but I assumed because you were looking at me that you were waiting to order." Shelby tipped her head to one side and continued softly, "I don't know what your expressions mean, and I don't want to be a bother. I know I'm sounding selfless, but in truth, I'm still just a little afraid of making you angry. So you see, I'm really doing it for myself."

"Thank you for telling me," Nikolai said sincerely. "As a rule,

I don't anger easily. You'll have to learn that since I've shown you differently, but if you'll just keep being as honest with me as you were just now, it will go a long way toward our future."

"Are you ready to order, sir?" a waiter, who had just appeared, asked.

"I think we'll start with something to drink," Nikolai said smoothly, "but we'll need a little more time with our menus."

Shelby ordered a tall glass of iced tea, and Nikolai asked for lemonade. They studied the menus in silence—the selection was vast—and eventually found meals that sounded good.

"Do you know what surprises me?" Shelby suddenly asked.

"What's that?"

"How easy it is to live at the palace. I dreaded it," she admitted. "I felt I would have no privacy and do everything wrong, but no one makes me feel that way. I can come and go in the kitchen any time I like. One thinks of that kind of thing as being taboo, but it isn't."

"It probably is in some royal households, but not in Pendaran. You're right, Pendaran is different that way. I for one am quite glad about that."

"I couldn't agree with you more."

"Do you miss home?"

"Yes, especially not having contact with my parents on a daily basis. Other than my two years at school, I've always lived at home. I miss them."

"Do you go home much?"

"About once every two weeks, and I talk with my parents on the phone, but it's not the same."

"I felt the same way when I moved into the north quadrant. I was so lonely at first that I had dinner with my parents at least three times a week."

Shelby smiled. It was so hard to imagine him lonely or at a loss.

"What does that smile mean?" he asked, still watching her closely.

Shelby told him and watched him shake his head.

"You're as bad as I am, Shelby. I assume you've accepted all of this with complete aplomb, and you think I'm rock steady."

Shelby laughed a little at the accuracy of his description, but neither admitted to the other that he was thinking about the future, and that if events followed a logical course, they would both know each other well enough not to be in doubt about such things. The prince simply couldn't handle opening himself up that much at the moment, and Shelby, because she'd never shared such closeness with a man, could not imagine it. They both felt relieved when the waiter came to refill their drinks and take their orders.

Nine

"Good morning, Princess Shelby, it's Murdock."

"Good morning, Murdock."

"I hate to impose on you, but could you manage a haircut? We've come into a small emergency because I made a mistake on the schedule, and I would be most grateful for your help."

"I can come right now. Will that work?"

Shelby heard him sigh. "Indeed, Princess Shelby, right now would be perfect."

"I'll come down to the kitchen, shall I?"

"Actually, it would be easier if you cut the prince's hair in his bathroom. Would you mind?"

"No," Shelby answered automatically, but all expression went out of her voice.

"Very good. I'll call up and tell him to expect you in say, five minutes?"

"Yes," she again answered in a resigned monotone. "Five minutes."

Shelby hung up the phone and sat very still. They had certainly gained ground over the weekend, but cutting the prince's hair was not part of the bargain. She was still too uncomfortable around him for that.

"What if I cut his ear off?"

The sound of her own voice helped to shake off the trance. After taking a deep breath, she stood, made herself get her scissors and comb, and resolutely walked out the bedroom door. She knocked briskly, telling herself to buck up and to ignore her shaking knees. It worked until the prince opened his door wearing only a pair of black denim shorts.

"Thank you for coming, Shelby," the prince said as a greeting. "I appreciate it." He stood back so Shelby could enter, something she did on wooden legs.

"I washed my hair. Is it going to work to have it wet?"

"That's fine," Shelby said so quietly that Nikolai looked down at her. Her face was a bright red, and he watched as her eyes skittered to his chest and back across the room. There was no missing her discomfort, but he opted to ignore her bright features.

"I've got a chair in here," the prince began as he led the way. "If it doesn't make me high enough, I can call for a stool."

"I'm sure it will be fine," Shelby said without thought. Had she been thinking, she would have known it was perfect. The prince was many inches taller than she was, making things much more even if he was sitting down—something he did the moment he entered the bathroom.

Shelby looked at him, swallowed past a dry throat, and spoke. "Maybe you could tell me what you like."

"You can trim all over or just get the hair off my ears. I like it longer in the back."

Shelby nodded. She had certainly noticed this and also how attractive the prince's hair was, but she never planned to touch it. Telling her hands to stop shaking, she started in the front and worked her way to the sides. His hair was a dream to cut. Long before she reached the back, she was into her job. Her eyes on her work, she forgot he was the prince and simply enjoyed working with his hair, which was thick and black with just the right amount of wave. Shelby loved the way it curled softly on his neckline.

Nikolai was in another place entirely. He hadn't counted on the effect of having Shelby's hands in his hair. They hadn't as yet had any physical contact, and now her soft hands were touching his head and neck with the utmost care. Nikolai found himself wanting to touch her in return.

And all the time he watched her. If she was in front of him, his eyes were glued to her face. If she was on his side or in the back, he watched her in the mirror. Her brow lowered in concentration a few times, and she had a tendency to purse her lips, all of which he found very distracting. At one point she glanced into the mirror to find his eyes on her and lost her composure, nearly dropping the comb. After a moment she pulled her eyes away and continued. She ended up cutting his whole head and then looking at him with anxiety.

"Thank you, Shelby. It looks great," Nikolai said, coming to his feet and barely glancing in the mirror. There was no point in looking; he wouldn't have shown his disappointment even if he had hated the cut.

"Are you certain? Maybe I can do something more if you don't like it."

Nikolai forced himself to look into the mirror. His brows rose. It looked good, very good.

"It's perfect," he was able to tell her honestly, looking down to find her still watching him. Before he could change his mind, he bent and kissed her cheek.

She looked surprised but not flustered. Her eyes stayed on him for a moment before they dropped.

"Why don't I get a broom and sweep some of this hair up?"

"Because I need to get into the shower and be on my way to a Council meeting."

"I can come back when you're gone."

"It's all right, Shelby. This isn't as easy a place to cut hair as the kitchen porch, but Arlanda will see that someone cleans it up."

Shelby nodded, knowing this was to be expected. She moved out the bathroom door and back the way she had come.

"Are you returning to your room?" Nikolai asked as he followed her.

Shelby turned and nodded.

"Go this way," Nikolai said, moving to the door that joined their rooms. He turned the knob and held it open wide. "This will save you a few steps."

"Thank you."

"Thank *you*. I may never go back to my barber."

Shelby smiled at him as he shut the door with a wave. For a moment Shelby stood and simply stared at the closed portal.

Something is happening here, Lord. I don't know exactly what, but things feel different. I don't feel ready for intimacy with this man, but lately he watches me so much. Please don't let him ask too soon. Please don't let it be all physical so that I feel used. I don't expect a miracle, but if he's still so much in love with Yvette, don't let him say or do anything that will hurt me. Shelby stopped. Her prayer suddenly seemed very selfish. *What about Nikolai's needs, Shelby? Are you thinking of those? The Bible commands husbands and wives to come together so as not to fall into temptation. If your husband needs you physically, you need to be prepared for that.*

Shelby knew that was going to be easier said than done. They had spent so little time together. They had begun to talk more, but in so many ways he was still a stranger.

I'm starting to worry, Father, and I can't do that. Please don't bring it to pass before I'm ready, and help me to be ready whenever You bring it to pass. It was a prayer that Shelby prayed off and on the entire day.

"Oh, Shelby," the queen exclaimed, "you look lovely. This blue is wonderful on you."

"Thank you," Shelby replied, accepting the compliment and the hug. The king was next, putting his arms around her and hugging her close before he bent to kiss her cheek.

"You look nice too, Nicky," Erica teased her son, who was standing back and waiting for his parents to greet his wife.

"Thank you, Mother," he replied dryly as he hugged her close.

"I hope you're hungry, because dinner is ready and Maisie outdid herself. We're having grilled sole and orange pepper rice, and because she knew Shelby was coming, dessert is peach cobbler and cream."

"I'm starved," the king proclaimed before Shelby could even express her thanks.

The four adults took chairs at the dining table, and just as soon as the king returned thanks, the food began to appear. It started with a wonderful lettuce salad, filled with all types of garden greens and topped with a light oil dressing. Small cups of onion soup were next. To go with both the soup and the salad, melt-in-your-mouth rolls arrived nonstop.

Shelby dug in. She knew full well that the staff in the north quadrant could produce such delights, but so often she and the prince were gone. Shelby rarely ordered anything with more than two courses because it seemed a waste for one person. She had to admit, however, that this was delicious.

"How is everything?" the king asked. "I know Maisie will want to know if you were pleased."

"It's excellent, isn't it, Shelby?" her husband asked.

"Yes," Shelby agreed fervently. "I was just thinking that Fran is capable of producing the same delights and that Nikolai and I ought to stay home more often."

"Are you out most evenings, Shelby?" the queen asked.

"Yes. Not so much on weekends, but during the week it's

about four nights out of five. People ask so far in advance that I look at my clear calendar and think I'm completely free. Then the time rolls around, and I have nonstop appointments. I'm in the process of slowing down a little."

"You don't want to get tired," the king said with kind concern.

"No," Shelby agreed, glancing at her husband to see that he was smiling.

"I think we missed something," Erica observed.

"Shelby wishes she'd missed it too," Nikolai said rather dryly, and Shelby found she was able to laugh over this.

Dessert was served in the yellow parlor with coffee and wonderful, warm conversation. Shelby still felt shy around her husband, but the banter among the four of them was fast-paced enough to help her over the awkward moments. The evening was still in full swing when the king mentioned the fair.

"Three weeks from tomorrow," he told Shelby. "It's an annual event that runs from Saturday morning to Monday noon."

"I've read about the King's Fair, but I'm not sure of the schedule."

"We start with games for the children on Saturday morning followed by a big lunch. After lunch we have a skeet-shooting contest. There will be a concert after dinner on Saturday night, and we always take off on Sunday morning so we can get to church. Sunday afternoon is the tug-of-war before an early dinner in the evening. Monday morning we present the awards to all the winners of the games and go home after a big brunch."

"It sounds delightful," Shelby said honestly. "My brother has been on two tug-of-war teams. I'll have to tell him so he can come watch."

"Watch?" Nikolai sounded outraged. "If he can pull, we

need him. Toby always brings men who try to tear our arms out of their sockets."

"Would you really want him to participate?" Shelby asked in surprise.

"Of course. He's family now, and we need him. Father and I both pulled in school, but my uncles don't have a good grasp of the technique."

"And two of them are quite small," Erica added.

"So one team is family?" Shelby confirmed.

"Yes. Toby sets up a team that he pulls on, and so do Council members Royden and Lindell," the king went on. "It's the best two out of three pulls."

"I'd better get Brice's number from you, Shelby." Nikolai was taking a piece of paper from his pocket. "Or do you want to call and ask him?"

"You can ask him," she said, thinking it would be a nice surprise for her brother, who had had very little opportunity to speak with the prince. Shelby gave him the number and then listened as the conversation went back to the subject of the fair. After a moment it stopped making sense. The king had just said he would be making breakfast.

"You do the cooking?" Shelby asked.

"At the Palace Fair, yes."

"Oh, the Palace Fair. Is that soon too?"

"A week after the King's Fair. We used to schedule them farther apart, but the whole point is to give the staff a break. What could be better than that after they've worked so hard at the King's Fair?"

"The King's Fair is always the last weekend in September, Shelby. And the Palace Fair is the first Saturday in October."

"The Palace Fair is just one day?"

"The actual fair, yes, but the staff has off until Tuesday at noon."

"What can I do?" Shelby asked.

"Any of a dozen jobs. We'll be worked hard, but it's fun, and the staff and their families adore it," said the queen.

"Don't forget the children," Rafe reminded her.

"Oh, yes. Anton's mother does a magician's act. It's a scream. Her sleight of hand isn't as polished as it used to be, so she ends up turning it into a comedy routine."

Shelby's mouth was still open. "The queen mother?"

They laughed at her expression.

"Yes, as a matter-of-fact, she's so popular that she performs at both fairs," Rafe added.

"There's more," Nikolai continued. "My grandfather juggles soccer balls."

Shelby's eyes had grown to immense proportions. The three other family members all laughed hysterically at her.

"I won't need to do anything like that, will I?"

"Well," Nikolai surprised her by speaking up, "I think we could set up a hair-cutting booth. That would be fun for a change. You could just use your scissors all day and throw in a shave or two as well."

Shelby, not seeing the gleam in his eyes, fell for it hook, line, and sinker. She swallowed convulsively and nodded in the sweet way they'd come to expect.

"All right. I could try that if you think it will help."

"Oh, Nicky," the queen said with a soft voice, one that was lost on Shelby. Shelby's eyes were on the coffee table, and she appeared to be lost in intense thought. She actually jumped a little when Nikolai reached over and took her hand. Shelby's eyes came to him.

"I'm teasing you," he said softly, his eyes contrite. "You don't have to do anything you don't want to do."

Shelby nodded, her face going red even as she realized how soft and warm his hand felt on hers. She forced herself not to look down on the sofa between them, but his hand felt very nice. He held hers until his mother offered him a warm-up of his coffee. With the teasing incident behind them, the conversation moved on, but Shelby felt the pressure of Nikolai's hand on her own for some hours to follow.

~

"We certainly enjoyed having you and Shelby dine with us on Friday night," Rafe told Nikolai on Monday morning. Council had not been called into session yet, and the two men had just had breakfast with King Regent Anton.

"We enjoyed it too."

"Shelby was as relaxed as I've ever seen her."

"Yes, she was. It was better before I teased her about cutting hair."

"I think she took it all right," the king said. "She still blushes easily, that's for certain."

Rafe watched Nikolai's face for a moment. He had nodded in agreement but then looked rather pensively across the room.

"How are *you* doing, Nick?"

Nikolai sighed and answered without looking at his father. "How can I still miss Yvette and yet be drawn to Shelby?"

"Because Shelby is here and needs you. Yvette doesn't."

Nikolai turned and stared at his father. It was said so simply, but it was also glaringly on target. Yvette didn't need him anymore; it was time to face that fact. Shelby, on the other hand, needed him very much, and Nikolai was never more aware of that than at this moment.

"Does that help issues, Nick, or just make them more painful for you?" the king asked.

"I think it helps. I'm feeling things I didn't know were possible. I don't love Shelby, but I do care. I care if I think she's going to get a sunburn or if she isn't getting enough rest or time with her family."

"That's where love begins, Nick. I felt as though I loved your mother the moment I set eyes on her, when in reality I was probably just infatuated. When I learned she had the flu and I couldn't get her from my mind, I knew that the initial feelings, whatever they were, were going deeper."

"I care if I think she's afraid, especially of me," Nikolai continued, almost as if Rafe hadn't spoken. "I want the staff to give her extra care but also for her to feel free to come and go as she pleases. I find myself lying in bed at night sometimes wondering if she's all right. She's on my mind so much lately, and when I see her, I just want to stare."

"May I give you a word of advice, son?"

"Yes. Anything."

"Don't fight it, Nick. If you're falling for your wife, allow yourself the privilege and enjoy it. Romance and court your wife until she feels all the tenderness, support, and security your love will bring to her."

Nikolai looked at his father again, seeing him with new eyes. He knew his father was passionately in love with his mother, but he tended to be a nuts-and-bolts type of man. There was no denying the fact, however, that Nikolai had just heard him say "romance and court your wife."

"Thank you, Father." Nikolai smiled at him, his heart feeling a bit lighter. "I don't know how I'm going to go about this, but I won't know unless I try."

Rafe's brows rose. "Considering how distracted Shelby was after you held her hand on Friday night, I think you'll be able to come up with something."

A soft chime sounded down the hallway. The time had slipped away from them; Council was starting. Without another word, both men exited the king's Council Building office and moved to the Council chamber. At least for the moment, Nikolai and Shelby's relationship had to be placed on hold.

~

The evening was progressing as it usually did. Shelby was at an evening function, dressed in one of her many stunning gowns and surrounded by people who wanted to speak to her. Some of them she knew and others she had only just met. There was one major difference this evening: Nikolai was with her.

Dinner was over, and the dance would be starting soon. Shelby hoped with all of her heart that her husband would remember to come and claim her for at least one dance. So far no one had asked her for the first dance, something that had never happened before. She thought there might be rules about this. Maybe the only reason she'd been asked before was because the guests knew she was on her own.

The first strands of a waltz started up just then, and everyone turned toward the floor. Their host and hostess, Major and Mrs. Walker, walked to the middle of the ballroom floor and danced for several minutes before the orchestra leader gave a signal for everyone to join in. Shelby was not left standing alone, but the women in her group were silent as the floor filled up. Shelby kept her eyes on the dancers. She didn't think anyone would cast a pitying look in her direction, but if they dared, she might be tempted to say something unkind.

If Nikolai doesn't come to dance with me, he has a good reason. After all, there's more to life than balls and parties. People are much more important, and if someone here should fail to recognize this, well it's not my—

"I'm sorry I'm late." Nikolai was suddenly beside her, taking her hand and leading her onto the floor. "I was tied up in a conversation, and the music started before I realized."

Shelby didn't speak. All she could do was look up at him.

"Are you all right?"

"Yes," she said softly, not sure it was true. It was the silliest thing in her mind, but she suddenly felt he'd rescued her by coming to dance with her. The last time they had done this had been at the King's Ball, and she'd been terrified of him. For a moment she tried to speculate on the change.

Knowing this was not the place to press her, Nikolai wondered if she was really all right. He simply pulled her a bit closer as they danced. He had never known anyone whose eyes seemed like mirrors to the soul. At times he thought Shelby looked like a child, lost and alone. At other times he saw her capable and strong, not seeming to need anything or anyone. But the woman he saw most often was just Shelby—sweet, unassuming, intelligent, talented, and caring Shelby. His wife.

The music ended just then. Nikolai clapped with everyone else, but he took Shelby's hand for the next dance as soon as his hands were free. Again he held her closer than was needed for the dance, and with the way she looked up at him, he was certain she noticed.

"Are you having a good time?" he asked.

"Yes. How about you?"

"I am, thank you."

"I forgot to ask, Nikolai, but how do you know the major?"

"His brother was in school with my father, and I went to school with his nephew. As a matter of fact, the major's brother was just telling me about Mark—that's his son—and how he's living in the United States these days."

"Where in the U.S.?"

"California."

"I've been to New York."

"Have you really?"

"Yes. On a school trip."

"What was it like?"

"Interesting but hot. It was summertime, and I thought we would all melt. The sights were spectacular, but the traffic and crowds were a little hard to take. It's difficult for me to believe that not all of America is like that."

"Pendaran spoils us—it's so small and consistent."

"It didn't feel small to me until I visited New York and realized that our whole country is smaller than that one state. To think of the rest of the United States stretching out for thousands of miles was a bit overwhelming."

"You were glad to get home?"

"Tremendously. The flight was long and tiring. I guess I'm not much of a traveler. By the time I sit in the car for the two hours to the lake house, I have ants in my pants."

Nikolai smiled.

"What did I say?"

"I just haven't heard the phrase in years," Nikolai admitted, "but my grandmother used to say it to me all the time."

"Were you a rambunctious child?"

"I could be, but I also liked to read. I could disappear into a book for hours. I still can."

"If I recall from your letters, you like the classics."

"You have a good memory. Did I ever ask you what you like to read?"

"I don't think so. I like history but also an occasional romance."

"I don't mind a romance myself. I've read all of Jane Austen."

"What was your favorite?"

"*Persuasion.*"

The dance ended the moment after Shelby said, "Mine too."

Nikolai let her go, because his father came to request her hand, but he told her he would be back and to reserve the last dance. Shelby nodded without speaking, seemingly as composed as any woman could be. If she were questioned, however, on half of what her father-in-law was saying to her, she would have failed miserably.

Ten

Shelby sank into the rear seat of the limo and stifled the sigh that threatened to escape her. Had she been alone, she would have felt free to express herself, but Nikolai's presence—he had climbed in on the other side—held her in check. Nevertheless, that didn't stop the ache in her feet or the hollowness of her stomach. She certainly hoped she could raid the kitchen without waking anyone as soon as she got home.

"Did you have a good time?" Nikolai asked out of the darkness.

"Very much. The major's daughter knows my father, and I didn't realize that until we had talked for some time."

"She's a fascinating woman. I don't know if there's a country she hasn't visited."

"She told me about some of them."

"How does she know your father?"

Shelby chuckled. "He cuts her hair when she's home."

"You're kidding."

"No. She's been to hairdressers all over the city and finally found my father in Henley. She misses him dreadfully when she's abroad."

Nikolai was still chuckling when he noticed something

odd. Not having ever cared to use the phone in the limo, he hit the button and lowered the window.

"Ivan?"

"Yes, sir?"

"Can you tell me where we're going?"

"Burger Haven, sir, to pick up some food for the princess."

"Oh no, Ivan," Shelby spoke up, her face heating instantly. "We can go home."

"Did the princess ask you to stop?" Nikolai questioned. He wasn't upset, just remarkably curious.

"No, sir. Hank informed me."

Shelby was rattling on again, but both men ignored her.

"Do as Hank asked," the prince said quietly and put the window up, at the same time putting an end to the conversation.

She thought she was beyond this horrible blushing, but right now she couldn't speak or even look in Nikolai's direction. There was so much he didn't know. There were so many little things the staff did for her, and for some reason, his learning of the way they spoiled her was mortifying to her. It didn't lessen when she felt the car come to a halt and knew that Ivan was getting out and coming around to see her. She still hadn't looked at her husband when the chauffeur opened her door.

"The usual, Princess Shelby?"

"Yes, please," she said softly, hoping just to get it over with.

"Anything for you, Prince Nikolai?"

"Some fries sound good, Ivan, and maybe an orange drink."

"Very good. I'll be right back."

"I'm sorry, Nikolai," Shelby said softly, just as soon as the door was shut.

"Why are you sorry?"

"Because you must want to get home."

He was silent for almost a minute, his eyes on her profile. Shelby could feel his gaze but didn't shift her own.

"You're too hard on yourself, Shelby. If you were hungry and the staff didn't see to your needs, that would be something to be upset about."

Shelby nodded but still kept her eyes averted. She might as well have told Ivan not to bother; she didn't think she could eat a thing.

Why does it feel this way? Why do I think the staff spoils only me and that Nikolai would be angry? Surely they must spoil him as well. They've known him years longer. Some of them probably watched him grow up.

"I had a long conversation with your brother today," Nikolai said conversationally, breaking neatly into Shelby's tortured thoughts.

"Brice?"

"Yes," Nikolai said on a chuckle. "How many brothers do you have?"

"Five!" she said defiantly, feeling tired of trying never to be a bother to him.

"Well, let's hope they all want to pull."

"Does Brice?"

"Yes. He sounded quite pleased to be asked and even wanted to know the practice days and times. I'm not sure whether he's made up his mind to like me yet, so maybe this will help."

"Why would you say such a thing?" Shelby asked as her head turned swiftly. "Did he say something to you?"

"No, but I get the impression that the jury's still out where I'm concerned."

Nikolai had been watching her and saw her mouth open in surprise.

"I take it you haven't said anything."

"Of course not! If Brice has been rude to you, Nikolai, I must know about it."

"He hasn't. Not in the least. But I did steal the sister, whom

I suspect he adores, and I'm not certain he thinks me worthy of her."

Shelby relaxed a little. She had also gotten that impression from Brice, but just one time. It had been at her birthday celebration, and it had been so fleeting that Shelby thought she had imagined it. She didn't think her brother had been discourteous, but she now understood what Nikolai was speaking of.

"I'm glad he wasn't rude to you. I would be surprised if he had been, but I would still expect him to apologize."

"There is no need."

"Were you rude to him?" she asked before she thought.

"I hope not," Nikolai said with some surprise. "Why did you ask that?"

Shelby shrugged, but for just a moment he'd sounded so lordly and superior that she wondered if he hadn't put her brother on the defensive.

"You didn't answer me," Nikolai said out of the darkness.

"I shrugged," Shelby told him, but her voice said more—it said that was all he was going to get out of her right now.

Nikolai watched her until their food came. He honestly hadn't seen the shrug. The only thing that was illumined in the deep recesses of the limo was one side of her face, a face that was turned in profile to him.

They ended up not speaking while they ate, but Shelby was no longer tense. She was a little angry at herself, but only because it seemed that all she did these days was try to act as though everything were fine.

Where is the balance? she prayed as she finished the last of her burger and shake, a combination she'd found herself hungry for the moment Ivan handed it to her. *I need to be the woman this man needs, but I'm not myself when I'm around him. I'm not given to impulsive speech or actions, but I'm almost afraid to speak at all. It's not fair of me to think he might have been impolite to my brother. I have no solid reason to accuse him of that.*

"Thank you, Ivan," Shelby said. It was nice to have her thoughts interrupted by their arrival back at the north quadrant. Ivan had opened the door, and because it was late, she headed inside with the intent of retiring. The plan worked until she was in the green parlor on the way to her bedroom door. She was on the verge of saying goodnight when her husband spoke.

"May I ask you a question, Shelby?"

Shelby turned to him, her feet throbbing. "I'm rather tired," she admitted.

"I don't think it will take long."

Shelby nodded.

"Did you not enjoy the food at the party tonight?"

"What I had was delicious, but it's hard to eat when so many people have questions."

Nikolai blinked. This had never occurred to him. His head tipped as he asked, "What do they want to know?"

"Oh, the usual. Where did I grow up? How did I meet the prince? Are my parents alive? That type of thing."

"What do you say about meeting me?"

"That it was through your parents."

Nikolai just barely kept his mouth closed. There was so much he wanted to say, so much more he wanted to know, but her fatigue was obvious now, and unless he missed his guess, the almost constant shifting of her feet meant they hurt.

"Thank you for telling me," he said simply. "Sleep well, Shelby."

"Thank you," Shelby said, too tired to add anything else.

Nikolai would have been pleased to know that she did sleep well, and almost as soon as her head hit the pillow. His night wasn't quite so restful.

～

To look at the prince on Sunday morning, his gaze intent on his wife, no one would suspect that he had stood in front of Yvette's picture that morning and cried.

Never had his heart been in such a quandary. Never had he been so confused and unsure of himself. His new wife was lovely, poised, and talented. Why then did he feel that she desperately needed him? And not just that—he was beginning to desperately need her in return. He felt different, comforted somehow, when she was around. He knew she was angry with him at times, but even then he wanted to be near.

He realized suddenly that he had been watching his wife but not really listening to the words she was signing for Pastor Allen. He turned his mind toward the sermon, and just in time.

"I remember the first time it occurred to me that anxiety was a sin. I was a teen at camp, and the speaker was telling about when he'd come to Christ. He had wrestled and fought against the Lord for years, and when he finally came to Christ, his children wanted nothing to do with him. One went so far as to pack his bags and move out.

"I remember sitting there as the man described the scene. The 18-year-old son went storming from the house, his father going after him and trying to speak with him, but the young man would have none of it. The father was forced to stand and watch as his son threw his bag into the back of his car and tore down the street with enough speed to kill someone, maybe himself. The speaker said he stood there and felt worry crowding in but made himself stop. I'll never forget his words. 'In my newfound faith I knew that worry was a sin. I had no choice but to give my son to God, even if I never saw him again.'

"There I sat," Pastor Allen went on, "just a teen mind you. But even in my youth I asked God how that could be. I sat there and said, 'Not even then, Lord? Not even when someone I love might be hurt? Do You mean I can't *ever* worry?' I remember my heart crying out those words to the Lord. You see, I had been worrying myself sick over college. How would I pay for it? Should I sell my car? Should I attend now or save for a while?"

The pastor paused and looked out at all of them. "I saw that day that worry was a sin. Our text here in Matthew 6, Jesus' own words, makes that perfectly clear, but I hadn't read my Bible very much at that time. After that experience at camp, I dug deeply and learned that when it comes to worry, God is very serious.

"When we worry we say to God, 'I can't trust You. You're not doing Your job, so I'm going to step in and take over.' We can't just call that arrogance and foolishness—it's sin."

Nikolai's eyes had been closed for some time, but he was still listening. For weeks now he had done nothing but worry about his relationship with Shelby. He opened his eyes and watched Shelby as she signed these next words.

"God is able to bear all that you are fretting about. He has made a plan. He has made provision. There are no shoulders larger or more capable than His. Give that worry, whatever it is, to God."

Help me to do this, Father. Help me to give Shelby to You. I believe as my parents do that this marriage was the right thing for us, so I know You will work this as well. I know she doesn't know what to do with me at times, just as I'm at a loss with her. Help me to give of myself and help Shelby to give of herself as well. Work in both our hearts, and help me to believe that no matter how far we have to go, You'll be with us every step of the way.

The service was coming to an end. They stood for the closing prayer, and Shelby was already headed his way. They sat closer to the front when she interpreted, and he had noticed that she liked to be back in her seat by the time the service ended. He was beginning to enjoy the familiarity of opening his eyes to find her standing next to him.

"Tell me something, Shelby," Nikolai said almost immediately as he turned to her. "Do you get as much out of the sermon when you sign it?"

"No, but Pastor Allen allows me to keep the notes, so I'll go over them this week."

"And what do you do if something isn't clear to you?"

She looked uncertain and then shrugged. "I just hope he'll cover it the next week."

"I hope you'll check with me," Nikolai said with quiet modesty. "I can't promise to help, but if I'm in the dark too, maybe we can find out together."

"All right," she agreed, her heart pounding a bit. "Nikolai?"

His brows rose in expectation.

"It's terribly late notice—I mean, I should have said something to you before now—but my mother's birthday is tomorrow, and we're going out to dinner." Shelby came to a painful halt and swallowed once. "You probably have plans," she continued with a red face. "I'm sorry I neglected to ask you sooner."

"Did you say tomorrow night?"

Shelby nodded.

"I do have something on the calendar, but I'll do my best to get out of it."

Shelby blinked. "You would do that?"

"For your mother's birthday? In a flash."

Shelby was speechless.

"What time will you go?" Nikolai asked, sorry that she was so shocked by his courtesy.

"Um . . ." Shelby answered foolishly, every logical thought flying out of her head.

Nikolai couldn't stop his smile as he said, "Do you want to let me know about the time?"

Shelby felt rescued when she had only to nod. The church was clearing out as they left, but several people still stopped them for conversation. By the time they got to the day limo, Shelby's brain had kicked back into gear.

"I'm leaving for Henley at five," she told Nikolai. "It's pretty casual, and we'll leave for the restaurant as soon as I arrive."

"I'll try to go with you, but maybe you should give me the name of the restaurant in case I run late."

"We'll be at the Electric Company. Do you know it?"

"Yes. My mother went to school with the owners."

"Should I have invited your parents?" Shelby asked, suddenly thinking she'd been remiss.

"Did your mother want you to?"

"She only asked me about you."

"Then don't worry about it. I can assure you my parents won't give it a thought."

Shelby nodded, trying to take in his advice.

"What are you giving your mother?"

"Oh, I haven't found anything yet. I've plans to shop tomorrow."

"What will you look for?"

"A book probably, and maybe a nice blouse or jewelry."

"Sounds as though she likes everything."

"She does, and she won't make a list or even hint. She likes to be surprised."

"How about you, Shelby—do you like surprises?"

"Only if I know the surpriser very well. One day the women at the hospital surprised me for my birthday," she said as she gave a small shudder. "I blushed for an hour."

Nikolai's head went back as he laughingly said, "And of course blushing is the worst thing you can do."

"You can only use that teasing tone because you've never been embarrassed."

"Oh no, I've never been embarrassed. I'm just the man who tried to introduce himself to the redheaded woman sitting in the kitchen, only to learn she was my wife."

"I'd forgotten about that."

"I never will."

Shelby turned her head to look at him, and Nikolai did the same to look at her. For several moments they studied each other. Shelby, a little confused by what she saw, was the first to look away. She was surprised when Nikolai's large hand cupped her jaw and brought her eyes right back to his. Shelby watched as he opened his mouth to speak, hesitated, and removed his hand.

"I'll talk to you a little later," he said softly, turning his gaze to the front.

But he didn't. Shelby didn't see Nikolai again until they left for evening church, and although she waited for him to mention the incident, he never did.

~

"Happy birthday, Daria," Nikolai said as he shook his mother-in-law's hand. "I'm sorry I'm late."

"We haven't even ordered, Nick," she assured him warmly. "Please sit down."

"Thank you," Nikolai replied as he shook Brice's hand and signed a few words to Josiah, who smiled in delight. He had no more than taken his chair when a waiter arrived and spoke to Josiah and Daria; Nikolai took a moment to address his wife.

"I told Ivan to leave because you have your car. May I have a ride back to the palace?"

"Certainly," she told him easily enough, but her eyes dropped to the way he spilled over the small wooden chair. "It's not a big car," she felt a need to add.

Nikolai's eyes twinkled, and for the first time he tried a flirtation. "Afraid I'll be too close?" he asked softly.

Shelby's face was glowing in a matter of moments.

"Well, Red," Brice prodded from her other side, "want to share?"

"Red?" Nikolai asked, his brows rising nearly into his hairline. "Did you call her Red?"

Brice smiled wickedly. "Don't tell me you haven't noticed."

Nikolai turned very amused eyes to his wife, whose own eyes were telling her brother that he was in for it.

"Red." Nikolai tested the name. "I like it. It fits you very well."

Shelby refused to look at him. She was still blushing and decided the menu needed her attention.

The waiter left for a moment, and Daria turned her gaze to the young people at the table. Her son and son-in-law were on the verge of laughter, and her daughter's face was buried in her menu.

"Something tells me you two are in trouble," Josiah spoke up, having noticed as well.

"I'm getting ready to flatten Brice," Shelby, setting the menu aside, informed her father quite calmly.

Nikolai laughed when Josiah smiled.

"Actually," Daria inserted, "it wasn't that long ago that she could."

"Come on, Mom," Brice teased, "it's been at least six weeks."

"Yes," Shelby said in a low voice, "Brice has even been dressing himself for two whole months now."

Nikolai saw Brice's hand move but didn't know the intent until his wife jumped from the pinch she'd received. Shelby's own hand moved, but Brice caught it in both of his. As though everything were completely normal, he began to speak to Nikolai.

"What time do you need me on the thirtieth?"

"We don't pull until two on Sunday, but you're welcome to come for the entire weekend. In fact," he continued, turning to his in-laws, "you're all welcome to stay at the palace. Henley isn't a long drive, but we'll have many guests, and it's a very fun time."

"We'll plan on it," Josiah wasted no time in saying.

"Great," Nikolai responded, meaning it. "I think you'll have a good time."

"What else goes on besides the tug-of-war?" Brice asked as he let go of his sister's hand.

While Nikolai answered, Shelby put her hands in her lap and worked to pull her emotions under control. Why did it bother her that her husband was getting on so well with her family? Wasn't that what she wanted?

I'm crabby right now, Lord, and I don't even know why. There is always so much to thank You for, but I'm being a grouch. Thank You that Nikolai was willing to change his plans to be here tonight. Thank You that he's making such an effort. Help me not to be afraid of the change in him. That this was the crux of the matter did not occur to Shelby until she uttered the words to God. The concept took her by surprise, even as she realized she was going to have to deal with it.

It was a relief to have the waiter come back for their orders. For the moment Shelby put her tumultuous thoughts aside and tried to remember that this was her mother's birthday.

～

Daria had loved her gifts, a mystery novel and small spray bottle of her favorite cologne, and although Shelby had prayed almost constantly, she was still a bit disgruntled when she and Nikolai exited the Electric Company and made for her car. It never occurred to her to ask Nikolai if he wanted to drive. Shelby unlocked her door, hit the unlock button so Nikolai could get in, climbed in herself, and started the engine.

In a matter of moments Nikolai was shown yet another side of his wife's personality. A confident, almost aggressive driver, she shifted with the ease of breathing and launched into traffic like a racecar driver. Nikolai was crammed rather tightly into the passenger seat, or he would have held onto something.

"Have you had this car long?" he asked to take his mind off the way she zipped through traffic as though she'd lived in the capital city her entire life.

"Two years."

"A friend of mine has a car something like this, but it's black."

"I don't like black," Shelby told him honestly but was immediately sorry for her tone. To make up for it she asked, "Do you have a car you drive much?"

"No. I've been driven all my life and never gained much of

an interest." The last word escaped on a small gasp as Shelby avoided a truck that stopped suddenly.

"I love to drive," she volunteered as she changed to a lower gear and the car shot up the long drive to the palace. To Nikolai's amazement, Shelby did not stop at the front door but scooted around their home to the car barn.

"Has Murdock told you that the staff will put your car away for you?"

"He has, but everyone already spoils me to death, and I think this is the least I can do."

Nikolai fell silent as she brought the car to a halt. He had to bend nearly double to get his legs out from under the dash and emerged to see that his wife had not waited for him. His long-legged stride made it easy to catch her, but other than thanking him for holding the door, she spoke not a word.

Nikolai was on the verge of asking her about the silence when her almost irritated pace slowed. She was crawling along when she spoke his name.

"Nikolai?"

"Yes?" he replied softly.

"I was crabby at you when we drove home, and I'm sorry."

"Thank you, Shelby. May I ask you a question?"

"Yes."

"Did I do something?"

"No," she said so softly that Nikolai had a hard time believing her.

"You're sure?" Nikolai tried again.

Shelby kept walking but didn't answer. They were to the green parlor now, and Nikolai, afraid she would just keep walking, caught her hand.

Shelby looked up at him.

"Why were you crabby?" he asked quietly, his eyes more than his voice telling her he wanted to know.

Shelby swallowed and admitted, "I'm angry at both of us. My own brother had things to talk to you about, but when I'm with you I can't find ten words. I know you're trying, and I'm trying too, but when my own family seems to have more common interests with my husband than I do, it bothers me more than a little."

"I'm glad you told me. I've been asking the Lord about this very thing."

"What exactly?"

"How to get to know you and have you know me."

Shelby softened on these words, and her face revealed this.

"What did I just say?"

"That you want me to get to know you."

"You thought otherwise?"

"Yes, but I understood why you might not."

"Thank you for that, but this marriage is going to be empty and lonely if we don't work on the walls that divide us."

Shelby only nodded, but she could have told him that her marriage was already a lonely place for her. She hadn't expected it to be so, but it was. At the same time, she was afraid to let him get any closer. It was the most complicated situation she had ever been a part of.

She was very glad when, just moments later, Nikolai wished her a good night, and she could go alone to her room. She had quite a bit to think about.

Eleven

"Have I missed Shelby?" Nikolai asked the next morning as he walked into the kitchen.

"She hasn't been here yet," Fran told him, "and unless she's not hungry this morning, she should be here soon."

"How often is she not hungry?"

Fran's head tipped to one side in thought. "Maybe once a month, twice at the most."

Nikolai nodded and took a seat. The newspaper was already waiting for his wife, but Nikolai did not pick it up. His mind was too busy working out how many months they had been married. The way Fran said it made him feel as if he'd lost track. A few mental calisthenics told him it would be five months on the day of the King's Fair. When he felt Yvette's absence keenly, it felt much longer. When he thought of how little he knew his present wife and how far he had to go, it seemed but days.

"I'm starving," Shelby announced as she came sailing through the kitchen door and right for Fran. She put a companionable arm around her shoulders and said, "What can I have in about four seconds?"

"Ham-and-egg quiche, cereal, or muffins."

"Can I have all three?" she asked playfully as she turned and saw Nikolai. "Hi," she said with soft surprise.

"Good morning. You sound hungry."

"I am. I don't know why after that big meal last night, but I'm starved," Shelby said as she sat opposite him and tried not to touch her heated face. Without looking at him, she poured herself a small bowl of cereal but didn't add the milk because Fran set a hot piece of quiche in front of her at the same time.

Nikolai watched her pray and then thanked Fran for his own warm plate that held a piece of quiche and two muffins. He waited only until Shelby picked up her fork before speaking.

"Did you tell me last night that you don't care for the color black?"

Shelby nodded and said nonchalantly, "It's never been my favorite."

"So you don't mind it?"

Shelby's head tipped. "I can live with it, I guess." She took a bite of food, completely unaware of where this was headed.

"Your entire room is black," Nikolai said, watching her grow very still.

Shelby licked her lips. She had been in such a bad mood the night before and now saw that she had let her tongue run away.

"That's true," Shelby said softly.

"Would you have decorated it that way had it been your choice?"

Shelby wanted to hedge and say "probably not," but that would have been a lie. She forced herself to shake her head no.

"Did no one tell you that you can redecorate to your heart's content?"

"Yes, I knew that, but—" Shelby stopped. How could she say this and not hurt or upset him? She had to make herself go on. "Nikolai, I thought Yvette decorated my room."

She hadn't been looking at him but now glanced up to see his look of surprise and then recovery.

"And you thought it would upset me to see the room changed?"

Shelby nodded, feeling miserable.

"I appreciate that, Shelby, I honestly do, but the truth of the matter is that my grandmother did that room. When my parents lived here, they shared my room, as did Yvette and I. My mother isn't that crazy about black, but her own mother loves it. She left it that way because her mother had liked it. My mother would be vehement about your changing it if you don't like black, and I would agree with her. Change the room, Shelby—do anything you want with it."

Shelby nodded and thanked him softly before making herself go back to her food. She was still hurting inside from realizing how lonely her marriage was, and now to be reminded that at least two couples had not even needed her room but had been happy to share one bedroom was like salt in an open wound.

"What will you do with it?" Nikolai asked as he started on his own meal.

"I'm not sure. I might ask my mother for some ideas. She's good with that type of thing."

Shelby was glad that Nikolai only nodded and continued to eat. She didn't want to talk about this. She didn't have time right now to think about redecorating. Indeed, having her bedroom and sitting room torn apart was the last thing she wanted at present.

The royal couple managed to talk during breakfast, but Shelby could feel the strain in herself. They shared the paper, and she smiled and laughed in all the right places, but just as soon as she was able, she left the room. She didn't need to leave for an appointment for more than two hours, but she still felt a need to escape. She lasted only about 20 minutes before she went back to the kitchen, intent on finding Nikolai and asking him if he had noticed her unsettledness at breakfast. He was gone. Murdock informed her that he'd gone out to the skeet area. Shelby was forced to go to her appointment, not certain whether she needed to apologize or not.

⁓

"Of all the cookies you've made me, this batch of cookies was my favorite," the queen mother told Shelby the following morning. "I think I could have one of these every day."

"Well, do, and when you run out I'll make more."

"It's a deal," she said in her elderly voice, her eyes, still quite bright, smiling at Shelby where she sat holding the photo album. "Now this," she said, her bent finger pointing, "is Rafe. You probably recognize him. And this little head at the edge of the picture is Nicky."

"Where are they?"

"They're skeet shooting."

Shelby only nodded, but the queen mother was the second person in two days to mention skeet shooting, and she was becoming curious. She knew nothing about it, only that it was scheduled to be part of the competition at the King's Fair.

The queen mother sat next to Shelby on the deep sofa and watched her profile. That she had lost the younger woman was evident, and as she was tired, she let the silence linger.

I don't believe we've ever had a redheaded king, she told the Lord. *I do hope it will be a boy, tall and strong like Nicky. But You know me well, Father; I'll gladly take a great-great granddaughter.*

"Queen Miranda," said Beckett, who suddenly appeared at the door. "Your son is here. May he join you?"

"Of course," the queen mother said with a smile.

"Am I interrupting?" Anton asked as he entered the room.

"Not in the least. Come and sit with us."

Anton kissed his mother and granddaughter-in-law and then took note of what they were doing.

"A walk down memory lane?" he asked with a twinkle in his eye.

"Indeed." The queen smiled right back. "Shelby is the only person I've ever known who doesn't tire of old family photos or slides from vacations."

Anton laughed, but he could see that his mother was flagging. Shelby probably didn't know her well enough to recognize the signs. He knew he must keep his visit short and somehow take Shelby with him when he left.

"I'm here about the King's Fair, Mother," he wasted no time in saying. "Did you remember that it's coming up soon?"

"I did. I had my locking rings out last night to see if I could do a little something with them."

"How did it go?"

"Fine for a few minutes, but my arms tired quickly."

"In that case I think I have good news for you. Toby's neighbor does magic tricks. He's 11 and a rather somber child, but very intelligent and respectful. I thought the two of you could figure out a way to work together."

"Would we need to meet today?"

"No, I can see that you're tired," Anton came right out and said. "If you're interested, I'll ask him to come in the morning."

"Good," the old queen replied. "Do that. I'll look for him about nine, shall I?"

"Yes. Shelby and I will go now and let you rest, and if you change your mind about the morning, you need only call."

"Anton, what's the boy's name?"

"Peter. Peter Owens."

"And you say he's 11?"

"Yes."

The old woman nodded and smiled before putting a hand on Shelby's arm. "Thank you for coming, my dear. We'll visit again soon."

Shelby smiled as she leaned to kiss the well-seamed cheek that smelled of wisteria. Anton rose when she did, and the two made their way from the west quadrant.

"I didn't know she was tired," Shelby admitted softly. "I'm sorry."

"She hides it very well," Anton said sternly of his mother. "She shouldn't do that. I've told her many times, but she can be stubborn."

"She's so special. She told me all about the way she married into the royal family. I feel I've learned a lot."

"She would be just the person to talk with, but you're doing splendidly, Shelby. I hope you realize that."

"Most days I'm afraid I don't, but it's nice of you to say."

"Is something bothering you right now?"

"Yes, but it's something very foolish."

"Tell me anyway."

Shelby stopped and looked up at him. "I don't know anything about skeet shooting, and I've been told that Nikolai will shoot at the fair and so will the king." Shelby shrugged awkwardly. "I just wish I knew more."

"I'll tell you what you can do." Anton's voice dropped in a conspiratorial tone. "Head out of town on the B48. Take it to the lake crossing and go right. You'll stay on the road for about two miles, and then you'll be at the skeet club."

"I can go out there?"

"Anytime. They'll show you around, let you shoot, answer your questions—anything you want."

Shelby's smile started slowly but grew huge. The king grinned back at her and fairly beamed when she went up on tiptoe to kiss his cheek. Watching her walk away for several seconds, he wondered if his grandson had learned yet that she was one girl in a million.

~

Shelby glanced behind her to see if Kris was flagging. He looked strong, so she kept on toward her destination. Normally she would not have been concerned, but he'd been a bit under the weather during the weekend. Gilbert had accompanied her on two excursions.

Today was Thursday. This morning she'd been given the restful news that because of a cancellation she had no appointments all day, and because the King's Fair was just ten days away, she had immediately made other plans.

Shelby was beginning to think she'd misunderstood the directions when she saw the area ahead. "Royal Skeet Grounds" the sign read, and Shelby turned and pedaled along the road, Kris still trailing her. Not many minutes later Shelby pulled to a stop and surveyed the acres in front of her.

It was a lovely section in the capital city's east end. Flat, wide-open fields stretched before her, and dotting the acres in a remarkably straight line were the shooting areas and the boxed mechanisms that released the clay pigeons. Kris rode up beside her as she sat, still astride her bike, both feet on the ground.

"I had no idea it would be so big," Shelby said softly. She was not overly familiar with Kris and not surprised when he recited for her the total acres and said nothing more. Shelby smiled at him in thanks, knowing he would know, and then looked to see two men coming toward her.

"Princess Shelby," the taller of the two spoke as soon as he was near, "King Anton's minister called and said you might be coming. I am Matthews, and this is my assistant, Austin. May we show you around?"

"Thank you," Shelby replied graciously, climbing from the awkward position on the bike. "I don't want to be in the way."

"Not at all. We have a small clubhouse with a cafe and gift shop. We would be most honored if you would join us."

"And the prince's gun is here," the assistant added. "You may shoot if you wish."

"Oh, I wouldn't want to use the prince's gun. I might break it."

They were all denials and smiles over this, but Shelby's

mind was quietly made up. She had a wonderful time seeing the clubhouse, cafe, and shop, but when they went out to show her how the competition worked and offered her a shotgun, she would not take Nikolai's.

"We have another one," Austin offered. "I'll just run and get it for you."

Shelby smiled at his enthusiasm but felt a need to remind Matthews that she hadn't done this before.

"I've never shot a gun."

"The gun Austin is bringing is very basic. Feel free to try it."

He was so eager to please her that Shelby knew she would have to try. She glanced at Kris, who had moved a discreet distance away, and wondered how she'd gotten herself into this.

"Here we are," Matthews said joyfully as Austin came with the gun. He took it from his assistant's hands and held it across the palms of his own. "Feel free, Princess Shelby."

Shelby swallowed and lifted the gun. She was rather intimidated by the feel of it and the fear that she would hurt someone.

"It's not loaded," one of the men told her, but Shelby was still very careful. She turned out to look across the fields and even thought about raising the gun to her eye. She was looking down at the barrel, surprised by the length, when one of the men spoke to her husband. Shelby hugged the gun to her, the barrel next to her ear, and spun to see Nikolai towering over her.

"Hi," he said softly as he gently removed the weapon from her grasp.

"It's not your gun," Shelby told him breathlessly, only too happy to relinquish the weapon. "I didn't want to break your gun."

"I'm not at all worried about your breaking my gun, but I'd rather you didn't hug any gun close to your face."

She watched him break the barrel, check the chamber, and close it again.

"It's unloaded, as I was certain it would be, but you still shouldn't point it toward your ear."

Shelby nodded and bit her lip. How did he know she was here? She turned to question Matthews and Austin, but they had both started away.

"Did you want to try to shoot, Shelby?"

Feeling panicked, Shelby looked back at him and shook her head. Nikolai watched her and tried to find some words to take the fear from her face.

"Shelby, I'm sorry if—"

"I'm so embarrassed," Shelby whispered, cutting him off. "I just wanted to see what it was like. I just wanted to watch. I didn't know the gun would be so scary in my hands, but they wanted me to take it. They were so eager to show me, and I didn't know how to say no."

Had Nikolai not been holding the gun, he would have hugged her. "I'll tell you what," he said kindly. "Why don't you sit here, and I'll show you how this works."

He took her hand and led her to a bench nearby. Shelby sat down and watched as he went to the box of shells, loaded the gun, and placed earplugs in his ears. Just a minute later he took position, shouted "pull," and shot at the clay pigeon that was released. Shelby watched as the dishlike object burst in the sky. Nikolai then turned to look at her.

"That's all there is to it," Nikolai said easily. "Would you like to try it?"

"I think I'd rather watch you."

Without a word, Nikolai turned and raised the gun again. He shot several more targets in the next few minutes, missing only the last one.

"I must be nervous with you watching me," he said, his eyes on the reloading of his gun.

Shelby smiled. "I somehow doubt that."

Nikolai slanted her a sidelong glance. "You might be surprised."

Shelby couldn't pull her eyes from his. He was devastatingly handsome to her right now, his eyes so blue and probing that Shelby felt her breath leave her in a rush. After a moment he turned back to the open fields.

"I think we're making progress, Red. You didn't even blush."

Shelby bit her lip to keep from laughing even as she felt her face heat.

"But I won't turn around right now," Nikolai said with his back to her, "or I'll be proved wrong. *Pull!*"

Nikolai took several more shots, sometimes calling for two pigeons at a time, before setting his gun aside, removing the plugs from his ears, and waving to Matthews at the controls.

"You can still try to shoot if you'd like."

"No, thank you. My family has never even owned guns, and I just wanted to see what skeet shooting was like before the fair."

"I'm glad someone called me."

"Is that how you knew?"

"Um hm."

The couple was walking toward Nikolai's car now, and Shelby glanced sideways up at him.

"What did that person say?"

"Oh, he was very respectful, but the gist was simple: The princess is out here and looking quite lost. Does anyone want to claim her?"

Shelby looked away, feeling very much a fool. It had all seemed so innocent. She just wanted to learn of the sport. Never was she hounded by people or pursued in any way, but having everyone know who she was had its keen disadvantages, not to mention the fact that the king regent had asked his minister to call ahead.

"I'll see you back at the palace," Shelby said, her own path parting from his. "Thank you for showing me, Nikolai."

"Where is your car?" Nikolai asked her retreating back.

"I rode my bike," Shelby answered without turning.

"Ride home with me," he called, needing to raise his voice to be heard. "I'll send someone back for your bike."

"Thank you, but I need the exercise." Shelby had stopped and turned to say this, but as soon as the words were out of her mouth, she continued on toward Kris. She had just sat down in the bike seat when Nikolai reached her. Shelby continued to strap on her bike helmet, put her hands on the handlebars beneath the seat, and put one foot on the pedal, her message clear.

Nikolai stared. "This is your bike?"

"No, Nikolai, this is my swimming pool. I ride it everywhere."

He was so astounded by her sarcasm and the recumbent style of the bike that all he could do was laugh. Shelby sat in bemused silence over his outrageous response.

"I'm sorry, Shelby," he finally gasped. "You just took me by surprise."

"Have you really never seen this bike before? I ride a couple of times a week."

"Never. I've seen you on your skates, but not this bike. I'd like to try it sometime."

"Anytime except now is fine. I'm getting hungry for lunch."

"Why don't you come back with me in the car?" His offer was most sincere.

"Because I want to ride."

Nikolai thought it was her way of saying she needed some space. He was happy to oblige her.

"I'll see you at home."

"All right. Thanks again."

Nikolai waved as she took off, amazed at how swiftly she covered the yards to the road and then started back toward town.

"No wonder Kris looks like he's dropped weight," Nikolai

observed as he watched the companion stay at an exact distance behind the princess, and seemingly with remarkable ease.

Ivan heard the remark but kept silent. Kris had lost weight, but he was loving it. He claimed to have more energy than he'd had since his school years.

"Let's go home, Ivan. If we don't hurry, she'll beat us."

"Yes, sir."

Ivan was as faithful a servant as any royal could hope for and not given to gossip, but if Arlanda should ask, and ofttimes she did, the report he would give would be very positive indeed.

~

The clock read 2:15 the next morning when Nikolai woke from a startlingly real dream. He lay looking into the dark, his arms aching to hold his wife.

Something is happening here, Lord. I've never dreamed of Shelby. I've even tried to have her in my last thoughts before sleep so I could, but it's always been Yvette. Nikolai's chest rose and fell. *It was so real, Father. I still can't believe she's not here.*

In a single move he sat on the edge of the bed, his eyes on the door that separated their rooms. He knew it would only frighten Shelby if he checked on her, but the temptation was strong.

She might be your wife, Nick, but you've got to go slow here. You've got to give her time. She still looks at you with too much apprehension and doubt.

The prince rose. The water he splashed on his face from the bathroom sink felt very good, but his heart was no more settled.

Show me, Lord, he prayed as he lay back down. *Show me the next step. Help me to be more approachable, and help Shelby to move toward me too. Show us how to do this. Show us in Your time.* Nikolai was still asking God for wisdom when he finally drifted back to sleep.

Twelve

Shelby watched the old man next to her as he pushed his food around his plate with a fork. Her eyes, which darted about the dining room, took in what she was accustomed to seeing in that room of the care center. Not one of the staff members ate with the residents, nor did any of the directors save herself. Shelby also took note of the fact that visiting family members only sat with their beloved—they did not eat with them.

The princess felt the time for a confrontation had come. The directors' meeting was to start in less than ten minutes. Shelby had a few more words with the people at her table and then rose to freshen up in the bathroom. By the time she took her seat at the huge table in the meeting room, she was ready. The old minutes were read and a few changes were made, but just as soon as the floor was open for new business, Shelby's pen went into the air.

"Princess Shelby," the head director acknowledged.

As was the custom, board members presented new business at the small podium set up at the head of the table. Shelby grabbed her notebook, hoping her knees would carry her, and took her place behind the smooth oak stand.

"It has recently come to my attention that I am, as a member of the royal family, allowed a certain measure of influence, within reason, in this facility. Is that correct, Mr. Chairman?"

"Indeed, Princess Shelby. You may add or adjust rules that only the king can change."

"Thank you. I have not as yet felt a need to take advantage of my status as the princess, but today I will. Effective November 1, just a little more than a month from now, no employee or director of the care center may bring food onto the premises, including the parking lot."

As Shelby expected, Mrs. Radford, the center's administrator, put her hand into the air.

"Yes, Mrs. Radford?"

"Princess Shelby, I find a need to remind you that the staff has only 30 minutes for lunch and 10 minutes at break time. There is no time for them to go out to eat."

"Precisely," Shelby said with no triumph in her voice. She went on quietly. "Which means they'll have to eat what the kitchen prepares."

Shelby knew exactly which directors had known where she was headed and which were surprised by this announcement. Mrs. Radford was dumbfounded. Her face was a deep shade of puce, and had she been wearing a corset, Shelby was sure the stays would have creaked.

"I don't think you know what you're asking," she began, but Shelby cut her off.

"On the contrary, Mrs. Radford, I know just what I'm asking, and that's why I'm giving you five weeks to implement the change. Today was the last day I will be forced to watch the residents in this home push tasteless food around on their plates. Not even visiting family members will eat the food provided."

"I'm not sure you understand, Princess Shelby," Mrs. Radford cut back in. "Food prepared in great quantities and in an institution such as this tends to have a certain institutional-type flavor."

"I do understand. There will be certain limitations, Mrs.

Radford, and I have appreciated your efforts to keep costs down, but you will no longer trim costs in the kitchen. I want fresh fruits and vegetables served whenever possible. I want meat served on its own, not smothered in sauces that disguise all taste. I want fresh desserts every day, not something baked on Monday and served all week."

Shelby's eyes met those of everyone around the table. Some were furious and some held respect.

"I have gone over the books repeatedly. This care center can well afford better food. We spend a small fortune on the grounds, which most of the patrons cannot even go out to enjoy. They look beautiful, but something simpler would be just as appreciated. Three delicious meals a day will go much further for the hearts and lives, no matter how brief, of our elderly patients."

Again Shelby studied their faces. "You have five weeks to make the changes. If this is not enough time, you may see me about an extension, but the rule stands."

Shelby took her seat, still trembling inside. The table was quiet for a few seconds, and Shelby kept her eyes down. When she did look up, it was to see one of the sternest men at the table staring right at her. Shelby had to force herself not to look away. The table erupted in argument just a moment later, but not before Shelby watched one of those stern eyes wink at her. It gave her just the courage she needed to stand her ground.

~

Shelby skated down the hallway to her bedroom, sweat dripping down her back. The morning's meeting had been long and heated, and she had felt a great need to skate into the park for some time alone. She took a chair right inside her bedroom door and took her skates off. A moment later Shelby dampened a hand towel and put it around her neck, then walked into the middle of her bedroom and stood still.

I believed with all of my heart that You wanted me to do that,

Lord. I've tried so many times to get Mrs. Radford to improve the food, but she always makes excuses or says she'll do it and then doesn't. I felt I had no choice. I didn't want to go to all the other directors and start a conspiracy behind Mrs. Radford's back, but maybe this wasn't the way either.

Shelby thought for a moment about who had been opposed. The people who had been against the change, Mrs. Radford and four others, had never had family members in the care center. So many people believed that the elderly couldn't taste anything. Shelby knew that some of the tongue cells grew dull, but she had yet to see an old person who couldn't taste the difference between sour cream and ice cream.

Shelby paced around a bit, still feeling hot and miserable. She was just about to open the window when a startling thought hit her.

What if I've gone too far, Lord? What if I've put the crown in a bad light? What will Nikolai's father say to me? How will I explain? Maybe I should have gone to him first.

Shelby was still in a quandary over this when someone knocked on the door.

"Come in," she called absently, turning to see Nikolai enter. She waited until he'd shut the door and then blurted, "Nikolai, can the princess be fired?"

Nikolai stopped short. He blinked and stared at his wife.

"No," he finally said slowly.

Shelby nodded but still looked distressed.

"Shelby, is there something you want to discuss with me?"

She opened her mouth but ended up shaking her head. "No, but thank you for offering. I still have some thinking to do on my own."

"You're sure?"

"Yes."

"All right," Nikolai said but continued to watch her.

Shelby's brows rose after a moment, and her husband seemed to come out of his trance.

"Here is that list of names Murdock said he would get to you."

"Oh, that's right, thank you," Shelby said as she took the paper from his hand.

"You're sure you're all right?"

"Yes, Nikolai, thank you again."

Not until after he went out the door did Shelby wonder if she should have talked to him. Thinking she'd missed her chance, she mentally shrugged and went to take her shower.

～

"Well, hello there," Nikolai called as he walked into the large parlor in the west quadrant and greeted the small boy he found sitting there.

"Hello," the lad returned softly, watching him with huge eyes.

"Are you here to see the queen mother?" Nikolai asked, taking a seat across from him.

The boy nodded. "We do magic together."

Now it was Nikolai's turn to nod. He had not heard of this but found it plausible.

"What sort of tricks do you do?"

"Oh, things with cards and rings and such."

"Have you been at it for some time?"

"Years and years," he said with quiet modesty.

Nikolai smiled. "Is my grandmother teaching you, or are you teaching her?"

"We're sorta working together. She's pretty good."

"Yes, she is. I've been watching her magic acts since I was your age at least."

The boy's eyes grew round. "Are you the prince?"

"I am. What's your name?"

"Peter, sir. Peter Owens."

"It's nice to meet you, Peter. Do you live near the palace?"

"I live next to Toby."

"Oh, I know Toby," Nikolai said calmly, but things were beginning to fall into place. Toby had been asking for prayer for his neighbors for many years now. Nikolai's heart softened instantly, just knowing who this was.

"How is it you came to work with my great grandmother?"

"Toby told King Anton, and he told Queen Miranda."

"Maybe you can perform for me today."

The boy nodded, looking old beyond his years. "If the queen wants to, we can." Peter paused. "Sometimes she gets tired."

"And she needs her rest for Saturday."

"We're going to do a magic show at eleven."

"I'll look forward to it. What would you say is your favorite trick?"

Peter's head tipped a little. "I think separating the rings. I like how smooth they are and the sound they make."

"I'll look forward to seeing that one," Nikolai said. Not for the world would he have told him that his great grandmother had shown him the trick to that one when he was ten.

"Well, Nicky," the queen mother spoke as she entered the room, "I'm glad you made it. Lunch is just about ready."

"Good. I was just talking to your partner here. It sounds as though the two of you are going to delight us."

"Peter will," the queen mother said as she sat beside him. "He has marvelous hands."

The little boy smiled shyly up at the queen, and Nikolai's heart turned over. He adored his grandparents, all of them, and was delighted to see this young man with some of the same feelings.

"Prince Nikolai was hoping we would perform for him," Peter now confided to the queen.

"What do you think?" she asked without looking at her great grandson.

"Maybe just one," Peter said softly.

The queen nodded solemnly, not once letting her eyes

roam to Nikolai. She had lost her heart to this hurting child and knew that speaking to him like an adult made all the difference in their relationship.

"Actually," the queen mother remembered, "Beckett and two others of the staff were hoping we would give them a little performance. Why don't we do one trick right after lunch and invite them to join Nicky?"

Peter smiled, a shy smile that didn't last long but lingered in his eyes as Beckett called them to lunch.

At the table Nikolai sat opposite his great grandmother, Peter between them.

"Now, Peter," the queen said kindly, "whenever Nicky eats with me he thanks God for the food. I just wanted you to know."

"I don't have to pray, do I?" Peter asked, his look becoming guarded.

"No, but I like Nicky to."

"Since you don't care to pray, Peter," Nikolai added, "is there anything you would like me to ask God when I pray?"

Clearly the question caught the boy off guard. Not surprisingly he said no.

Nikolai nodded and bowed his head. "Thank you, Father, for this food. It looks very good, and I know we'll enjoy it. Amen."

Both Nikolai and the queen immediately reached for the food set out for them, although they were both very aware of Peter's intense scrutiny. That he had been expecting a different sort of prayer was obvious.

"I hope you're hungry, Peter. I ordered extra because you were coming."

"I like these chips," he admitted as he put some on his plate. He already had a sandwich and his root beer. The queen took this as a good sign and told him to save room for dessert.

The conversation picked up where it left off, Nikolai asking questions about tricks of illusion, and Peter answering them with serious confidence and dignity.

The lunch was a delightful hour, and whether or not the queen mother planned it, Nikolai's heart was hooked. He left the west quadrant for his next appointment, asking God to put him in touch with Peter Owens again.

~

There was a blonde woman in the kitchen. She was dressed in a royal blue pantsuit and baking cookies. Nikolai stood quite still as he watched her take a pan from the oven and nearly laughed when she turned and he could see it was Shelby. This wig was curly, shorter than her own hair but still touching her shoulders.

"Bible study today, Shelby?" Nikolai asked as she let the door close.

"Yes," she said with a smile in his direction, the hot tray in her hand going onto the counter.

Nikolai approached.

"How many are in the study?" he asked, his eyes on the sheet.

"There are six of us," she replied, a smile in her voice as another batch of cookies went into the oven.

"Are any of them watching their weight?"

Shelby had a good laugh over this. "I take it you'd like a sample."

Nikolai turned innocent eyes to her. "Only if you have enough."

"I have plenty, but they have nuts in them."

"Does that matter?"

"It would to Fa and Brice. They want my mother to warn them."

"Well, I guess my favorite chocolate chip cookies would be without nuts, but since I'm begging, I can't be choosy."

"Would you like a hot one or one that's cool?"

Nikolai gave a sad shake of his head, his voice positively tragic as he said, "That you would offer anyone a cold chocolate chip cookie when there are hot ones available is nothing short of a crime. I'm ashamed of you, Red."

Shelby bit her lip to keep from smiling as he continued to wag his head and at the same time sweep three cookies from the pan. The first one went down in two bites, and she waited for the verdict.

"These are good," he managed before another cookie disappeared. "I think you might be in the wrong line of work."

"Some days I would agree with you," Shelby admitted.

"Like when?" Nikolai asked, instantly alert. He leaned against the table as though he had all day.

Shelby shrugged. "Like tomorrow at the King's Fair."

"Why then?"

"I don't know," Shelby admitted. "I'm just very nervous about it. I wish I had a job to do."

"Shelby, you work hard all week long. It's supposed to be a time of fun."

"The queen mother will be working."

"True, but she doesn't do what you do all week long. Not anymore, that is."

Shelby still looked unconvinced.

"I hope you know that you might change your mind a week from now."

"Why?"

"The Palace Fair. This weekend you need to try to relax. We'll be working hard next weekend."

Since Shelby didn't know what that would involve, her doubts were not dispelled. She knew, however, that if they continued to speak of the fair, she would start stammering and blushing in an attempt to make herself understood. It was nice to have the timer go off and to have an excuse to turn her attention to the cookies. She also had to keep moving for other reasons—five of them to be exact: The women in her Bible study were waiting.

～

"How are you?" Shelby asked Natty where she lay in the hospital bed. The women were meeting in her room this day.

"It was worse yesterday, I'll say that much, but I can't promise that I'll stay awake, even for Second and Third John."

"If you fall asleep, we'll just fill you in later," Grace offered.

"I'm not sure I can study with a cookie in my hand." This came from Deb, the character of the group.

"You could consider putting it down," Natty suggested.

"Spoken like a woman who isn't in the mood for cookies," Deb continued as she took one more.

Natty only laughed and tried one. Shelby was quietly pleased when Natty went on to eat two. Shelby kept study short and spent extra time on prayer requests, but seeing Natty so ill made her feel drained. She returned to the palace, her mind full of questions for her Lord. Without even changing her clothes, she took a walk on the grounds and ended up near one of the trees that had been a gift from the garden club.

"You know me well, Lord," she prayed softly, glad to be alone and unheard by others. "I planted these trees close by so I could be reminded not to fear, but I must tell You that I would much rather be stung by a bee than lose my Natty. My father told me when I took over the study that the price might be steep, and even though I understood, I didn't really grasp it. It's hard to see her so sick. She was so pale, and I know she felt a little vulnerable without her wig."

Shelby's hand went to the blonde hair on her own head. Just the feel of it caused tears to flood her eyes. This time she prayed in her heart.

She won't need one of these if You take her home, will she? The only question that remains is whether or not the rest of us will survive. You suffered for us, and I forget that so easily. Now I see

Natty, and I can hardly stand the thought of what You went through on the cross. I want to ask You to take her soon, but that's telling You what to do. My heart just hurts so much.

"Shelby?"

The princess turned to see Nikolai standing just ten feet away.

"Are you all right?"

A single tear slid down her face as she shook her head no. Without permission, Nikolai came forward and put his arms around her. Shelby, desperate to be held, clung to him. The prince ached to tell her everything would be all right, but he couldn't do that. Knowing that she had been with her Bible study ladies, it could have been any number of hurts that brought on her tears.

"I'm sorry," he finally heard her gasp. Up to then she hadn't been making any sound at all.

"Did something happen?" he asked, his arms still around her.

"No, not really. I mean, Natty's in the hospital, and she just looks so—" Shelby couldn't go on.

"You don't have to explain," Nikolai said, his head slightly bent so she could hear. "After you left, I was sorry I didn't ask you if I could come long enough to meet the women."

Shelby moved back in his arms, her own falling from his back, but his hands remained locked behind her waist.

"You wanted to meet my cancer ladies?"

"Yes. I'm sorry I keep forgetting to tell you."

"Oh, Nick, they would be so thrilled to meet you—especially Natty."

"We could see her tonight. I'm free."

Shelby blinked fast but still felt tears come on again. She made no argument when Nikolai pulled her close once more. He hugged her for a long time, and when he let go, he kept an arm around her to lead her to the house.

"We'll go right after dinner. Will that work for you?"

"Yes. Thank you, Nick."

Nikolai had everything he could do not to pull her back into his arms. Whenever she dropped his full name, he felt they were making progress. Some weeks before, his father had told him he would think of a way to court Shelby. Nikolai felt as though he'd done just that. He had cleared his schedule as much as he was able and simply looked for times and opportunities to be with his wife. When he had looked out and seen her on the grounds, he had been content just to watch her. Then she had put her hands over her mouth, and he knew he had to join her.

A few hours later he was very glad that they'd gone to see Natty. Shelby walked with great familiarity to her friend's hospital room, and when she slowed, he put a hand on her arm.

"I'll wait here, Shelby, so you can see if she's up to meeting me."

"Oh, that's a good idea. I'll be right back."

Nikolai leaned against the wall, sure he would be waiting some minutes, but Shelby was back in just a matter of seconds.

"Come on in."

Nikolai joined his wife in the spotless hospital room and saw a small woman on the bed. She had a golf cap atop her bald head and smiled as soon as her eyes met his.

"Natty," Shelby began, "this is Nick. Nick, this is Natty Carlson."

Nikolai put his hand out. "It's good to meet you, Natty."

"Thank you for coming. My husband just left. He'll be sorry to have missed you."

"Maybe I'll meet him next time. Do you have children who visit, Natty?" Nikolai asked as he took a seat.

"Yes. They're all grown, though. We have an empty nest."

"Natty's daughter is a nurse here at the hospital," Shelby filled in. "They see each other a lot."

"Does she actually work in this ward?"

"No, she's on the children's floor, but when I'm admitted she comes after work each day."

"Do they want to keep you for a while?"

"About a week total. I go home Monday or Tuesday."

Nikolai smiled.

Natty's gaze shifted to Shelby, and she smiled.

"I had forgotten how pretty your hair was, Shelby. All we ever see are the wigs."

"I have my eye on a new one." Shelby's smile was mischievous.

"What color?"

"A strawberry blonde, all curly and wild."

Natty crowed with laughter.

"Where is it?"

"At Bergdorf's. They also have a gray one I like, but I don't think I can pull that off yet."

"Give me some warning," Nikolai chimed in dryly. "If anyone ever spots me moving around town with all of these different women, my reputation will be shot."

The women clearly took no pity on him. They teased him for a while before one of the interns wanted to check Natty. The exam held the possibility of being quite lengthy, so the royal couple said their goodbyes.

"Thank you, Nick," was all Shelby said when they arrived back at the car.

Nikolai only kissed her cheek, unable to speak. So many things were starting to make sense about his wife—her kindness and way with people, her tender, compassionate heart. Something was happening to him, something scary and exciting all at the same time, and he didn't know what to do with it. He wanted to tell Shelby that the trip to the hospital was his pleasure, but at the moment he couldn't have spoken if he'd tried.

Thirteen

The day of the King's Fair dawned lovely and warm. Shelby dressed according to the schedule on her desk. The children's games were first. After lunch came skeet shooting. Following dinner that evening they would attend the concert on the palace grounds. All of the events were fairly casual, but Shelby wanted to look nice. Her family would be arriving that morning and staying for the next two nights. She was very excited about this but also a little nervous about their having a good time.

She need not have worried. They arrived when she was getting some last-minute instructions from the queen, and Murdock saw to their comfort. She didn't see them until the children began to gather for the games, and the first thing they told her was how comfortable and beautiful their rooms were. Shelby was able to move on and not worry.

"Shelby," Nikolai called to her almost as soon as she left her parents. She turned to see him with a boy.

"Hi. Did you need me?"

"Yes. I want you to meet Peter Owens. Peter, this is my wife, Princess Shelby."

"Hello, Peter," Shelby said warmly as she put her hand out to shake his. "How are you?"

"I'm fine."

"Are you excited about the games?"

"Yes, but I can't do some of them. I have to perform."

Shelby looked to Nikolai.

"He's doing an act with Great Grandma."

"That's fabulous!" Shelby told Peter. "I'll bet you're good."

He smiled a little and ducked his head.

"Peter, the queen just gave me a schedule of all the games, and the magic act isn't for a little while yet. Can you come and meet my parents and my brother?"

"They're here?"

"Yes. They just arrived."

"Do they live here?"

"No. They live in Henley, but they're going to visit me for the weekend."

"I get to stay too."

"With the queen mother?"

Peter nodded.

"Did you bring some of your family with you?"

Nikolai held his breath on this question, but Peter just shook his head.

"They can't come."

"You'll have to tell them everything you did. You can even have your picture taken and take it home." Shelby saw the look on his face but went on as if everything was normal. "In fact, I hope you'll have at least one picture taken with me."

"We can do that?"

"Yes! You'll want pictures of the magic act too."

Peter nodded, a little dumbfounded by all she was offering.

"Come on. My folks are over here, and then you'll need to meet the king and queen."

Nikolai followed along, a smile on his face. It was good to

know he wasn't alone. There was something very vulnerable and yet appealing about Peter Owens. Nikolai didn't know if he was to play a major part in the boy's life or not, but it was good to see Shelby just as taken with him as he was.

Her family was no different. They all questioned Peter about his magic and delighted in the serious little way he explained himself. When Brice decided to get a little closer to where they were setting up the food tables and invited Peter to go with him, Shelby took an opportunity to speak to Nikolai.

"Who is he, Nick?" Her eyes searched his in appeal.

"He's Toby's neighbor. His mother deserted all of them when he and his sisters were very small. His father is in a wheelchair; he was injured at work. They have the money from the settlement, but he's a very bitter man. Peter's world is a very cheerless place."

"How old are the sisters?"

"Both older. One is out of the house, and she's even willing to take Peter to live with her, but the father won't allow it."

Shelby nodded, her face intent.

"Don't let it ruin your day, Shelby. It's a step ahead that Mr. Owens even allowed Peter to come for the weekend. Just pray with the rest of us."

"I'll do that."

Ten minutes later the whistle blew and the games began. Shelby did pray for Peter whenever she saw him, and as she hoped would be the case, the magic act was the highlight of the morning.

~

Nikolai and Shelby opted for one of the blankets. They had been held up for a few minutes inside, and the bleachers and chairs were pretty full by the time they came out for the concert. The staff had spread thick quilts on the lawn, and the prince and princess sat down as unobtrusively as possible. They were toward the back of the crowd, and although the music had started, Nikolai wanted to speak to his wife while they had a semblance of privacy.

"Have you had a good day?" Nikolai whispered. His chest was close to Shelby's back, one hand stretched out to support him. Shelby turned to find his face very close.

"Yes. How about you?"

"Very. It's been fun to see the fair through your eyes."

Shelby's brow lowered. "I'm not sure I know what you mean."

"I probably take parts of this for granted, but you've never seen my grandmother perform or had the pleasure of cheering at the finish line. Your face reminds me how special this is."

The face he spoke of went a bright pink within seconds. Nikolai studied it for several heartbeats.

"Is your skin as soft as it looks?"

"I don't know," Shelby said with a nervous laugh.

Nikolai took a breath and plunged into new territory. "Are you afraid for me to find out?"

Shelby's own breath became labored. All she could do was nod in the affirmative.

As was becoming a wonderful practice for Nikolai, he leaned and kissed her cheek.

"Don't give it another thought," he said softly.

Shelby looked into his eyes, and Nikolai just smiled at her. She turned back to the singers up front. Their songs and voices were wonderful, but it took a little time to do as her husband directed. Not giving someone like Nikolai Markham another thought was nowhere near as easy as it sounded.

~

"How are you?" Daria asked her daughter right after lunch the next day. They had gone to services—Shelby had signed the sermon—and enjoyed Sunday dinner afterward. The tug-of-war was not scheduled for two more hours, so mother and daughter slipped into the park for a walk. They didn't get far. The first bench looked very inviting, and they opted to sit.

"I think I'm all right. Is there some reason you asked?"

"Yes. Not because of you, but because of Nick. He's different toward you."

Shelby nodded. "I'm starting to notice that. What do you think it means?"

"That he's starting to care, at the least."

"What do you mean 'at the least'?"

"Maybe he's starting to love you, Shelby."

Shelby shook her head. "I don't think so, Mother. I really don't."

Daria didn't try to argue with her but simply asked, "Are you ready for what's ahead?"

Daughter looked at mother. "You mean intimacy?"

"That's exactly what I mean."

"Not right now, " Shelby answered honestly, "but then I'm not convinced we're to that point."

"Are you happy, Shelby?"

"Most of the time. You've always told me that joy is a choice, and I have that, but this job has its lonely moments."

"So it still feels like a job to you?"

"Yes," Shelby answered without hesitation. "I'm open for changes, but I still feel that my heart would be intact if I had to leave here. I'm not planning on leaving—I know I never will—but I wouldn't be brokenhearted. That's the type of thing I ask myself, just to see where I stand."

"Since you don't feel Nick loves you, it's probably easier on your heart that you don't love him."

"I think you must be right, but I might be more willing to give of myself to my spouse if I did love him already."

The words were no more out of Shelby's mouth than she thought, *Or am I afraid of being in love alone?*

Not for the first time Daria Parker thought her daughter the most precious in the world. She was not a selfless, sinless individual, but she was in very good practice of putting others ahead of herself. Indeed, Daria remembered that the first verses Shelby learned after salvation were Philippians 2:3,4: "Do nothing out of selfish ambition or vain conceit, but in humility consider others better than yourselves. Each of you should look not only to your own interests, but also to the interests of others."

"May I ask you a very personal question, Mother?"

"Yes."

"Is Fa ever interested in you, you know, in that way, and you're not interested right then?"

Daria smiled. "Yes."

Shelby nodded, her face getting warm.

"Don't you want to ask me what I do?"

"I want to, yes, but I feel as though I've pried enough."

"Go ahead and ask me."

"What do you do?"

"If I'm tired, I simply tell him, and we plan another time. If not, I get interested as soon as I can. If I feel irritated, I see that as sin, confess it, and work to give myself to my husband selflessly. Not an easy task at times, but always worth it."

Shelby nodded, her face still a bit pink.

"I hope you know that he's going to fall for you," Daria said suddenly, still studying Shelby's face.

Shelby only looked at her.

"Do you know how I know?"

"No."

"Any man who's delighted when his wife blushes will keep finding ways to make it happen. He'll have to get closer and closer to do that."

Shelby's eyes closed.

"I frightened you, didn't I?"

"Yes. For so many weeks he avoided me and even apologized for it. Now he's getting into my world, and I'm scared to death."

"Have you tried getting into his world?"

Shelby looked pained. "With his family, but not with him. I never want to upset him or mention Yvette, so I keep my mouth shut and hope he'll talk."

"Does he?"

"No. He only asks about me."

"You're going to have to ask some questions, dear. I don't know how else you can show him you care."

"Just the thought makes my heart feel like a stone in my chest."

"You'll find a way," Daria spoke with confidence.

Shelby hugged her mother. "Thank you," she said softly.

"Anytime," Daria said, meaning it with all her heart.

~

The marvelous fun of the tug-of-war, the early dinner Sunday evening, and the awards ceremony on Monday, all lingered in Shelby's thoughts for the rest of the week, but her husband had been correct. All too soon she found herself at the Palace Fair, which was set up under huge tents by the river, and working hard to do her part.

"Now, Toby," she said sternly to the man whose intervention had brought her to this place, "I've handed out tickets and helped with the pony rides. I want a real job this time."

"The others have been pretend?" he teased her.

"You know what I mean. I want to work hard and feel that I contributed. I almost wonder if Nikolai came and told you to take it easy on me."

"Actually it was the king; Nikolai was right behind him."

Shelby's mouth swung open. "Are you serious?"

Toby grinned as he nodded, and Shelby's eyes narrowed.

"I won't need you to give me a job; I'll find one of my own."

"Now, Shelby—" Toby began.

"I mean it," she said sternly. "If anyone wants to know where I am, I'm *working!*"

Toby opened his mouth, but she'd already turned away. He moved to follow her, intent on seeing where she went, but he lost sight of her when another worker interrupted him. By the time he looked for her again, she was nowhere to be seen.

∼

"You missed a spot," the young man working with Shelby teased, handing a pie pan back to her.

"Where?" She squinted as he pointed to a minuscule piece of food that Shelby flicked off with her finger.

Seventeen-year-old Luke Grant, one of the queen's nephews, grinned unrepentantly at her.

"You're pickier than an old woman, Luke."

"Well, we can't put these pans back unless they're clean." Shelby made a face at him.

The princess and Luke were working in the pots-and-pans tent. Huge tubs of hot, soapy water had been set up, and they were taking turns washing and drying the pots, and emptying and refilling the tubs with clean soap and rinse water. Shelby's back was screaming at her, and her arms were starting to feel like wet noodles, but doggedly she kept on. She had wanted a job and found one. Luke's older brother Andrew had been on dish detail with them, but he had been needed elsewhere.

The Palace Fair was set up differently than the King's Fair: This fair was less scheduled. The palace staff and their families were able to eat all day long. For this reason the pots and pans never stopped. Some weren't so large, like the pie pans, but the boilers they used for the corn and hot dogs were huge. Nevertheless, she did not complain.

The day was wearing on when Andrew came back with food for them and they took a few minutes to eat. Shelby had just started on another tubful of large pots when Nikolai found her.

"I wondered where you'd gone," he said mildly, reaching for the pot she was trying to hand to Luke.

"I can do this," she told him.

"I can see that," he responded, his voice again deceptively mild. Her face showed that she was tired, and her arms shook as she lifted the pot. No one had meant to baby her, but he could see that she'd misunderstood Toby's words. What his father had asked of Toby was that Shelby be in a place of high visibility. The children all loved her, and so did the staff members from all four quadrants. In the pots-and-pans tent she hadn't seen anyone but Luke and Andrew all day.

The prince had been evading the question as to her whereabouts for hours. It didn't look good to have him shrug in ignorance. The staff was supposed to be taking the day off. If they thought the princess was missing, it would have put some in a state of anxiety. "Oh, she's working hard around here somewhere" had been his reply, but all the time he had wondered where she could be.

"I'll help you dry, Luke," Nikolai offered, picking up a towel.

"Actually," Luke responded, setting his down, "it's my turn to wash."

"Okay," Shelby said, telling herself not to look at Nikolai. If he was too kind to her right now, or for that matter scolded her, she was going to overreact. She was getting tired, and there was nothing like fatigue in Shelby to bring on the tears. She did notice that Nikolai was taking the largest pots to dry. She should have ignored it, but she didn't.

"Have you been working hard all day?" she asked.

"I think I have, yes."

"Then why do you take all the large pots? You must be just as tired as I am."

Luke turned completely away from the soapy water to watch this conversation. He loved his older cousin but never missed an opportunity to tease him.

"Well," Nikolai began, his gaze taking in both his wife and cousin, thinking anything he might say to his wife right now would be taken wrong. "I'm just trying to be chivalrous," he blurted, thinking he'd had a moment of genius.

Shelby did not look convinced.

"I can do this," she repeated.

Nikolai felt it was safe to nod. Even that got him frowned at. He looked over to find Luke grinning at him and had all he could do not to laugh. He was still working steadily when Shelby picked up a stack of pie pans and took them to the clean table.

"Has she been in here all day?" Nikolai whispered.

"Since about ten this morning."

Shelby was on her way back, so Nikolai gave a surreptitious glance at his watch, glad to see they had less than an hour to go. The fair ended in ten minutes, and cleanup never took that long.

"Did you two get some dinner?" he asked conversationally.

"Andy brought us some." This came from Luke.

"It was delicious," Shelby added. "Who did the cooking for dinner?"

"I think Luke's parents were in that tent," Nikolai filled in. "Toby and my grandfather helped as well."

"Don't forget the queen," Luke added. "She always does dessert."

It was the last word anyone said for a while. Fatigue was beginning to grind on all of them, and when the last of the mess was cleared away, everyone was out of words. The next day after church the royal family would get together, prepare their own meal, and talk about the fair; but for tonight, everyone headed home as soon as possible.

Because the staff was off, Nikolai and Shelby took her car. Nikolai didn't even ask Shelby if she had a preference. He took the keys from her hand, saw her safely into the passenger's seat, and drove them home. He let her off at the front door and took the car around.

By the time he got upstairs, she was nowhere to be seen. He

knocked on her door but there was no answer. Risking embarrassment for both of them, Nikolai went in. The room was dim, but Shelby could still be seen. She had lain face down on the bed, not bothering to remove anything or cover herself.

Nikolai approached. He put his hand on Shelby's shoulder and even said her name, but she didn't stir. Moving to the foot of the bed, he removed her shoes and socks. The moment he did this, she turned on her side, curled into a ball around the other pillow on the bed, and slept on. Nikolai took a blanket and covered her.

When the blanket was tucked close around her, Nikolai stood looking down at her. He was gaining small glimpses into her personality, but there was still so much that was unexplained. Even her need to work hard that day and not be given preferential treatment was a mystery to him. She was always a hard worker, and he had a hard time seeing why she'd been so tense.

After a time Nikolai used the door that joined their rooms, slipping quietly away to let her sleep. Long after he'd showered and climbed into bed, he could still see her in his mind, curled peacefully around that pillow, and he wished she'd been holding him instead.

Fourteen

A week after the Palace Fair, Shelby stood alone, licked her lips, and rubbed her sweating palms together. She hadn't been invited to this park, but she was here. Nikolai had been asked by Ryan to participate in a pickup game of field hockey. Nikolai had made a point of telling Shelby where he was going but didn't invite her. She had sat for a long time after he left, trying to figure out if he wanted her to join him or not. In the end she had opted to go. Now her eyes scanned the field at the city park, looking for signs that other wives had come along and quite unaware that she had been spotted.

"Well now," Ryan said to Nikolai from their place on the sidelines. "Did you just say you weren't sure how it was going?"

"Yes."

"If red hair is any indication, I think things might be looking up."

Nikolai followed Ryan's gaze across the field and smiled. Shelby was making her way slowly toward the field. She looked lost and uncertain, even when she spotted Nikolai approaching.

"Nikolai, you can tell me if I shouldn't have come and I'll go right home."

Nikolai realized there had been no "Hello" or "How is the game going?" —just immediate panic over whether or not she was wanted.

"I'm glad you did. I wasn't sure if you had time."

Shelby nodded, looking relieved. Even if there were no other wives, she was not intruding.

"Come over and see Ryan."

"Hello, Shelby," Ryan greeted her. "Beth will be sorry she didn't come."

"Oh, tell her I said hello."

"I'll do it. Feel free to sit on the bench. We'll be headed back into the game the next quarter."

"Thank you."

Shelby turned to the field and watched the players in action. The quarter break came faster than she anticipated, and in no time at all she was watching Ryan and Nikolai play. They moved well together and their team even pulled ahead before the half.

Shelby had taken a seat on the bench to watch, and Nikolai joined her as soon as he was able.

"Brice was here when I arrived."

"Was he really?"

"Yes. He and some guys were skating the trails."

"I can believe that. He's the one who got me started."

"He's strong on the skates. Actually, he's strong, period. It's not a surprise to me that we won the tug-of-war."

"Do you really think Brice made the difference?"

"Yes, I do."

Shelby looked very pleased but still said, "Do you still think he's uncertain about you?"

"As a matter of fact, I don't. Now his sister . . . " Nikolai drew the word out. "She's another story."

Shelby looked at his teasing eyes and told herself not to blush. It was a relief to have Ryan join them, if only long enough to tell Nikolai that he had to run to his car.

What happened next was hard to recount later. Shelby only knew there was no warning. Nikolai was answering a question she had about the park when a ball flew right at him. His head was thrown to the side a little, and for an instant Shelby didn't know what happened.

"I think I'll lie down," Nikolai said in a strange voice. Reaching for his right temple, he slid off the bench unconscious. Shelby was on her knees beside him in a flash.

"Nicky!" She put her hands on either side of his face and leaned close. "Nicky, can you hear me?"

Ryan seemed to come out of nowhere and dropped to his knees as well.

"Nick!"

"Nicky," Shelby tried again, her hands moving on his face.

His lids fluttered for a second and then opened. Things were blurry, but there was no missing Shelby's concerned face so near his own. She continued to smooth his hair back and even laid her cheek against his for a moment.

"Can you hear me?"

"Yes. Did I get hit?"

"It must have been a ball. I didn't really see it."

"Sorry, Nick," a voice said from above them. "It was my shot."

"Who is that? Tom?"

"Yeah."

"You always were a wild one," Nikolai joked as he sat up.

Shelby remained next to him, her hands still trying to hold his face. He looked over at her.

"I'm all right."

"You were knocked out."

Nikolai's grin was lopsided. "It's not the first time."

Shelby still leaned close, her hands framing his face for a moment.

"Do you have a headache?"

"Yes. I think I'll just head home."

"Here, buddy," Ryan offered, bending over him. "Let me help you up."

Nikolai didn't so much as sway when he came to his feet, but Shelby was still shaken. Both Ivan and Kris had come in very close, their eyes glued to the prince.

"Can I get you something?" This offer came from Tom.

"No, thanks, Tom. I'll be all right after a few aspirin."

Ryan gathered Nikolai's gear and walked with them to the car. Ivan and Kris were the closest Shelby had ever seen them, and this gave her more alarm. She had been driven by Hank, but she climbed into Nikolai's day limo, her eyes going to his face.

"Nicky, maybe we should call the doctor."

He took her hand. "I'm okay, Red."

Shelby looked into his eyes and shook her head.

"I just need to go home," he reassured her as he slouched a little and laid his head back against the seat.

Shelby waited only until Ivan was behind the wheel.

"Go to the hospital."

Ivan looked at Nikolai, whose head had come away from the seat.

"*Now,* Ivan," Shelby ordered in a tone he'd never heard. Even Nikolai blinked.

"Shelby—" Nikolai began.

"We're going to the hospital," she stated, her eyes straight ahead as she brought his hand into her lap and held it with both of hers.

Ivan did as he was told, pleasing Shelby with how swiftly he moved. They were pulling into the parking lot outside the emergency room in a matter of minutes.

Nikolai's head was pounding, and he wanted nothing more than to lie down, but he climbed out of the car and started inside. What he was not going to do was argue with his wife, so he allowed Shelby to see him to a chair but knew the doctor would say he was fine.

~

"Mild concussion," the doctor said about an hour later. "Nothing to panic over, but you need to take it slow for a few days—no field hockey—and if your vision should become blurry or you have intense pain, come right back in."

"Is it all right if he sleeps?"

"Yes. He shouldn't head off anywhere alone for a few days, but just using common sense and not overdoing will do the trick."

"Thank you," Nikolai said respectfully as the doctor took his leave. He looked to his wife. He thought she would be pleased, but she looked even more concerned.

"You heard the doctor, Red. I'm fine."

"I heard him say you have to take it easy. I'm wondering how busy your schedule is next week."

"I don't have any more field hockey scheduled."

"You're not going to have a lot of things scheduled."

Nikolai frowned at her, and Shelby frowned right back.

They were rather quiet on the way home. Shelby was not sure if he was telling her the whole truth, and Nikolai just wanted to sleep, something he did as soon as he'd showered. He had dinner in his room, as he was in no mood to converse, and went to bed early.

Not knowing if she was needed or not, Shelby paced in her room. She had asked Murdock if he'd checked on the prince, and he had, but not talking to Nikolai was most unsettling. That he hadn't wanted to talk to her was clear, but Shelby still felt they'd done the right thing in going to the hospital.

Feeling at a complete loss, Shelby took herself to bed at a late hour but was awake by two with Nikolai on her mind. Genuinely concerned for his welfare, she knew she wouldn't sleep again if she didn't check on him, so she grabbed her robe and went out to knock on his door. There was no answer, and Shelby became alarmed. She eased the door open and stepped in.

A light was on in the bathroom, and for the first time Shelby was sorry they did not have a more intimate relationship. The last thing he would want would be to come from the bathroom and find her there, but if he needed something, she wanted to get it for him. As it was, Shelby took so long in figuring this out that Nikolai came from the bathroom and found her standing in his bedroom.

"Are you all right, Shelby?"

"That's what I'm trying to find out about you."

"I'm fine. I just took some more aspirin."

"Your head still hurts?"

"A little."

Anxious and upset, Shelby twisted the front of her robe, not sure what to do.

Nikolai moved to the bed. "Come talk to me," he said as he climbed beneath the covers.

Shelby hesitated but went forward. Nikolai scooted toward the middle of the mattress so she would have room to sit. She did so, perching so close to the edge that she was half off.

"You usually don't wake in the night, do you?"

"No, but I was worried about you."

"Why were you worried?"

Shelby hesitated for several seconds and was startled when a dim light came on above the bed. When her eyes adjusted, she found Nikolai still watching her in question. Her chin came up a bit before she answered.

"I guess I was worried for the same reason you came to the pots-and-pans tent, saw my tired face, and tried to help out without being too obvious."

Nikolai's eyes filled with understanding as he nodded. For several minutes they sat in silence, Shelby's eyes in her lap, Nikolai's eyes on Shelby.

"Tell me something, Shelby," Nikolai said, waiting for her to raise her eyes. "Do you think you could be intimate with your husband, even if you didn't love him?"

"I'm not sure that's the issue, Nick." Shelby had not hesitated at all.

"What is?"

"Could you be intimate with me when you're in love with someone else?"

There was a brief silence this time.

"I'm committed to this marriage, Shelby," he said finally. "And I do care for you. Very much. I would also like for us to have children."

Shelby swallowed. "Are you thinking of something right now or in the future?"

"If you mean right now, as in this instant, no, not now, but I would like you to consider a change in that part of our relationship. I would want you to feel ready and safe, so this is not intended to press you too soon, but you're not going to know what I want unless I tell you."

"And you want intimacy between us?"

"Yes."

Shelby nodded, looking more serene than she felt.

"I think I'd better get back to sleep now," Nikolai said, seeing that she needed to be rescued.

"Is there anything I can get you?"

"No, but thank you for checking on me."

Shelby stood. "Goodnight, Nick."

"Goodnight, Shelby."

Nikolai was not certain he should let her go with things so unsettled, but he had no idea what the next step looked like. At least he had been telling the truth; he needed to go back to sleep. Not long after she left he did exactly that, all the while praying that they would both know what to do.

Shelby was not in such good shape. She lay for the next hour trying to pray and thinking about what her husband had asked. Without his having to say it, Shelby believed Nikolai had left the next move up to her. Shelby found herself wishing she could turn back the hands of time. If she could, she wasn't sure she would have gone to Nikolai's room at all.

~

"Something occurred to me this morning," Nikolai began without preamble. They hadn't had much time alone on Sunday—Nikolai had done a lot of resting. Now it was Monday, and the prince was raring to go.

"What's that?" Shelby asked, opening her door a bit wider so he could come in.

"Intimacy with someone you don't know would be very uncomfortable, so I want you to get to know me. Ask me anything you like."

Shelby blinked. "All right," she said slowly but then came to a halt; her mind was totally blank.

"What are you going to do today?" Nick volunteered.

"Oh, right!" She looked relieved. "What are you going to do today, Nick?"

Nikolai smiled. "I wasn't priming you, Shelby. I honestly want to know what you're doing today."

Shelby didn't even try to speak; she just looked away in embarrassment.

"Do you have a busy schedule?" Nikolai tried again.

"As a matter of fact, I don't," she said softly, her eyes still on the floor. "I was going to go shopping."

"Alone?"

"Yes."

"I'll go with you," Nikolai offered, bringing Shelby's eyes to his. His face was like that of a puppy's—dying to please. Shelby didn't have the heart to deny him. She also didn't want to. She had come to one solid conclusion in the last 24 hours: They needed to start acting like a normal couple. She knew that was not something she could turn on with a switch, but they had to start somewhere.

"What time is good for you, Nick?"

"Any time."

"Nine-thirty?"

"Fine. Do you drive or order the car?"

"When I want to go all day, I drive so Hank doesn't have to wait."

Nikolai suddenly frowned. "How does Kris get there when you drive yourself somewhere?"

"It varies. I'm sure he'll drive himself today, or he'll come with Ivan when he finds out you're coming."

And this was just what happened. Shelby drove them in her car, but very close behind were their companions. The shopping plaza was quiet for a Monday morning, and Shelby found a parking place with ease. Once in the plaza they drew looks from various people, and Shelby was reminded of how few appearances they made in public places together. She was also reminded that she needed to tell Nikolai something. Shelby wished it was dark to cover her blushing face, but determining to keep her eyes forward, she plunged in.

"There's something I need to tell you, Nick."

"All right. Do you want to sit down?"

"No, that would only make it more difficult."

Nikolai nodded, a small smile coming to his mouth.

"I'm going to shop off my list today, just like I planned, even if I blush."

"That's fine." Nikolai enjoyed her profile for a moment. "I, um, take it you have some personal items to shop for?"

Had he not been looking at her he wouldn't have seen her brief nod. This taken care of, Shelby led the way into Bergdorf's and straight to the lingerie department. She addressed her spouse without looking at him at all.

"I'll meet you back here in about an hour. Is that all right?"

"Yes," he said softly.

She started to move away, but he called her name. He remained silent until she looked at him.

"Thank you," he simply said.

"For what?"

"For shopping off your list."

Shelby nodded and moved on her way. Nikolai turned toward the men's department, all the time wondering if she had any idea how kissable she was.

~

"Are you going to try it on?" Nikolai asked as he took in the curly, strawberry blonde wig that was displayed on the counter.

"I'm tempted."

With that, Nikolai sat down on one of the stools as if he had all the time in the world.

"Try it on."

"Princess Shelby," the woman behind the counter greeted as she came over to them. "Good morning."

"Hello, Julie," Shelby smiled.

"Still thinking about the curls?"

Shelby laughed.

"I want her to try it on," Nikolai spoke up.

"Of course. Come on back, and we'll get you all set. Can I get you a cup of coffee or something else, Prince Nikolai?"

"No, thank you. I'll just sit here and relax."

"You'll have to come back in when I call you," Shelby suddenly said softly.

"What was that?" Nikolai missed the words and leaned close as she was doing.

"I can't come out here in a wig," she said in a desperate whisper. "You'll have to come back to the changing room door, okay?"

"Okay. Just send Julie. Was that her name?"

Shelby nodded and moved off. Julie had already picked up the wig and taken it back.

About 15 minutes passed before Nikolai heard his name. He set the newspaper he'd found aside and headed toward the door. Julie stood off to one side and the princess, already a bright pink, waited just out of sight. Nikolai stepped around the corner, took one look at her, and smiled hugely.

"She'll take it," he told Julie before stepping close to Shelby. Julie took her cue and exited.

"Your ladies are going to love this."

"I don't know."

"Trust me."

"You told her I would take it."

"Because you should. It's perfect."

"I look like that little cartoon character with the big eyes."

Nikolai laughed but still said, "Take this home."

"Are you sure?"

"Yes. If you want to give it to me, I'll purchase it. As soon as you're ready, I'll take you to lunch."

Shelby pulled the wig from her head and handed it to him. Without looking back she slipped back to the dressing room to fix her hair. By the time she came out, the wig was in a box and Nikolai was waiting. Shelby had little appetite but accompanied her husband to lunch anyway. It was time to ask some questions, and she was going to make herself start now.

~

"Nick, may I ask you a question?"

"Yes, anything."

"You seem to be home a lot right now. Is this a slow time of year for you?"

"No. It seems slower to you because I was so deliberately busy right after we were married, but the main reason you're seeing more of me is because I've cut back on my engagements."

"Can you tell me the reason?"

"You're the reason."

Shelby stared at him.

"To be with me?" she said at last.

"Yes. Our relationship got off poorly, and I'm trying to do what I should have done weeks ago."

Shelby nodded. They didn't talk like this very often, and it took some getting used to. She saw him as a busy, important man, and he was, so his taking time to be with her felt a little odd. It didn't occur to Shelby that as his wife, she was more important than his work, and Nikolai was just starting to see this.

"I'm going to ask you a question now, Shelby. It's a normal husband/wife type of question."

Shelby nodded. "All right."

"What did you find when you shopped today?"

Shelby swallowed but managed to answer. "I found some panties and nylons and a new nightgown. Then I bought those bike shorts I was looking at and the T-shirt you liked."

"All right. Is there more on your list, or are you just going to browse?"

"I need to find a gift for one of the women in my Bible study and a card for your great grandmother's birthday." She hesitated but then admitted, "If I see some dresses or shoes that catch my eye, I'll look at those too."

"Good" was all he said, and Shelby had a thought.

"When do you shop for yourself, Nick?"

"I usually wait until I'm at the lake house. There's a small shop up there that carries a lot of things I like. They also have mail order, so I take advantage of that."

"What size are you?" Shelby asked before she thought.

Nikolai laughed. "Large, Shelby, very large."

The waitress came to take their order, and Shelby felt instantly sorry for her. She could not take her eyes from the prince. Nikolai didn't seem to notice in the least and gave his order in a kind but impersonal manner. Shelby couldn't stop her compassionate smile when the woman walked away.

"What?"

"Oh, nothing."

"That smile doesn't mean nothing, Red—now give over."

Shelby shook her head. "I was just taking pity on the waitress. She was quite taken with you."

Nikolai stared at her and then looked in the direction of the kitchen. When he looked back, his face told Shelby that he was completely at sea.

"You didn't notice the way she stared at you?"

He shook his head no.

"It's nice to know you're not conceited." Shelby went ahead and said what she was thinking.

"About what?"

"Your looks."

In an instant Nikolai realized he wanted to know what Shelby thought of his looks but also saw that asking would make him seem full of himself. He had to let it go, but Shelby's opinion of his looks and all else concerning his life lingered in his mind for a long time afterward.

Fifteen

Shelby was not certain how she would be received at the care center, but she went anyway. Her change in procedures made it difficult to visit unless it was in an official capacity, but knowing that she could brighten the day of some of the residents sent her on. It wasn't as bad as she might have expected. Mrs. Radford's manner was a bit cool, but she did greet Shelby respectfully and even thanked her for coming.

Shelby had some papers to return to one of the secretaries, and finishing that task, she set out toward the recreation hall to visit for about an hour. As Shelby hoped, Mrs. Rose was there. Mrs. Rose was from Shelby's neighborhood in Henley, and the younger woman was always glad to hear stories about when she was growing up. Mrs. Wills, her roommate, was also in attendance this day, and the three of them settled in for a visit.

"I remember when the factory that makes those baked goods was built," Mrs. Rose said with a nod. "We all would stand in the street and just smell the goodies they made. And when they had the parade during Henley Festival Days, they would drive trucks down the street and hand out little cakes and such."

"I could live on Fairy Cakes," Shelby admitted, and the older women smiled at her.

"How is life at the palace?" Mrs. Wills asked, as she always did.

"Just fine. The prince is meeting with the Council today, as are the king and king regent."

"So what do all the ladies do on those days?"

"Well, I came here to the care center, but I haven't talked to anyone else."

"Don't you remember what she told us, Ida?" Mrs. Rose put her oar in. "The palace is all split up like apartments. They don't see each other unless they purpose to."

Shelby only smiled. If the north quadrant was an apartment, it was the largest in the world. She knew, however, that the best part of discretion would be to keep this to herself.

"Princess Shelby," Kris said, suddenly at her side. "May I see you a moment?"

"Of course. Excuse me, ladies."

Shelby rose and moved to the edge of the room with him without question but found his behavior rather confusing.

"What is it, Kris?"

"There is a fire in the kitchen."

"Oh, no." Shelby grabbed his arm. "What can I do?"

"What you can do is leave with me immediately."

"That's out of the question," she said, blinking in surprise. "We've got to help."

"The prince would not thank me if you were harmed, Princess Shelby. We need to leave."

"Why aren't they moving the residents out?"

"They will if they can't contain the fire, but right now it's small. We must go."

Shelby looked him in the eye. "We're not leaving until we learn what's going on."

The words were no more out of Shelby's mouth than Mrs. Radford stepped in the door and blew a whistle.

"I need everyone to come into the hallway please." Her voice was raised in order to be heard. "If you can move yourselves, do so in an orderly manner. If you need assistance, someone will be with you shortly."

Shelby was off like a shot. She made it to Mrs. Rose's side in a moment and began to wheel her to the hall.

"Kris, get Mrs. Wills' chair, will you please?"

That he was not happy with her was more than obvious, but he followed close behind, wheeling Mrs. Wills' chair as he went.

"Go ahead and move them to the front lawn," Mrs. Radford directed as she passed, and Shelby made a beeline for the front door.

"Shelby," Mrs. Rose said when they were outside. "I didn't want to come outside. It's too cold these days."

"I'll get you a blanket."

Shelby found her wrist caught in a steel grip.

"You'll do no such thing," Kris commanded in a voice Shelby hadn't heard before.

"Kris, I might be needed inside," she began, but he only shook his head.

With one hand he held her, and with the other he reached for the phone at his waist. He could have howled with frustration when it didn't work. He pushed several buttons, but the phone was dead. His next thought was to check the batteries, something he proceeded to do. It took less than a second to see his mistake. The moment he let go of the princess, she headed back to the door of the care center. Thinking he would have plenty to answer for, he put the phone back in its holder so his hands would be free and went after her.

∼

Not in all the years he'd lived in the north quadrant did Nikolai ever remember Murdock coming to get him from a Council meeting. The man's face gave nothing away—it never did—but Nikolai couldn't help but be alarmed.

"Yes, Murdock, what is it?" Nikolai questioned as soon as they were in the hall.

"I thought you should know that we just heard a news report. There is a fire at the care center."

"Is Kris with the princess?"

"He is, but we can't raise him on the phone."

Nikolai thought fast. "Get word to my father, explain to him what you've heard, and tell him I'm headed there."

"I'll do it, sir."

Nikolai moved for the front door, thankful for Murdock's efficiency. Ivan was already waiting with the car, and a moment later he was on his way.

~

It was tragic that it sometimes took an emergency to show people what they needed to do. Mrs. Radford had meant well, but by not evacuating everyone as soon as the fire started, they now had a full-blown panic on their hands as they rushed the old and infirm to the doors, working as they went to keep everyone calm.

Kris was not a lot of help, as all he would do was shadow Shelby. She was quite exasperated with him, but knowing what his job required, he ignored her frustration. He had only just stopped wasting his breath telling Shelby to come with him. When the firemen would allow no one else in, he simply followed her as she moved about the lawn, calming fears and giving away her coat and anything else she had to make people more comfortable. This was the way Nikolai found her. She was bent over an old man who was crying for something he'd been forced to leave behind. She had no coat, vest, or shoes, but seemed otherwise unharmed.

"I think it will be all right, sir," he heard her say. "The fire is under control. I don't think it touched your wing."

Shelby spoke to the man for several minutes before she noticed her husband. She had not been aware of him or his conversation with Kris but had been very glad to see him. On Nikolai's part, he was so glad to see she was safe that nothing else mattered—almost nothing.

The next two hours were spent helping out wherever they could, but many people had to be transported to other facilities, and there was little the royal couple could do. When Nikolai finally said it was time to go, Shelby was ready. For the moment Nikolai just wanted to see her safely home—something he did without fuss. He made a call to his father to inform him of the situation and then asked him to pray.

"Can you be specific?"

"Shelby said no to her companion."

"I'll pray," the monarch promised just before his son rang off.

~

Nikolai chose a quiet spot for his talk with Shelby. She had showered and dressed comfortably, and they had eaten a light meal. Nikolai then took her hand and asked her to join him in the blue parlor, over by the windows. The table they sat at was a game table, not very wide, but sturdy and smooth in a deep rosewood. Nikolai felt a hunger to touch his wife and reached for her hands as soon as she set them on the tabletop.

"I was proud of you today," he said softly, looking into the velvety depths of her dark brown eyes. "You comforted a lot of people, and I know they appreciated you."

"I don't feel I did all that much. So many people were frightened."

Nikolai nodded, weighing his next words.

"You've fit into the palace so smoothly, Shelby, that I sometimes forget you didn't grow up in the royal family."

Shelby studied him a moment. "I think that might have been a compliment, but I feel a 'but' coming on."

"You're right." He was glad she sensed it. "Shelby, you can't say no to your companion."

The princess blinked. "I had no choice, Nikolai. Kris wanted me to leave."

"Shelby," he said, repeating her name firmly, "you can't say no to your companion."

"I can't live like that—" she began, but Nikolai gave her hands a light squeeze and cut her off.

"The companions chosen by the crown were picked with extreme care. It's a rare situation, but they are here to protect our lives. Am I making sense to you?"

"Yes, Nikolai, but I'm not a child. Unless I've been knocked unconscious, I feel I'm able to make judgments on my own."

Nikolai reached up now and very tenderly held her face between his hands.

"What if someone with a vendetta against the royal family had started that fire? I'm not sure you realize that over the years we've had more than our share of Pendarans who opposed us. What if you don't see the situation for what it is and decide you can handle it on your own?"

"It's not the same thing."

"It is, Shelby." Nikolai still managed to keep his voice level, but he was ready to pull rank. "I've given Kris new instructions. He has my permission to bodily remove you from any situation that he deems dangerous."

"You can't be serious," his wife whispered.

"I'm very serious. He even has my permission to knock you unconscious if you fight him."

Shelby's mouth dropped open.

"Shelby," Nikolai cut in before she could speak, "Kris' job is on the line here, not to mention your life. He has the right to see you to safety whether you like it or not. If ever he acts unwisely, and it's proven that he took advantage of his position, he'll be dismissed, but your saying no to him today was very serious. He's just glad he still has a job."

Shelby's eyes went from shock to looking like those of a lost child. Nikolai's heart broke a little, but this was too serious to relent.

"I didn't know."

"I realize that."

"You didn't fire him, did you?"

"No, I understood the situation as soon as he explained it." His mouth quirked into a lopsided smile. "What he described was just like you. I would have been surprised if you'd have left without a qualm."

"They needed me," Shelby said softly.

His eyes drilling into hers, Nikolai said, "I need you more."

Shelby took a shuddering breath. "Oh, Nicky, I honestly didn't realize."

Nikolai bent over the table and pressed a kiss to her brow, dropping his hands back to hers.

"I don't want you to beat yourself up over this. I just want you to be more aware for next time."

"I need to apologize to Kris."

"As a matter of fact, you don't. He spoke to me about that. He could tell from the get-go that you didn't understand. And as you've probably already guessed, he's a most patient and understanding fellow."

"He's certainly proved that with me."

"Don't ever forget, Shelby, that he loves his job."

Shelby sat back, feeling utterly drained. Not even when she left the care center did she feel so spent.

"I think you need an early night."

"I think you might be right. I never thanked you for coming. I was glad to look up and see you there."

Again Nikolai smiled. "After seeing that you were all right, I had all I could do not to shout at you for giving away your shoes."

Shelby looked chagrined. "You should have seen them on the feet of the little old man I gave them to. His bathrobe was red, his pajamas were gray, and my shoes were a bright pink."

The description got Nikolai to laughing. "You gave them to an elderly gentleman?"

"Yes. He said his feet were cold."

Nikolai laughed for a long time, and Shelby just watched him. It had not been easy to have him tell her that she had been wrong, but when she saw past the embarrassment, she saw this as an act of caring. For this reason and one other, she smiled at him.

"What does that smile mean?"

"Do I really smile so little that you must question me each time?"

"No, but you have different types of smiles, and that's one I haven't seen before."

"Well, you'll have to get over it, since I'm not telling you what I'm thinking."

"Come on, Red," he coaxed, but she would not be swayed.

Nikolai, knowing she was tired but wanting more time with her, suggested a game of cards. They decided on Hand and Foot and played for the next two hours. By the time Shelby went to bed she was ready to sleep, but she still managed to drift off with Nikolai on her mind, most specifically his telling her that he needed her.

～

Now for matters you wrote about: It is good for a man not to marry. But since there is so much immorality, each man should have his own wife, and each woman her own husband. The husband should fulfill his marital duty to his wife, and likewise the wife to her husband. The wife's body does not belong to her alone but also to her husband. In the same way the husband's body does not belong to him alone but also to his wife. Do not deprive each other except by mutual consent and for a time, so that you may devote yourselves to prayer. Then come together again so that Sa-

*tan will not tempt you because of your lack of self-control. I say
this as a concession, not as a command. I wish that all men were
as I am. But each man has his own gift from God; one has this gift,
another has that.*

Shelby sat back after reading these verses in 1 Corinthians 7
and thought about them for a long time. She had read them before, but not since she'd married and certainly not since Nikolai
had told her he wanted their relationship to become intimate.

*It would seem that Nikolai and I have an obligation to each
other. I can't say that I feel tempted at this point, but maybe it's
different for Nikolai.*

Shelby had no more finished saying this to the Lord than
she realized how true it must be. Her husband had been married already; he knew all about intimacy. Most of it was still a
mystery to Shelby, but this one point was clear: Men viewed
such things differently than women.

What this meant for Shelby, she wasn't sure, but she
needed to stay open to the subject. She went back to her reading, still believing the ball was in her court.

～

"Prince Nikolai," Peter whispered softly in the quiet waiting room.

"Yes, Peter?"

"Will he die?"

Nikolai reached over and put an arm around the boy's
shoulders, glad that he didn't stiffen or pull away.

"I don't know, Peter. The doctors say he's pretty sick."

"I wish my sister had been home."

"You did the right thing in going for Toby. He's talking to
the doctor, and then he'll try to call your sisters."

"You came fast," the boy said quietly, and Nikolai saw no
need to comment. He had come swiftly, though. Peter had
asked for him, and Toby had called. Late as it was, Nikolai
left the palace ten minutes later.

"Would it be all right if I pray, Peter?"

The boy looked at him. "I tried that tonight for the first time. I don't think He heard."

"I was just reading my Bible this morning. Do you want to know what I read?"

Peter nodded.

"I read that the way to God is through His Son, Jesus Christ. I've known that for some time, but I need to be reminded often that I'm a sinner, that I can't get to God or even talk to Him on my own. First I need to believe in God's Son; then I know that when I pray, He hears me."

"So if you pray right now, God will hear you?"

"Yes."

"Will you pray for my dad?"

Nikolai pulled Peter a bit closer as he bowed his head. "Father in heaven, thank You for Peter. Thank You that he wanted to call me and that I was able to be here with him. Right now, Lord, I ask You to put Your hand on Mr. Owens. He's very sick, Lord, and I would ask You, in Your will, to heal his body. But I would mostly ask You to heal his soul. We all sin against You, Lord—Peter, myself, and Mr. Owens—and You are the only One who can save us from those sins. When we're hurting or injured, Father, our first thought is for You to ease our pain. Use this pain, Lord, to make us more aware of You."

A sharp thought snapped in Nikolai's brain as he prayed these words. He was speaking to God, but there was also a frightened 11-year-old tuned in beside him.

"Thank You that You love us, Father, and always want the best for us. Take care of Mr. Owens and Peter. Help them to know You care. In Christ's name I pray. Amen."

Nikolai looked into Peter's eyes and saw that he was calm. He even managed a small smile.

Nikolai was to later remember those few seconds of peace he saw in Peter's face. Nikolai clung to the memory when Toby

and the doctor returned not five minutes later. Peter Owens'
father had just died.

~

"Did you have a chance to speak to the sister?" Shelby
asked Nikolai on the way home from the funeral. "Does she
know we're willing to help her?"

"Yes. Pam is going to move back home, because there's
more room, and her boss has given her two weeks off work."

"Are they all right financially?"

"Toby is checking into that. He's going to help but also be
in touch with both Great Grandma and me. On top of that, I
am picking Peter up next Saturday morning so we can spend
some time together."

"What can I do?"

"We may end up visiting the palace. If we do, I'll want us to
do something normal like playing cards or baking cookies. If
we don't come by, you can just keep praying that he'll stay
open to me, as will his sisters."

Shelby did keep praying. This wasn't hard to do, as Peter
was on her mind for the rest of the day. She was greatly encouraged when Toby called to say that Peter and both his sisters had been in church on Sunday.

~

Nikolai had honestly not known she planned to golf, but
once he'd seen her car, he was not going to leave the country
club. He had been there only to personally deliver some papers
to Councilman Royden, but as had become the norm, he once
again had time to stick around.

Right after Peter's dad died, he had been on call quite often.
Things were still going well with Peter but had slowed down.
Nikolai now had time to court his wife again.

It had been more than six weeks since he had spoken with

Shelby in the middle of the night, but the subject hadn't resurfaced. The events of that past month had not been much help, but Nikolai couldn't help but wonder if she had given any more thought to the conversation.

"Well, Nikolai," Councilman Royden called as Nikolai worked his way past the clubhouse restaurant. "I thought you were leaving."

"Change of plans," Nikolai said.

The Councilman smiled. "She went that way."

Nikolai only grinned at being discovered before he headed out the indicated door. He wasn't long in spotting his wife. She was walking with two other women, all three pulling wheeled golf carts. Nikolai strode purposely toward them and knew the exact moment Shelby spotted him. She stopped in surprise, and the other women halted with her and followed her gaze.

"Hello," Nikolai said jovially. "Need a fourth?"

"No," she answered quietly. "We have four."

"Oh." Nikolai was momentarily defeated. "I'll caddie," he offered, recovering swiftly.

Shelby's eyes grew huge. "There is no need," she said, barely keeping her voice calm. "Really there isn't."

"I don't mind." He grinned like a schoolboy and reached for the handle of her cart. With his free hand he shook hands with the two other ladies, both of whom he'd known for years. Just after this, they were joined by the fourth in the party, a woman who also knew the prince and whose smile matched those of the first two women.

"Go ahead," Shelby said when greetings had been exchanged all around. "I'll be right along." Shelby waved and smiled as if all was fine. "Don't you have something else to do, Nick?" she asked pointedly.

"Not for at least four hours. Isn't it nice that I saw you?"

Shelby's look was telling. "So nice that I could pinch you," she muttered.

"Feel free," Nikolai said quietly, a smile lighting his eyes as his wife turned away. "But I might pinch back."

~

"Enjoy it, Shelby," Vickey said on the thirteenth green. "Most women would kill to have such an attentive husband."

"I don't know what's come over him."

"He certainly seems to be enjoying himself."

At this point Shelby had to smile. It was very clear that Prince Nikolai *was* enjoying himself. For all of his huge size, he would study the fairways like an earnest child and then solemnly hand Shelby a club, practically hugging her when she did well.

The other three women, all councilmen's wives, looked on in clear enjoyment as the prince's eyes followed Shelby's every move.

They played the full 18 holes. Shelby was bemused for most of the time, until she remembered that Nikolai had been moving closer to her before Mr. Owens' death. All she could think was that he must be making up for lost time. She didn't know if she was flattered or intimidated.

"Thank you, Nick," she said as the women finished and prepared to eat lunch. The two had a moment alone.

"You're welcome. You played well."

Shelby smiled a little.

"Maybe sometime you and I could golf together."

Shelby had never seen him look so vulnerable. It was heartbreaking. With a hand to his chest, she went up on her toes to kiss his cheek.

"We'll do that," she said softly and smiled into his eyes.

Shelby went in to lunch and even enjoyed herself, but her mind was a tad preoccupied. Deep in her heart she knew that the time had come.

Sixteen

Nikolai was sitting against his headboard the next night, a book in hand, when the knock came. Thinking he was hearing things, he paused. Before he could go back to his reading, it sounded again.

"Come in," he called, watching in amazement as the door between his and Shelby's room opened. The only light shining was over his bed, but he could still see the way she came in, shut the door, and leaned against it. Nikolai stared at her for a moment, got off the bed, and went to stand before her.

"I didn't know if I should call or just come in," Shelby admitted softly.

"You're welcome either way."

Shelby nodded, and Nikolai took in her attire. She had shorts on and a long baseball shirt. He thought she looked adorable.

"May I tell you something, Nikolai?"

"Certainly."

Shelby took a deep breath. "I'm terrified," she barely whispered, effectively breaking her husband's heart.

"Oh, Red." Nikolai's voice was low, and a moment later he

reached for her. Shelby sighed when his arms went around her. It was so much easier to have him touch her.

Nikolai found it easier too. Until she'd admitted that she was frightened, he hadn't wanted to assume why she'd come to him. To finally have her permission to hold her was one of the sweetest things he'd ever known. And when he kissed her, it was sweeter still.

Shelby was amazed at his gentle touch and found herself smiling up at him.

"I should have known you would be nice."

Nikolai's smile matched her own. He spoke with his hand on her hair. "I should have known you would be amazingly soft."

Shelby laughed a little, thinking it was a lovely note to begin on. She was also very glad she had come.

～

"The prince gave me this as he left this morning," Murdock said as he handed a note to his wife.

First studying her husband's face, Fran opened it slowly and read. *Murdock, Princess Shelby is in my room. Please let her sleep.*

Fran raised shining eyes to her spouse. Murdock smiled down at her before he leaned to give her a kiss.

～

Shelby stretched luxuriously, a groan escaping her, before she remembered where she was. Turning to look at Nikolai, she found herself alone save for the note that lay on his pillow. After Shelby pushed up against the headboard, she opened it.

Do you ever notice the timing of things? It had been on my mind several times yesterday to tell you I had to be away for a few days, but I kept forgetting. I had just about decided to call you when you knocked on the door.

Please know, Shelby, that leaving you this morning was
very hard. I'm in Enstrom, meeting with the committee
on budget cuts and taxes, but remembering your
sweetness is going to make it very hard to concentrate.
Looking forward to seeing you Friday or Saturday . . .

Nick

Shelby read the note over twice and sat thinking about the
changes that would follow in the days and weeks to come. She
suddenly didn't want to stay in bed much longer. The princess
had an urge to see her mother.

~

"What's this?" Shelby asked as Daria put a large wrapped
box in her lap.

"Something I bought you before you married, but the timing was all wrong."

This was all Daria would say, so Shelby opened the box. She
pulled out the two loveliest peignoir sets she had ever seen.
One set was a soft peach; the other, a pale mint green.

"Oh, Mother."

"Do you think Nick will like them?"

Shelby smiled. "He didn't seem to mind my shorts and
baseball shirt, so he'll probably love these."

Daria's smile was huge. "You knocked on his door wearing
shorts and a baseball shirt?"

Shelby shrugged, trying not to blush but not succeeding.
She laughed a little and said, "I don't think he cared."

"Of course he didn't." Daria's voice was gentle. She studied
Shelby's bent head for a moment. "Are you all right, Shelby?"
she asked quietly.

The princess looked at her mother. She knew the question
stemmed from what she had shared that morning, but Shelby's
mind went elsewhere.

"I don't have anyone to talk to."

Daria nodded. "Your father and I realize that. Your loyalty to the palace keeps you from coming home to us with your questions and concerns, but then you haven't had a husband you could talk to either." Daria couldn't stop the tears that filled her eyes. "We can see the loneliness written all over you, Shelby. I can only hope and pray that it's coming to an end."

Shelby reached to hug and kiss this woman who was so dear to her.

"Shelby," Daria said as soon as they separated, "loyalty to the crown or not, you must tell me if you're all right."

"I am, Mother, honestly. Nikolai had to leave town, but to be frank with you, I'm glad for a little time on my own. It's a lot to think about."

There was so much Daria could have said, even more questions she could have asked, but this was not something she could do. Shelby must lead the way in this issue, and right now she was ready to be silent. It did her heart good to have Shelby come to her. They enjoyed a meal together and talked of plans for the holidays. When Shelby left, Daria reminded her that the door in Henley was always open.

~

Nikolai had worked hard on Thursday, bending his mind to the tasks of the committee and even into the dinner conversation that evening, but now he was in his own room at the chairman's house and able to give way to other thoughts, namely, Shelby's words from the night before.

I think I am ready for this change between us, Nick—as much as I'm able to discern. And like you, I'm committed to this marriage and also desirous of children. But there's one thing you must know. I won't say "I love you" until I'm sure I mean it, and I want you to do the same for me.

Nikolai had certainly agreed and thanked her for her wise words, but now, this evening, he was left alone with his thoughts. These two women, Yvette and Shelby, both of whom he'd known such a short time and who had played and did play such major roles in his life, were like warring factions within him.

Nikolai's eyes closed with a sigh. *Yvette is receding from my mind, Lord, and yet I still feel I love her. I can't honestly tell You what I feel for Shelby.* Nikolai sat by the open window and looked over the lights of the city, his heart in a quandary. *I care, Father. I care so much. I want to take such good care of Shelby. I want to see her obedient, blessed, and happy, but I'm not able to say those three little words. She was wise to put the subject right on the table. If we keep it open, I think we'll make it.*

Nikolai suddenly realized how tired he was. He had a full day ahead of him, possibly two, and he owed it to the committee to be at his best.

I would love the luxury of talking to You all night about this, but right now I must rest and be at peace in You.

Nikolai was ready for bed and asleep less than 20 minutes later. He wasn't anxious, but Shelby was still very much on his mind.

~

"What are you thinking?" Erica asked Rafe softly, but she received no answer. The queen stared at her husband in the reflection of the mirror, but he still didn't notice. She had been readying for bed when he joined her in the bathroom, kissing the top of her head and then sitting on the edge of the bathtub without speaking. Erica was at her dressing table, thinking he'd come about some particular issue, but he only sat, seemingly in another world.

"Rafe?" she tried again.

"Yes?"

"Did you need something?"

"No. I was just lost in thought."

Erica turned from the mirror to look at him. "Anything you can talk about?"

He finally looked at her. "Do you know how Nick and Shelby are doing?"

"I think well. They're trying to spend more time together; I know that."

Rafe nodded. "I planned to talk with Nicky this week, but he's in Enstrom right now."

"And you're concerned because they didn't travel together?"

"A little. None of the men take their wives to the committee meetings. It's too intense. But I am wondering how much time they are spending together."

"Maybe Shelby did go with him."

"No, she didn't. I saw her on her bike today."

Erica had no reply. She had spoken with both Nikolai and Shelby separately within the last week, and both seemed very fine, quite happy even. Their conversations, however, had not ranged to the personal.

"Why don't you give Nicky a call? He always stays at the chairman's house."

The king shook his head. "No. I'll see him when he gets back." Rafe's eyes now went to his wife's attire. She always looked beautiful to him, but tonight she had on red. He liked red.

"You look nice," he said, knowing it was an understatement.

"Thank you," she smiled. "I didn't think you noticed."

"I must remedy that," he said softly as he went to her. The queen's doubts flew as the king's lips touched her own.

~

When Shelby had awakened and found herself alone in Nikolai's room, she had exited through their adjoining door, innocently leaving it wide open. Because Nikolai had not been home, that was the way it was left. This was also the way the prince found it when he came home very late on Friday night.

Indeed, after putting a light on, it was the first thing he noticed.

Not troubling to do any more than set his case down, Nikolai found a flashlight and went through the door. As he expected, Shelby was asleep in bed. Careful not to shine the light in her face, he went toward the bed and set the light on the nightstand to cast a glow over her. Because she was in the middle of the mattress, he was able to sit on the edge. She did not move, but that was all right. Nikolai was happy just to stare at her face and watch the way she curled around a pillow to sleep.

He didn't know how long it was before he realized he needed his own bed, but one thing was certain: He took his cue from his wife and left the door open.

~

The next morning Shelby came from the bathroom wearing only her underthings, her mind already on the day. Nikolai might be home anytime, and she didn't know if she should go out or cancel her appointments. She moved to the desk and checked her calendar, seeing that things were very free. She was scheduled to interpret the next morning in church and knew she would need to be fresh for that, so she was relieved the day was a relaxed one.

Shelby was turning from the desk when she saw him. Leaning one shoulder against the doorjamb between their rooms, his hands stuffed into the pockets of his jeans, the prince stood and watched her.

"Nikolai!" Shelby cried in soft surprise as she backtracked and reached for the robe that was draped on the desk chair.

Nikolai pushed away from the jamb. In the time it took for him to come forward and kiss her, Shelby had knotted the belt at her waist.

"You're blushing," Nikolai noticed after he stood to full height.

Shelby shrugged and tried for nonchalance. "I'm not very used to having a man in my room when I'm not dressed."

Nikolai was watching her very closely as he asked, "Even when the man is your husband?"

Shelby's blush only deepened.

Nikolai's heart sighed gently within him. On the way home he'd figured that they might still have walls to scale, and his wife's red face told him he was very correct. He wished there was some way to tell her that he did not have a hidden agenda; neither would he ever rush her.

"You haven't started to redecorate, I see."

Shelby looked back to see him taking in her room.

"No. I don't seem to have the time right now."

"What will you do?"

"I don't know." Shelby glanced around as well, glad for the change in subject.

"Maybe we should redo mine at the same time. Carry the theme through, if you know what I mean."

Shelby looked up at him but wasn't sure what to say. She suddenly remembered the way both Yvette and the queen had shared the same room with their husbands. Nikolai didn't sound as though he was all too thrilled about such a plan, the way he was encouraging her to decorate both rooms. Shelby tried to be logical about it, but she couldn't quite ignore the painful feeling of rejection.

"Shelby, what does that look on your face mean?"

"What look?" she asked back, trying to evade the question.

"That look of confusion or hurt—I don't know which."

Shelby was searching desperately for a reply when the phone rang. She brightened with relief.

"I have to get my phone."

"I'll get it," Nikolai said, reaching around her and even taking the handpiece from her. "Hello. Yes, she is here, Murdock. Is it urgent? In that case I'll have her call you. All right. Goodbye." Nikolai put the phone down and turned back to his wife. Shelby had angled her body away from him, but Nikolai moved to look at her face. When she wouldn't look up at him, he sat on the edge of the desk, dropping his gaze to her level, and with hands to her waist, brought her to stand directly in front of him.

"I did a lot of thinking while I was gone, and I've come to one solid conclusion: We have to keep talking. It's awkward and embarrassing at times, but we must keep at it."

Shelby nodded but still didn't speak for a moment. Nikolai was on the verge of ordering her, not that that would have been helpful, when she seemed to come uncorked.

"I have to tell you something, Nikolai; I have to!" Shelby looked almost desperate now. "I'm afraid to even mention Yvette to you. I'm terrified of even thinking her name, let alone saying it. I'm so afraid that it will upset you or that you'll tell me it's none of my business. I mean, it should be my business, I'm your wife, but I don't feel that it is."

Nikolai put his hands on the backs of her upper arms and rubbed gently. The pink in her face had gone pale, and her features were strained. Nikolai found that it hurt him to know she was so upset. In truth, he didn't want to discuss Yvette with Shelby, but that wasn't fair to either of them.

"Tell me if this will work for you, Shelby: When you have a question about Yvette, just check with me about asking. At some times I feel more vulnerable in that area than at others. If you can check with me, then I think it will be less painful and uncertain for both of us."

"I can do that," Shelby told him, thinking she would say anything not to hurt him or have him mad at her.

"Good. Now, what did I say that made you think of Yvette?"

Shelby played with the belt on her robe, wishing she didn't have to answer but still making an attempt. "It was just the way you mentioned the rooms. I don't know if I can explain it more than that."

Nikolai worked in his mind to grasp what she had said and finally asked, "Are you ready to move into my room, Shelby?"

The thought alone made Shelby blush. She immediately shook her head no.

"In that case," Nikolai said, not seeing a need to tell her he wasn't ready for that either, "we'll start by leaving the door open and see how we like that."

Shelby nodded, relief coming in slow waves. She had known there would be more bridges to cross and battles to endure, but she was still so uncertain and embarrassed in front of her spouse. Would she never feel completely at home and secure in this place?

"May I hold you, Shelby?" Nikolai suddenly asked. Shelby hadn't been aware of his scrutiny, but she could relate to what she saw in his eyes: need.

"If I can hold you back."

Nikolai's eyes slid shut as her arms went around his neck, his own encircling her to hold on tight. Their prayers, had they but known it, were quite similar. They both asked God to help them find their footing in this relationship.

～

"All right, Peter," Shelby instructed, "put your cup of flour in now."

"What about the chocolate chips?" the boy asked.

"They go in last," Shelby said as she moved the bag from her husband's reach.

Peter smiled at his affronted look, but Shelby just kept mixing.

"Okay, Nick. I'm ready for those eggs."

He did as he was told and then realized he should be stirring.

"Here. Let me do that for a while." Nikolai took the spoon from her hand and began to work. With his help, they were ready for the chips in no time.

"How long will it be?" Peter wanted to know after the first batch had gone into the oven.

"About 12 minutes. Can you wait that long?"

"I think so."

Shelby smiled down at him. He was doing very well. She knew from Toby's reports that Peter had days in school when he would not respond or even look at his teacher, but even that was getting better.

She also knew that it helped that Nikolai was able to see him about once every ten days. The little boy had come to adore the prince. The only person he seemed to love more was the queen mother. And an hour later, when a box of cookies had been put together for that lady, Peter's face showed his delight in getting to see her and present her with the gift. Nikolai walked him to the west quadrant.

"How have you been, Peter?" Nikolai asked as they moved along at a snail's pace, Nikolai's design more than Peter's.

"All right," the boy said, looking up sideways at him. He had been smiling, but now he frowned a little. "I don't want you to pray for me anymore," he said suddenly. "I'm going to tell Queen Miranda too."

"Can you tell me why?"

"I didn't like what you said last time about the gift part."

Nikolai took a moment to compute this. "You mean when I said that salvation was a free gift from God?"

"Yeah." The boy's voice was soft, his expression guarded. "You said God was so smart that He created everything, but I don't think it's smart to make your Son die. I can't think why He would do that, so I guess I don't believe He did. Anyone could figure out that it must all be a big lie."

Nikolai kept his calm with an effort. When he worked with adults who called themselves believers but who did not really care to grow in the Lord, Nikolai didn't waste his time. This child was different. This child was not a believer in Christ and needed to be treated differently. Peter's words, however, still made Nikolai feel as though he'd been wasting his time, and he had to fight his emotions on the subject.

"Well, Peter," he said at last. "You're certainly entitled to your opinion. I take it you think my belief is rather foolish."

Put so bluntly, the boy hesitated, even coming to a halt on their walk, but he eventually nodded.

"In that case I need to check something with you. Are you still going to want to spend time with the princess and me? We're still going to believe the same, and you don't agree. Are you going to want anything more to do with us?"

Peter's face paled on these words. He wished he had kept his mouth shut and put up with the prayers.

"I didn't mean I don't like you," he said, his eyes filled with fear.

Nikolai put a hand on his shoulder, still pushing his first feelings aside.

"I'm glad, Peter. I would have missed seeing you."

Peter looked into the prince's smiling face and let out his breath. For a moment he thought he'd lost it all. He managed a small smile now as he turned and went through the door to see the queen mother.

"Thank you," he remembered to say, the cookie box coming up a little.

"You're welcome. Have a good time, and I'll see you sometime next week."

Peter's smile told Nikolai he'd said the right thing, but the prince still felt a need to be alone. He went for a walk in the park and had a long talk with the Lord. By the time he returned, he'd remembered that he was not the one in control—something he was very glad of right now.

Seventeen

Shelby spent the morning at the care center. The residents were all moved back in, and most were settled again. The fire was still the main subject of discussion, and everyone who saw the princess wanted to speak with her about it. Shelby had been listening to their talk for more than an hour when Mrs. Radford approached her.

"When you have time, Princess Shelby, may I speak with you in my office?"

"Certainly. I'll be right along."

Shelby said a slow goodbye to the men she was visiting and made her way to the matron's office.

"Please have a seat," that woman said quietly when Shelby entered the office.

Shelby, thinking she'd never seen her so subdued, sat in a leather chair in front of the desk.

"Has anyone informed you that I'm retiring?"

"No, Mrs. Radford. I hadn't heard."

The older woman nodded, her expression unreadable. "My husband wishes me to, and I think it's time."

"We'll miss you and the hard work you do," Shelby said sincerely.

Again Shelby could not read the other woman's expression, but Mrs. Radford surprised her.

"I did want to tell you one thing before I go, Princess Shelby." The matron cleared her throat and continued, "I have had several comments on the food lately—positive comments. I thought you would like to know."

"Thank you for telling me."

"I would also like to thank you on behalf of the care center for helping during the fire."

"You're welcome. I'm glad I was here."

Mrs. Radford gave a ghost of one of her old smiles—the ones Shelby had seen before she caused waves—and began stacking papers on her desk. Shelby took her cue, leaving the matron's office and going to speak to one of the staff about plans for a send-off party. When she got her information, Shelby opted to head back to the palace. She was suddenly feeling rather tired.

~

Nikolai had not seen his wife all day. He had been out of the palace when she had been home and vise versa. They had not even had dinner together, but now he was home and delighted to see a light still on in her room. He started that way but didn't enter when he saw that she was sitting quite still by the window. Her profile told him she was not asleep, but she looked contemplative. Nikolai shifted a little on his feet, and Shelby heard.

"Oh, hello," she said softly, turning her head to see him.

Nikolai felt better about joining her.

"How was the evening?" she asked as he approached.

"It was fine," Nikolai said. *I wanted to hurry back to you* was what he thought. "How was your evening?"

"Nice and quiet."

Nikolai smiled at the relief in her voice.

"Ready to head to bed?" he asked.

"I am." Shelby's voice dropped a little, and her gaze shifted away. "I think I want to be in my own bed tonight, Nick. Is that all right?"

"Of course," he answered without hesitation. "I hope you sleep well." With that he bent to kiss Shelby's cheek and tell her goodnight. He returned to his own room, his mind racing frantically to figure out whether he had done something wrong. Save for the nights he'd been away, he and Shelby had shared a room for some weeks now. That something was amiss was very clear; the specifics, however, were not. With a rather confused heart, Nikolai headed into his own bathroom to get ready for bed. He was in the middle of brushing his teeth when reality hit. Mouth still full of toothpaste, he went back to the adjoining door but heard Shelby in the shower. Not even this would deter his plan.

Five minutes later he was dressed in his pajamas and removing his pillow from the bed. He grabbed his book and reading glasses, turned all the lights off in his room, and headed to Shelby's bed. He made himself comfortable on the one side, light on, pillow at his back, and opened his book. He was attempting to read when Shelby came from the bathroom, spotted him, and stopped still. Nikolai looked up and smiled.

"I thought I would join you in here," he explained.

Shelby only nodded and then spotted the pillow he'd placed on the chair.

"I'm more comfortable with my own," Nikolai said; he'd been watching her every move.

Again Shelby only nodded. She came toward the bed and climbed in, and although Nikolai had gone back to his book, he noticed she lay as far from him as she could get. She then reached for her own book. By shifting ever so slightly, Nikolai could watch her without being obvious. Shelby's eyes moved across the page, but she blinked often and slowly. Nikolai wondered if she would have turned the light off right away if he hadn't been reading already.

Without pomp or ceremony, he set his book aside and turned off his lamp. He leaned close, kissed Shelby again, and then settled on his pillow.

"Goodnight, Shelby," he said with his eyes closed.

"Goodnight."

Nikolai could tell that her head was turned and she was looking in his direction for some time. When she did move, he heard her put the book aside, and a moment later he could tell from behind his lids that the room was dark. The bed was just different enough that it took some time to gain sleep. Never a sound sleeper, Nikolai eventually nodded off to the sound of his wife's breathing, never suspecting the kind of night that lay ahead.

∼

The clock read 4:15 when Nikolai heard Shelby get up for the fifth time since she'd turned the light out. The shower in her bathroom came on almost as soon as she shut the door. It wasn't a long shower, but the noise was enough that Nikolai was still very awake when she returned to bed. He waited for her to get comfortable again and knew somehow that she had not immediately fallen back to sleep.

"Is it this rough on you every month, Shelby?"

Shelby sighed. "Did I wake you all night?"

"Yes, but that's all right."

He was met with silence.

"Is it this bad each month?"

"No. My system is not very regular. It's not at all unusual for me to go five or six weeks between cycles. On occasion I'll go seven weeks. That's what happened this time."

"Should you see a doctor?"

"I have, and he's told me that it's pretty normal for some women. If I don't have a period for more than seven weeks, I'm to come back, but it's been this way since I was 14."

"How busy is your day today?"

"I don't think I have anything planned, and if I did, I would probably cancel."

They fell silent for a time, and Nikolai thought Shelby might have gone back to sleep.

"I should have explained to you last night," Shelby started again. "I was embarrassed."

Nikolai reached over and found her hand.

"Were you angry?" Shelby asked.

"No. Confused about what I had done wrong but not angry."

"You truly don't anger easily, do you?"

"Not as a rule."

"What does make you mad?"

"Let's see." He thought for a moment. "I think people who hate the crown for no good reason upset me pretty quickly. Or someone who does nothing but criticizes my father. No king is perfect, but I think he does a good job."

"What angers you on a personal level?"

"Like being upset with you or someone on the staff?"

"Yes."

"Offhand I can't think of anything, but I will admit to you that I was angry at Peter the last time we saw him."

"Peter Owens?" Shelby asked, certain she had misunderstood him.

"Yes. He didn't know it, and I had to confess it because I had no right, but a few weeks back I felt the door was open for the first time to explain to Peter how Christ died for us. This time I saw that it really seemed to bother Peter that God would do this to His Son, and then in so many words he said he didn't believe it—that only a fool would fall for such a story."

"I don't think you told me about this."

"I was too upset to talk about it. But after I calmed down and thought back on it, I realized Peter was defending himself. His father never gave him unconditional love, and even his sisters, although they don't treat him badly, have their own lives and friends. A little brother is sometimes in the way."

"And a God who would offer an unconditional gift of love certainly can't be trusted," Shelby concluded.

"You said that in a way that makes me think you understand."

"I don't know if I do or not. I was from the camp that says 'I'm good enough. Why would I need a Savior?'"

"What changed your mind?"

"Believe it or not, a low test score in school. I had always taken great pride in my academic ability, and then suddenly I didn't measure up. In an instant I saw myself standing before God trying to tell Him all the things I did well. I could almost see Him shaking His head and saying it wasn't good enough. For the first time it became clear to me that I was desperately lost. My parents and brother had already seen their need. It took me a little longer."

Shelby heard Nikolai move, and suddenly his arms were around her. With his lips against her temple he said, "I'm so thankful you saw the truth, Red. I can't tell you how much."

Shelby gladly turned in his arms, wanting very much to be hugged right now. It wasn't long before she felt relaxed enough to fall back to sleep, and she suspected Nikolai had, but Shelby didn't let herself. She lay still until light crept in from the edges of the curtains, praying for the man who held her close.

~

Shelby would not have chosen to spend the first two days after Christmas on her own, but Nikolai had been called away. Although she had been all ready to offer to go with him, she had learned that the king was to go as well. Shelby thought they might want a chance to be on their own.

With a few free hours, the princess took some time to think about redecorating her bedroom. She thought the idea of a central theme in both rooms worth looking into and went to her husband's bedroom to study the color theme. She liked the navy blue in the wallpaper and the contrasting light carpet. Her husband's room was also trimmed in light oak. Shelby liked that as well but wasn't willing to give up her mahogany trim, something she didn't like with the black wallpaper. If she did follow a matching motif, it would have to match both woods, and she knew the navy would do that.

While standing in the middle of the room, Shelby noticed that Nikolai had left a sweater and some socks and undershirts on the chair. Thinking to save the staff a little trouble, she scooped them up and moved toward the closet. Almost as large as her own, the prince's closet was surprisingly full of clothing. Nikolai always looked nice, but Shelby would never have said he was the clotheshorse she was.

Shelby was on the verge of hanging the sweater she found when she spotted Yvette's picture. The photo was displayed in full view on top of Nikolai's neat and orderly dresser. Shelby had seen her photo in newspapers before, so she felt no need to study the image, but finding the picture on his dresser was unexpected.

Shelby finished putting his clothing away, her heart thoughtful. She let herself out of the closet and even remembered to turn off the light, but she couldn't honestly say that she knew what she felt just then.

~

"I don't know what I feel right now," Nikolai told his father. They were in Enstrom together and had just gone to dinner alone. The two men, so alike in height and build, now walked on the banks of the Pierce River.

"Tell me something, Nicky, do you always feel loved by God?"

"Not as feelings go, no, I can't say that I do."

"So what do you do when that happens, when you don't *feel* loved?"

"I claim the truths of Scripture. I look at what Christ did on the cross and know that could only come from a heart of love."

"So what do you do with your feelings?" the king asked.

"If they're contrary to Scripture, I work to get them in line. It's not always that easy, but that's the process."

Rafe fell silent. Nikolai had answered the question, but his father did not comment.

"Why did you ask me that, Dad?"

"I just wanted to know the answer."

"But we were talking about Shelby."

"Yes, we were, weren't we?" Again, Pendaran's king fell silent.

Nikolai walked along studying his father's profile. The prince was not a dull-witted person, but this one took some thought. When he felt he'd finally caught on, he found he didn't want to talk at all.

～

Shelby looked at the pile of letters on her desk and shook her head. Why had she thought that life would return to a normal pace when the holidays were over? The holidays and even the prince's birthday had been wonderful times of fellowship and worship with family and friends, but Shelby had to be honest about wanting things to slow down.

Sitting here whining about this isn't going to help, Shelby. Start on your mail.

She had just begun to open envelopes when the phone rang.

"Hello."

"Hello, Shelby, it's Erica. Did I get the day wrong?"

Shelby took a moment to respond. "Oh, no!" she gasped. "I completely forgot. I'm so sorry."

"It's all right. Did you already eat?"

"No."

"Well, come over. I'll watch for you."

"Okay," Shelby agreed hurriedly, hung up the phone, and nearly ran from her desk. She didn't know when she'd completely missed an appointment, and with the queen no less!

Erica guessed the kind of state she would be in and refused to listen to any of Shelby's apologies. She assured her that she was not offended, only hungry. Shelby hugged her for understanding and realized she was hungry as well.

The meal started with garden-fresh salads and led to a rich cream of asparagus soup. A light pudding was served for dessert, and all the time the women talked. Erica told some lighthearted stories from the past and even shared with Shelby some things she was struggling with right now. She ended by asking Shelby some rather pointed questions.

"With whom do you talk, Shelby?"

"With whom do I talk?" Shelby echoed uncomfortably, not liking the turn in the conversation, although it had come about very naturally.

"Yes. When you're uncertain or upset."

"Well," Shelby began, thinking she was uncertain and upset at the moment, "I guess I just talk to the Lord."

The queen, who had suspected as much, put a hand on her daughter-in-law's.

"Shelby, no one in the palace expects you to be silent all the time. Your discretion is admirable—both the king and I have noticed it—but when you're hurting about something, you need to go to someone."

"And who would that be?" Shelby asked, feeling a little angry at this woman for the first time. "Whom do you suggest?"

In that instant, as she looked into Shelby's dark brown eyes, Erica saw how difficult it would be—really saw this time, not just imagined. Wanting to mention herself, the king, or Shelby's parents, Erica somehow knew, right or wrong, that

Shelby had already ruled them out on certain issues. With a prayer for wisdom, she made a suggestion.

"Pastor Allen," the queen said. "He knows all about your situation. He and Rafe have talked many times, as have he and Nicky. Pastor Allen is the soul of discretion, and he has one large advantage. He knows some of the details already."

Shelby nodded.

"I'm sorry, Shelby," the queen continued. "I asked you that question as though your situation were completely normal, and it's not."

"Some days it doesn't feel as though it ever will be," the princess said softly.

"Do you think it will help when things become more intimate between you?"

Amazingly, Shelby didn't blush. "I'm not sure," she answered honestly. "I'm finding that there is more than one type of intimacy. You can be intimate physically and still not have a meeting of minds and hearts."

"That's very true, Shelby, but then would you consider it true intimacy?"

Shelby's smile was a little sad. "When it's all you've got, I guess you take what you can get."

Erica told herself to breathe, even as her heart squeezed in agony. She still managed to smile very gently. Shelby was glad she had not been condemned, but she felt like a fake.

"I need to tell you," Shelby admitted, "that my own feelings for Nikolai are uncertain. I can't have you sitting here thinking he's been this unfeeling monster. Nothing could be further from the truth, but we do have a long way to go."

"Thank you for telling me, Shelby. I'll be praying. I've *been* praying," the queen corrected, "but it's nice to be specific when we can be."

"Thank you," Shelby said sincerely. She knew the queen loved her son, but she never made Shelby feel that he was perfect or that any problems between them were all her fault.

Long after Shelby left, she thought of their conversation. The advice the queen gave was not unwelcome. She had talked to her old pastor many times. The very thought of going to Pastor Allen about the things she had on her mind caused her face to heat, but she didn't disregard the queen's advice; she thought about it off and on for the rest of the day.

~

"I need to talk to you," Erica said on the phone to her husband the moment he picked up.

"Is it urgent?"

"I'm feeling as though it is, but it's not—not really. I'm just upset."

"I can be with you in about 30 minutes. Will that be all right?"

"Yes."

Erica forced herself to be calm. What she wanted to do was go somewhere and sob her eyes out, but her mother called just after she hung up and that helped pass the time.

"I just had lunch with Shelby," Erica told her.

"Isn't she the sweetest thing?" the queen regent asked.

"She really is, Mom. I could talk to her all day."

"Did she mention that Peter is having lunch with Grandma today?"

"No. I'm not sure she knows. Why isn't he in school?"

"A teacher's workday. His sisters gave him permission to come for the entire day. Your father is going to take him out to the skeet club. As a matter of fact, they just left."

"Oh, he'll love that."

The queen and queen regent talked almost to the moment Rafe walked in the door, and Erica found she'd greatly calmed. She was able to explain the impression she'd gotten from Shelby without bursting into tears.

"Help me to understand this, Rafe. How can Nikolai and Shelby enter into this union when they're not in love?"

"Rica." Rafe's voice was gentle but also matter-of-fact. "Shelby is a very desirable woman, and I know that Nikolai is being very kind and gentle with her. His desire is not hard to understand at all. On her part, she obviously cares and is responding to his gentleness. There's also one other aspect we have to consider."

"What's that?"

"That they're already in love and don't know it."

Erica blinked. "How could they not?"

Rafe looked a bit confused but still said, "I think our level-headed son is having a hard time distinguishing the difference between feelings and facts. He knows that love is a choice, but all he ever says about Shelby is that he doesn't know how he feels about her."

"What have you said to him?"

"Enough to make him think, but he must choose to deal with all of his feelings where they must be dealt with—within the realm of facts."

Erica stared into her husband's wise face; she needed to do the same work with her own feelings.

"I'm glad I talked to you. I'm sorry I called in such a panic."

"It's all right. I do need to go back to the office, but I'm glad you found me available." In the middle of his words, Rafe had a thought that showed on his face.

"What is it?"

"I was just thinking that we could be grandparents this year."

That Erica hadn't considered this was very clear. She drew her lower lip between her teeth, a sure sign that she was worried.

"Will you say anything to Nicky?" the queen finally asked.

"No. He's a big boy now, and for all we know, that's the very reason they've consummated the relationship."

Erica nodded. Again she was surprised by his logic.

"No worrying now," her husband commanded before he kissed her.

"All right."

"God is sovereign" were the king's last words before he left his wife alone.

~

Nikolai woke slowly the next weekend, something unusual for him; he had a tendency to awaken quickly. As he stretched and peeked one eye open to look at the clock, he thought he must be very tired. His eyes had already closed again when he realized something was amiss. He peeked the other eye open to confirm it. His wife was wide awake and staring at him.

"I can't sleep if you're going to watch me, Red," he said with a sleepy voice, his eyes closing again.

Shelby smiled at little.

Nikolai could tell she was still staring right at him.

"I mean it, Red." His voice was a growl. "You have to look away."

Shelby laughed softly but continued to study his face.

"Did you enjoy last night?" she asked suddenly.

Nikolai's eyes suddenly opened very fast. "You're doubting?" he asked, finding himself wide awake.

Shelby shrugged, wishing she'd stayed quiet. "Well, you didn't say."

Nikolai felt a bit impatient, although he covered it. "What is it I do, Shelby, that makes you feel so inadequate as a wife?"

Shelby could not keep the shock from her face, and Nikolai realized too late what he had just said.

"I'd better get up," Shelby responded, having already worked to school her features. "I'm golfing this morning with Vickey."

Shelby turned to leave the bed, but Nikolai caught her from behind. "Don't go just yet," he said quietly as he moved close and snuggled against her back. "It's early."

Shelby let herself be hugged and tried not to think about why she'd asked her husband that question or why she ached inside right now. She could not put her finger on one single point, but her whole being was telling her to go somewhere and have a good, long cry. Before she could stop them, a few tears fell.

"Shelby?" Nikolai asked. He'd felt a drop of moisture on his arm and begun to sit up.

"I have to get up," she gasped as she moved from his arms.

Not knowing if it was a mistake or not, Nikolai did not try to stop her. She nearly ran from the room, and the prince rolled to his back and stared at the ceiling.

I could speculate about a lot of things right now and let myself off the hook, but I would be willing to bet my last dollar that I have somehow caused those tears. Help me, Lord. Help me to find a way to love my wife as she deserves to be loved.

For the first time, Yvette's face did not swim into view the moment he thought about love. If it had, Nikolai would have pushed it away. Shelby was the woman who needed him right now.

Eighteen

"Well, Nick!" Daria said in surprise when she opened the front door and found him standing there. "Come in."

"Thank you. Is my timing awful?"

"Not at all. Josiah went back to the shop, and I just did the lunch dishes so I could sit down with a cup of tea. Will you join me?"

"I will, thank you."

Daria sent Nikolai into the living room while she went for the tea tray. He intended to sit down but found himself interested in the pictures on the walls. A young Josiah and Daria Parker looked out from one frame—she in a long white gown, he in a black suit. Shelby and Brice's graduation pictures were there, as were some baby photos. He wouldn't have believed his wife could ever be round, but there was no mistaking the redheaded butterball that smiled into the camera as a toddler. Nikolai found himself smiling at her in return.

"Here we are," Daria said as she entered the room. "I didn't know if you liked milk or lemon, so I brought both."

"Let me get that for you." Nikolai met her in the middle of the room and, taking the tray, set it on the coffee table.

Daria began a gentle dialogue about how fun the holidays

had been, and Nikolai was glad to have something to talk about. It didn't last long, however. She waited only until Nikolai had taken a few sips of tea to say what was on her mind.

"I think you've come today looking for something, Prince Nikolai. Are you going to tell me what it is?"

Nikolai looked into kind eyes, so like his wife's, and put his teacup down.

"It's been on my mind how you and Josiah trusted me to take care of your daughter. I don't know how much Shelby has talked to you, but I haven't always done a good job. I'm trying to rectify that."

Daria smiled at him. "I appreciate that very much. In truth, Nick, we have seen how lonely she is."

The words did strange things to his heart. In a quiet voice he asked, "Did you by any chance love someone else before you met Shelby's father?"

"No, I didn't, Nick, but believe it or not, my mother experienced what you're going through." Daria smiled at Nikolai's raised brow and continued. "My mother married my stepfather because she found herself widowed and alone, with two very little girls to take care of and no way to support them. He had adored her. It took more than two years for her to love him. They shared a bed and a life, but not love—at least not at first. When my mother did come to love my stepfather, it was with her entire being, but the pain of my father's death and his memory plagued her for a very long time."

Nikolai could not believe what he was hearing. The first question in his mind was whether Shelby knew this, but he realized that was foolish. Of course she knew.

"I've surprised you, haven't I?"

"Yes, but I thank you for telling me."

"If I can be so bold, Nick, I'd like to give you a little advice—something I think my mother would have said to you."

The prince nodded.

"Don't try to get *over* Yvette. Just make room in your heart for Shelby."

Without permission Nikolai stood. He walked to the window and stood looking out but didn't really see anything. He was having a hard time breathing but didn't notice. His mind saw Shelby's sweet face as she asked him not to say those three little words until he meant them.

Nikolai suddenly turned back to his mother-in-law. Just looking at her face reminded him that he must wait until he was certain. And even if he was certain, the timing for Shelby's sake must be right.

"I think I've lost you," Daria said.

"I'm sorry." Nikolai was instantly contrite and made a move to return to his seat. His hostess surprised him by standing up.

"I'm glad you came, Nick, and if you really want to stay, you're welcome, but I think you have some things to think about and probably want to be alone to do it."

Before he could consider otherwise, Nikolai went to Daria and gave her a hug. She hugged him in return. Thanking her sincerely, he made his way to the door. His hand was on the knob when he spotted a box addressed to Princess Shelby Markham. Nikolai turned back.

"Would you like me to take this to Shelby?"

Daria laughed. "Oh, you don't have to. It's just silly."

Nikolai smiled, picked it up, and weighed it in his hands. "Clothes?"

"No," Daria laughed again. "Fairy Cakes."

"*Fairy Cakes?*"

"Shelby is crazy about them." Daria shook her head. "A palace full of the finest desserts in the land, and she likes little packaged cakes."

Nikolai watched her for a moment. "You miss her, don't you?"

Tears filled Daria's eyes so fast that they were both amazed.

"I'll get these to her" was all Nikolai said, but his heart was assuring Daria that he would do right by her daughter if it was the last thing he ever did.

～

The events of recent weeks had united to make Shelby tired. Various encounters with her husband, some that hurt her and caused her painful confusion, had occurred. Shelby had not confronted him over any of them, making it all the more unsettling to have him turn around and treat her with such tenderness. Shelby was amazed. It was also puzzling to learn that he'd visited her mother. She was still trying to understand that one.

You could ask him, Shelby. Your mother may have read it all wrong. You've got to learn to talk to your husband. All you do is guess. You have no idea if you're correct or not. If you'll just talk to him, you might learn to love him as you should. You might even find a way to ask him about Yvette and tell him . . . Shelby shut down at that point. She didn't want to think about the possibilities, although her heart was telling her that was just what she needed to do.

Shelby was still in the midst of these mental aerobics when she heard a noise. The bathroom door opened, and Shelby, who was soaking in a tub full of suds, sank a little further into the water.

"Shelby?"

"Yes," she said as she tugged the curtain over.

"Hi," Nikolai said as he came in and shut the door. "It smells good in here."

"It's the bubbles," Shelby said, her red face peeking around the curtain. She watched Nikolai come all the way in and sit on the bench in front of her makeup table. He was in a perfect position to see her, but Shelby had pulled the curtain a little further forward and let the water cover her.

"How are you?" he asked, his eyes on her face.

"Fine."

Nikolai studied her. "Are you really?"

"I think so. Why do you ask?"

"I've just never known you to take a bath in the middle of the day."

"Oh, that. Well, I'm just a little achy."

"Could this be tied to your cycle?" he asked, knowing she would be embarrassed but trying to take down more walls.

"It could," Shelby said, her eyes averted.

"Shelby," Nikolai said, waiting for her to look at him. "What can we do to help you not be so shy around me?"

Shelby made herself look at him. "Do you think it's really that bad?"

Nikolai nodded. "You're the most modest individual I've ever known. You like the lights out and your bathrobe close at hand when the lights come on. You even prefer me to be covered, but you can barely take your eyes from me when I'm not fully dressed." He paused. "Right now, you're nearly drowning yourself to stay under those bubbles."

Shelby sighed. "We're a very modest family. I guess I've never thought about it, but it's true. I don't think I've ever seen my father without his shirt." She shrugged a little. "It's so lame to say that's the way I was raised, but in this case, it's very true."

Nikolai barely kept his mouth closed. That she had never seen her father's bare chest was amazing to him.

"Nikolai?" Shelby called his name and brought his attention back.

"Yes?"

"Do you think I'm pretty?" Shelby forced herself to ask.

"No."

Shelby nodded. She had figured as much, but hearing his admission was harder than she expected.

"I think you're beautiful."

All Shelby could do was stare at him, even when he rose,

came toward her, and bent low over the tub, his hands on either rim.

"Very, very beautiful. And I'm a fool for never having told you."

"Oh, Nicky, you've never said. You've complimented what I'm wearing but never mentioned me. I'm sorry it was so important to me."

"Never apologize for needing that affirmation. I think it every day, and I've been wrong not to tell you."

Shelby raised her face, eager to kiss him. Nikolai was just as eager to touch her.

"You are," he said softly, his lips still brushing hers, "the sweetest woman I've ever known. And you always taste wonderful."

Shelby smiled; he couldn't know the balm he'd poured on her heart. "When you give compliments, you go all the way, don't you?"

Nikolai only laughed and kissed her once again.

His touch was so soft. For an instant Shelby felt very cherished. Her heart told her to talk to her husband, to share her own heart and get close to his. But Shelby refused to do as she should.

~

"Thank you for meeting me," Nikolai said to Daria and Josiah as they walked in Henley's park. "She's so quiet these days. I ask her what I can do, but she just doesn't share."

The Parkers exchanged a glance, and Daria spoke, signing as well to ensure that Josiah could follow the conversation.

"We were just talking about this, Nick, and although there are things from the past that have to be worked out, right now we honestly think it's the baby. Shelby is even a little quiet with us, and we've just let—" Daria stopped when Nikolai came to a dead halt, his face mirroring shock and hurt.

Daria's hand went to her mouth. "Oh, Nick, did she not tell you?"

"No."

For a moment all three were silent.

"Come over here," Josiah directed at last, leading them to a bench that had a little privacy under one of the trees. He motioned for his wife and son-in-law to sit down while he sat on the bricks at their feet.

"Shelby didn't tell you she's expecting?"

Nikolai shook his head no. Tears had come to his eyes. "I feel like I love her," he said softly, "but she's so distant these days; I don't know how to tell her."

Daria wanted to sob. Even Josiah's eyes were suspiciously moist.

"She has to be the one to tell me about the baby," Nikolai said. "It has to come from her. I haven't gained her trust yet, that's obvious. When she knows she can trust me, she'll share."

"I could be wrong, but I'm not sure it's a trust issue, Nick," Daria had to tell him. "She told me that she can't stand the thought of this child knowing that he or she wasn't a product of your love. She knows that she'll love the baby and so will you, but the love between the two of you is missing. I tried to tell her love is a choice—she said Pastor Allen said the same thing when she went to talk with him—but she's not thinking clearly right now."

"She can't be," Josiah said, "or she would see how much you care. Does she know that you come here to see us?"

"I think so."

"Someone ought to tell her," Josiah went on, "that a man who will visit his in-laws in an effort to love his wife is very special. Shelby needs to understand that."

"Please don't tell her you've told me about the baby," Nikolai requested. "I want it to come from her. When we've talked it all out, I can tell her I knew, but not now."

"So you won't talk to her when you get home?"

Nikolai shook his head. "No. At least not for a while. If she waits too long, I'll need to say something, but my hope is that she'll come to me."

"We'll be praying for that very thing."

"Has she seen a doctor?" Nikolai asked.

"No. She did a home test and said it took only a few seconds to show positive. Beyond that, she says she feels different."

It didn't sound as though there could be any mistake. Nikolai thanked the Parkers for telling him. He desperately wanted to be alone, but he took some time to tell them how much he appreciated their efforts and support of him. Their conversation ended on a positive note, as their talk ranged to Brice's activities. By the time he said goodbye, Nikolai had his emotions under control. His plan to swing by Ryan's and talk with him, however, was changed. The prince just wanted to go home.

I have to remind myself that You knew all about this. I've dreamed of having children my whole life, and now my baby is here and I can't even share in it. I don't know when I've been so confused. I'm trying to show Shelby I love her, but she's not seeing it. She still holds me at arm's length. I've got to find out what I've done to cause that. Something is wrong here, Lord. Please show me what it is, or help Shelby to open up to me. The prince laid his head back, thinking that would be the sweetest thing of all.

He prayed all the way home, giving his wife, baby, and marriage over to God. Each time he worried and took them back. He debated about going to his father or Pastor Allen but decided to wait. The only person he really wanted to hear from was Shelby, and he thought the best way to promote that would be to spend time with her. Nikolai was forming a plan, even as he was let off at the front door and making his way inside the palace.

～

Two days later, Shelby walked onto the deck at the lake house and stood still in the crisp morning air. She hadn't bothered to make coffee or have anything to eat. She found she wasn't hungry at all—only hurting and confused. That most of her hurt was her own fault was not something she wanted to deal with.

As she'd been doing, she pushed all thoughts of the baby away. Looking out at the water, she realized that as soon as Nikolai woke, he would look for her. Without leaving a note any more specific than "Going for a walk," Shelby left the house and headed to the beach, all the time denying the knowledge of what she must do.

∼

Nikolai wouldn't have said that he could wait a week, but so far he had made it. As soon as he had arrived home, he suggested to Shelby that they head to the lake for the weekend. She hadn't been thrilled but had gone and, although she had slept a lot, seemed to have a good time. She had even seen and played with Jenny and Monty Stevenson and their baby brother, Ricky, but still she had not shared the news with him. He prayed all the way home that she would come clean, but it was not to happen. Nikolai thought he would give her a few more days and then make some gentle hints. Even if he hadn't known the facts, he would have started to wonder. Shelby's appetite had changed, and she was fatigued all the time.

He knew she was too tired to attend the dinner they were invited to that night, but when he suggested that they stay home, or at the very least, she stay home, she declined.

"They'll understand if you're tired, Red," Nikolai said gently, referring to the hosts.

"You're right, Nick, but they've both been so kind to me. I'd really like to go."

"We can make it an early night," Nikolai suggested, and Shelby was more than willing to comply with that plan.

What neither of them counted on was the man driving the large truck. He didn't see the red light as Ivan, taking the royal couple to dinner, crossed the intersection. The truck was on Shelby's side, and she spotted it just moments before impact. After that, she knew nothing for several hours.

~

Shelby struggled out of unconsciousness and squinted at the woman bending over her.

"Nicky," she tried to say.

"It's all right, Princess Shelby. You're going to be all right. She's awake," the woman said to someone else, and Shelby told herself to fight the pain and speak. A man had just bent over her when she found her voice.

"Where is my husband?" she whispered.

"He's being looked at right now, but he's fine. We'll bring him to you as soon as the other doctor finishes his examination."

"Ivan?"

"The driver? Not a scratch."

"I need to see Nick."

"You will."

"I have to talk to him," she said, working to lift her hands to plead with him. "It's so important." But Shelby's hands didn't come up; she only imagined they had. She was too weak and too full of tubes to realize. Sleep was crowding in, and she couldn't fight it. Somewhere in her mind she knew they were lying to her. Nikolai was dead, and she would never see him again. She began to cry just as she fell back to sleep.

~

Daria and Erica sat side by side next to Shelby's bed, their eyes on her white, bruised face. She'd been admitted to a regular room, not intensive care. The prince was in only for observation. Shelby had lost a great deal of blood and would be in the hospital for some days. The two mothers hadn't spoken much; they were content to wait for signs of life. Almost an hour passed before Shelby's lids flickered. The women stood as one.

"Shelby?" her mother spoke softly.

"Mother?"

"I'm right here."

"Where's Nicky?"

"He's right down the hall."

Shelby focused on her mother.

"Tell me he's not dead—please, Mother, just tell me he's all right."

"He's fine. The doctor just wants him to rest until you wake up."

Shelby tried to swallow, and Erica helped her with an ice chip. Shelby nodded her thanks before her eyes flew back to her mother.

"The baby!"

Daria quickly shook her head no and then watched Shelby's eyes go to the window. Although not crying, she lay very still for a time, staring unseeingly across the room. Neither of the older women knew what to say to her. As they sat together waiting, Daria had shared some of the past events with Erica. For this reason the older women allowed the quiet to continue.

"Mother," Shelby spoke at last, her eyes still distant.

"Yes, dear."

"May I get up and go see Nicky? Please."

"No, love. You've lost too much blood."

"He's aching to see you, Shelby," Erica put in. "Rafe and your father are with him, but he only has to stay in bed until you're ready to see him."

"I couldn't wait that long," said a voice from the door.

Shelby's eyes flew to the prince, scanning his person as best she could to see if he was all right. As he came forward, the mothers slipped from the room. Shelby didn't even wait for the door to close before she began to speak.

"I've done something awful, Nicky, just awful."

Nikolai came close, pulling up a chair to sit down. He was still weak and shaken.

"Do you want to tell me about it?" he asked.

Shelby nodded, thinking he was too nice.

"You deserve better than me for a wife, Nicky. I've just realized it."

"Nothing could be further from the truth, Red. And no matter what you say to me, I'll still feel that way."

Shelby licked her lips. "I've sinned against you, Nicky. I don't know if I can ever make it right." She paused, but Nikolai did not interrupt. "I was pregnant and didn't tell you," she said softly, making her eyes meet his. "I'm sorry. I never let you share in our baby, and now he's gone."

Nikolai smoothed the hair from her forehead, careful not to bump the gash over her left eyebrow.

"Is there a reason you couldn't tell me?"

"There is, Nick, but it's nothing but an excuse."

"Tell me anyway."

Shelby's eyes went to the ceiling again. "If it had just been us, Nick, I would have told you, but I wasn't willing to share our baby with Yvette. You still keep her picture in your closet, and one night you called for her." The princess looked at the prince, her eyes flooded with tears. "I've had to share you, Nicky, but I wasn't going to share our baby."

"Oh, Red," he whispered, "I'm sorry. So very, very sorry."

"You're sorry? No, Nicky, I—"

But Nikolai would not let her continue. He put his fingers over her mouth.

"I put Yvette's picture away a few weeks ago, but obviously not soon enough. And I do think of her, but she's not filling my dreams as it must have seemed."

Shelby shook her head. "I told you that was just an excuse.

I've sinned against you, Nicky," she cried now. "Don't you see how wrong I was?"

Nikolai stood and bent over so he could take her in his arms. He moved ever so carefully, the position awkward, but he had to hold her as she cried.

"We've both made mistakes," he said in her ear. "I'm sorry, and I know you are, but we survived the accident, Red. God is giving us another chance."

Nikolai backed off a bit to look into her eyes.

"Do you understand what I'm saying?"

Shelby sniffed as she nodded.

"I don't deserve to be forgiven by you."

"That's not true," Nikolai responded with deep conviction. "I've sinned against you as well. We need to learn from this, not let it tear us apart."

Shelby sobbed then. His forgiveness had seemed so unreachable. She had been disoriented when she first woke, but stark reality had not been long in coming.

Please help me, her heart cried out silently to God as she tried to hold Nikolai with bruised arms and hands. *Nicky's knowing about the baby would not have stopped the accident tonight, but at least I would have been blameless. He's so willing to give me a second chance. Help me not to take that away from us with my selfishness, fear, and pride.* Shelby could not go on. She wanted to cry and pray some more and hold onto Nikolai forever, but everything was fading.

"I can't stay awake," she just managed before her eyes closed and her arms went limp.

"It's all right," Nikolai told her. He was spent as well. Moving carefully, he withdrew his arms and sat back down. He reached over and brushed the damp hair and tears from her face.

"It's all right, Red," he repeated, knowing she could not hear him. "And as soon as you're ready to hear it, I'll tell you just how all right it's going to be."

Nineteen

"There's someone here to see you, Prince Nikolai," the nurse said quietly the next morning. Nikolai had just showered and finished his breakfast. "He says his name is Peter Owens."

Nikolai nodded. "Please tell him to come in."

Peter entered the hospital room moments later, his eyes huge and wary. That he was nervous about being back in this place was clear. It was also clear that seeing the strong, able prince of Pendaran in a hospital bed was not something that put him at ease.

"Hello, Peter."

"Hello."

"Come in and sit down," Nikolai said as he slowly swung his legs to the edge of the bed. "Who brought you to the hospital?"

"Toby. He came over while I was getting ready for school, and Pam," Peter continued, referring to his oldest sister, "said I could come."

"I'm glad you did."

Peter reached up to brush his too-long hair from his brow and continued to study the prince.

"Where is Toby?"

"He went to see the princess. He said she got hurt pretty bad."

"A truck hit the car" was all Nikolai said. He didn't want to go into details with this little boy.

"Did she almost die?"

"Well, she lost a lot of blood. And she'll be very weak for a while."

Peter nodded, his eyes dropping to his shoes.

"I need to tell you, Peter, that I would have been very sad if my wife had died, but Shelby believes as I do, that Christ died for her sins, so I know she would have been with Him."

"You mean in heaven?"

"Yes. Like we've talked about before."

"I was gonna ask you about that sometime," Peter said, his eyes on his shoes. "Not today, but sometime."

"Ask me what?"

He gestured with his hands, looking a little embarrassed. "You know, that stuff I didn't want to believe before, about God's Son and all that."

Nikolai tipped his head as he thought. "It's interesting that you should ask me about it here. After I understood my need to be saved, I prayed with my grandfather in a hospital room like this one. I was just a little younger than you are right now."

Peter licked his lips. "What did you say to God?"

"I told Him I believed that His Son died for my sins. I told Him I needed to be saved. And then I asked Him to come inside of me to live. God will do that, by the way—place His Spirit right inside of us when we accept His gift of salvation. And that's what He did for me, because He could see into my heart and knew that I believed that only His Son could save me."

"I don't know if I'm ready to say that to God," the child admitted.

"I'm glad you're thinking it over, Peter," the prince surprised him by saying. "It's a big commitment. Not something to be taken lightly, if you know what I mean."

"I figured as much. My sister was surprised when I tried to tell her, so I knew it must be pretty big."

"Did she make you feel that you couldn't?"

"No. She just didn't understand why I needed to."

Nikolai smiled. "Well, you can understand how she feels, can't you, Peter?"

Peter's brow lowered in confusion.

"The last time we talked, you pretty much said that it was a foolish thing to believe."

"I guess I did, but I've been thinking more."

"What have you been thinking?"

"That it would be nice to have Someone to talk to—like you said before—even when I'm alone or when I'm scared."

"It is nice, Peter—very nice. I love knowing God loves me and will never leave me. God doesn't make life perfect for those who trust in Him, but He does promise to always be with us."

The interest moved out of Peter's eyes, or was it panic that replaced the yearning?

"What do you think it is, Peter, that stops you from wanting Christ to save you and live inside of you?"

"I don't know," Peter said distantly, and again Nikolai felt the door had closed. "I need to go see Princess Shelby," Nikolai's visitor added.

"All right. I'll come with you. But before we go, Peter, remember one thing: You can always talk to me about this, and you can always go to Toby."

Peter nodded and even smiled a little before they left the room and started down the hall.

~

"Thank you for the flowers, Toby."

"You're welcome," Toby said sincerely, but his eyes were sad. "Rafe told me about the baby, Shelby. I'm sorry."

Shelby took a deep breath. "Thank you, Toby. I'll admit

that for a little while there I thought you had picked the wrong princess, but I'm doing better now."

Toby took her hand. "I'm glad to hear it, Shelby, because there wasn't anyone else more perfect for the job."

"You're too kind."

Toby smiled. "Is that what you call it? I call the whole business a rescue from God alone."

"Who needed to be rescued?" Shelby asked, her brow lowered in puzzlement. Before the king's closest friend could answer, they were joined by Peter and Nikolai.

"Hello, Peter." Shelby smiled at the boy but saw the shock on his face. For the first time she wondered what she looked like. "How are you?" she tried again, telling herself not to worry about her appearance.

"All right," he answered, but his voice was unusually subdued.

"I'm fine," Shelby felt the need to tell him. "I got bumped and bruised," she added, searching for the right words. "But I'm going home in just a few days."

Peter nodded but still didn't appear to be pleased. The adults filled in a little on the conversation, but Toby wasn't long in seeing that Peter needed to leave. They said their goodbyes about ten minutes later, leaving the prince and princess alone.

"Was he that nervous with you, Nick?" Shelby asked.

"Right as he walked in, yes, but then we had a pretty good talk. I think he wanted to come in here because I was asking him things that he didn't know how to answer. He gave something away for the first time, something about his sister. I think that might be some of what's going on right now."

"Maybe I should visit her sometime."

"That's not a bad idea."

"By the way, do I look horrendous?"

"I don't know if I'd go so far as to say horrendous, but you're a mess."

Shelby's mouth opened on his bluntness, and Nikolai smiled at her.

"Maybe you had better get me a mirror."

Nikolai shrugged. "I'll just tell you—you have a gash over your left brow, and your eyes are so black you look like a racoon."

Shelby stared at him in disbelief and then saw the teasing glint in his eye. "You obviously studied tact in school, Nick. You should be teaching classes."

Nikolai got a good laugh over her response while Shelby continued to study him.

"I think I'll take that mirror anyway, if you don't mind."

It took some doing, but Nikolai came up with a hand mirror.

"I do look like a racoon," Shelby agreed, studying her reflection with chagrin. "I didn't believe you." She looked again at the glass. "I don't know if my pride can take this. Maybe I won't have any more visitors."

"Actually, your visitors are limited anyway."

"Oh, how come?"

"Doctor's orders. He's not overly worried about you, but he's not taking any chances either. I know of several people who have been turned away."

Shelby nodded. She had worked in a hospital long enough to know the ropes. "How are you feeling, by the way?"

"Just a little sore."

"Are you going home today?"

Nikolai drew close before he answered. "Yes. It's not fair to take a bed and the staff's time when all the X-rays and tests have come back fine."

Shelby sighed. "I'm glad you're all right."

Nikolai leaned to kiss her. "I am too. Did you eat something yet?"

"No. I wasn't too hungry."

"How about now?"

"I could go for a Fairy Cake," Shelby said.

He surprised her by saying, "I'll see what I can do."

Shelby was still smiling when he left but was surprised when he didn't return. Indeed, her next visitor was Brice.

"Brice!"

"Hey, Red."

"Who called you?"

"Fa. I would have been here earlier, but I got word that you had a certain craving."

Shelby blinked at him and then laughed when a box of Fairy Cakes came from under his shirt. Just moments later Shelby had stuffed one into her mouth and was asking for milk. Brice managed to produce that as well, and Shelby's mouth was full again by the time the doctor walked in. Dr. Finley was a man she'd known for years. He felt free to tease her.

"That's a great breakfast," he said dryly.

Shelby grinned unrepentantly. "Want one?"

He appeared to consider it. "I think I do."

They didn't get down to talking about how Shelby was doing for several more minutes, but the prognosis was good. Yes, she had lost a lot of blood but was very strong physically. If she continued to improve, she would probably be home in about two days.

~

Erica's hug was delightfully long and warm when she came to see Shelby the second day she was home. It was a Sunday morning, and she had been assigned "princess sitting" duties by Nikolai. Shelby had showered and dressed but gone back to bed in Nikolai's room. Erica pulled a chair close to the mattress and then propped her feet up.

"Thank you for volunteering to come," Shelby said to her mother-in-law. "Much as he would have disagreed, Nick needed to get out."

Erica nodded. "Nikolai went with Rafe, who'll see to it that he stays out for a time. Rafe even planned to talk him into having lunch. Because I'm with you, I hope he'll agree."

"It was my turn to sign in church today." Shelby's voice was wistful.

"I'm sure they'll miss you, but everyone understands. Rafe is going to bring us the tape of the service this morning too."

Shelby nodded and then fell silent.

"How are you doing inside, Shelby?"

"Pretty well. I still regret not talking to Nicky, but I'm not beating myself up over it. I do think about the baby, though. A lot."

Erica nodded. "We've never talked about my efforts to have a baby, have we?"

"Nick has mentioned it, but I don't think you and I have discussed it."

Erica shook her head. "It was such a painful time. I learned a great deal about God's sovereignty during those years, but for a long time I thought I was defective."

"Did you really?"

"Yes. My mother had had my sisters and me, and before her, Grandma had given birth to my father and all his siblings, and I felt I'd dropped the ball. If I hadn't gotten pregnant at all, Shelby, it would have been easier. Then Rafe could have shared the load. But to get pregnant time after time and then lose the baby was unbelievable pain and loss."

"Did they ever figure out why?"

"No. I had five miscarriages in three years. I was put to bed as soon as we knew I was pregnant for the last two pregnancies, and that finally worked. Nikolai was born to us. You can't believe our joy."

"I think maybe I can."

Erica smiled. "Of course you can. I wasn't thinking when I said that."

"What if we can't have another?" Shelby voiced her thoughts.

"God will give you the strength, but unless there's something the doctors missed, Shelby, God will have another child for you. Your miscarriage was clearly a result of the accident. As I said, they never did figure mine out."

"I keep telling myself the same thing, but I do have my doubts."

"This is the real testing ground, isn't it, Shelby? When life is going along easily, when we're in harmony with God and our mate, when no one we love has died or is hurting—those are the times when life can seem grand. Some people would say that if that's the criteria, life is never grand. Those people especially, and eventually all of us, have had to learn to praise God when they hurt or when life changes and becomes confusing. It seems to me that you are in just such a time. It even seems to me that you've been in such a time since you married my son ten months ago."

Shelby stared at her, so many things rushing through her mind. This *had* been a time of growth for her. She was learning to trust as she never had before. Indeed, life had seemed ideal before the king and queen sat across from her in her parents' living room.

"I never thought about it that way before. Sometimes all I can see are the mistakes I've made."

"That's just what Satan wants, but deep inside you know better, don't you?"

"Yes," she said softly. "I do hurt over the baby and over the way I treated Nick, but I'm not destroyed. I think that must be God's work in my life."

Erica picked up Shelby's hand. "I'm sure of it, dear. I won't tell you I didn't experience some anger when you didn't let us all share in the baby, but you're a different person now than when you married Nicky. I didn't think I could love you any more than when we first met, but I've learned otherwise. You are so precious to me, Shelby. You're the daughter I couldn't have. Even if I had tried to dream you, you're the daughter my imagination wouldn't have done justice to."

Her comments made Shelby feel cherished and just a little tired. It was on Shelby's heart to tell the queen what she meant to her, but she didn't have the emotional energy. Instead Shelby thanked Erica and asked her to share about growing up in the palace and with her sisters. Somewhere in the story, she fell asleep. Erica left her to rest, moving to a seat by the window with her Bible and a study book. This was the way Nikolai found them almost two hours later.

"How was lunch?" Erica asked as soon as he took a seat.

"It was good. We just went to the grill. Father is probably close behind me, but Wallace had some news for him when we got in." Nikolai glanced toward his wife, even though he'd just been next to the bed checking on her. "How did she do?"

"Fine. We talked for a while, but she's been sleeping for some time now."

"Did she complain of any discomfort or pain?"

"Not beyond saying she was sore and wobbling a little on the way to the bathroom."

Nikolai nodded and looked back toward the bed. The room was huge, and their voices were hushed. Shelby usually slept soundly, but he noticed that she was beginning to stir.

"Feel free to head home," Nikolai offered. "I plan to be here the rest of the day."

Erica nodded. "Shelby said you needed to get out."

Nikolai smiled. "I appreciate her concern, but I'm not feeling a hundred percent either. I'll probably crawl in beside her and sleep for a while myself."

"In that case, I'll be off."

Erica kissed Nikolai on her way out. Rafe met her in the hall, but as soon as she explained Nikolai's intent, he went home with his wife. Had Nikolai known, he would have been thankful for his father's choice; the prince was asleep beside his wife just ten minutes later.

~

Shelby made it to the bottom of the stairs, a triumphant smile on her face. She was headed to Nikolai's office to surprise him. She had yet to venture from the bedrooms or the green parlor since she had come home six days earlier, but this morning she felt strong enough to make the effort. It was very deflating to find Nikolai's office empty. She was certain that's where he said he would be.

With no more energy to search further, Shelby took a seat in her husband's desk chair. It was too large for her but still comfortable, and for a while she just sat and stared out the window into the courtyard. She thought a walk in the sunshine might be nice but couldn't summon the energy.

"I found her."

Shelby opened her eyes to the sound of her husband's voice. He was speaking on the phone.

"In the office," he continued. "I'll let you know if I need you."

"I came down to surprise you and you weren't here," Shelby told him as soon as the phone was back in its cradle.

"Well, you surprised the staff instead." His voice was mild.

"How did I do that?"

Nikolai sat on the edge of the desk, his legs close to the desk chair. "Arlanda couldn't find you. They were in something of a panic."

"Oh, no. I didn't see anyone when I came down, but I didn't think anything of it."

Nikolai nodded but didn't speak. He was watching her so closely that Shelby began to feel uncomfortable.

"Are you angry at me?"

"Not at all. I'm trying to gauge if you're strong enough to walk to the main salon."

Shelby's brows rose. "What's in the salon?"

Nikolai didn't answer, but Shelby would not let the subject drop. With a decisive move, she pushed from the chair and headed out the door. Nikolai came after her, still debating whether he should have said anything.

"Oh, my" was all Shelby could manage as she opened the double doors and stared.

The main salon in the north quadrant was ablaze with flowers. Every conceivable blossom, size, and variety was present.

"It seems that the people of Pendaran heard of your accident and wanted you to know they cared."

Shelby turned to look at him, her mouth slightly agape.

"The staff is saying that we haven't had this many flowers at the palace since my mother was finally able to give birth to a child." The prince smiled. "I've been upstaged."

"Oh, Nicky," Shelby whispered. "Do you ever feel completely unworthy?"

"Often."

Shelby shook her head. "I haven't been such a great princess, Nick. If only they knew."

"If they knew everything I did, the flowers would never stop coming," he said gently.

It was too much for Shelby. Tears filled her eyes.

"This is why you asked if I was strong enough."

Nikolai didn't need to reply. He lifted her in his arms, Shelby's arms going around his neck, as he stamped down his alarm over how slight she felt and bore her gently back to bed. Arlanda was hovering with hot tea and blankets, but Shelby was almost asleep again.

"I'm so tired of tired, Nicky." The words came out on a sigh.

Nikolai only smiled as her face turned into the pillow and she fell asleep. It was amazing to him what he felt for this woman. The protectiveness inside of him was fierce, but the

love was of the gentlest kind. It also made him patient—a good
thing right now. If the sight of flowers made her cry, he feared
what the declaration of his feelings might do.

~

"There's been a change in plans," Nikolai mentioned to
Shelby about three weeks later. "We'll be leaving for the lake in
about two hours."

"All right," Shelby agreed, but she was confused. They were
breakfasting together in the small dining room with plans to
drive to the lake house immediately after.

"Are you all ready to leave?"

"Yes. I just have to grab my Bible and the book I'm reading."

"All right. Do that as soon as you're done eating, so we can
leave right after they go."

"Right after who goes?"

"The women."

"What women?"

"The women who are coming."

Shelby stopped, a small smile at her mouth. That Nikolai
wasn't going to come right out with it was obvious, but Shelby
wanted to know.

"Someone I know?"

"Yes."

"Do I know them well?"

"Yes."

"My mother?"

"Yes."

Shelby bit her lip. Who would be coming with her mother?

"Your mother?"

"Yes."

Shelby's smile was huge as she asked, "Are there more?"

"Yes."

"May I have a million dollars?"

Nikolai caught himself just in time, smiled, and said, "No, you may not."

Shelby laughed. "Please tell."

Nikolai shook his head.

"Tell me why they're coming."

Again the shake of his head.

"I'll scratch your back when we get to the lake," Shelby said, her voice at its most coaxing.

Nikolai's eyes lit with little flames as he looked across at her. "You do know how to tempt a man, don't you, Red?"

"Well, one man anyhow," she said with a smile.

Nikolai leaned close, and Shelby, thinking he was going to tell, leaned toward him.

"No," he whispered in her ear.

Murdock appeared before Shelby could cry in outrage. His presence, however, seemed to be some sort of signal.

"Are you done eating?" Nikolai asked solicitously.

"Yes. Am I going to find out now?"

"Yes. Just head into the dining room. They're waiting for you."

Shelby stood to leave, but Nikolai grabbed her for a kiss before she could get away.

"Have fun," he bid her with a smile. Shelby followed Murdock from the room.

What she found in the dining room was the last thing she expected.

"Surprise!" the women shouted.

Standing around a huge table stacked with decorating supplies of every kind were her mother, her mother-in-law, the queen regent, all the ladies from her Bible study, and even the queen mother. In a matter of seconds they had brought Shelby into the room, each one talking thirteen to the dozen. It wasn't two hours before she and Nikolai left for the lake; it was more like four.

Twenty

"So what did you choose?" Nikolai asked almost as soon as they were in the limo, his hand already having claimed Shelby's. Even though it was just before noon, they were in the formal limo, giving them added comfort and privacy for the drive to the lake.

"Well, I like the navy in your room," Shelby began.

"Our room," Nikolai corrected.

"Our room," Shelby rectified. "So I'm not making many changes in there, but my old bedroom will have a contrasting navy print on the walls and windows, with cranberry accents to go with my mahogany trim and furnishings. How does that sound?"

"Beautiful. I was thinking that enlarging the door between the two rooms might be nice. Would that work with your plans?"

"I think so. I hadn't thought of it, but a double door would be lovely."

"Oak on my side and mahogany on yours."

"Can they do that?"

"With veneers, yes."

The word veneer stopped Shelby for a moment. She had

just that morning been asking the Lord to help her talk to her husband about some things that were on her heart. At times she didn't feel she was completely herself with Nikolai and wondered if that constituted a veneer.

She glanced in his direction, but he wasn't looking at her. There was no way he couldn't know that she held back from him; he was too astute for that. But how did she tell him she wanted to change?

"Feel free to take a nap," Nikolai said as he laid his head back against the seat. "I'm going to."

"Tiring morning?"

"Um hm" was all Nikolai had to say on the subject. In truth, he thought the evening might be more tiring and knew he would need every ounce of rest he could get. He only hoped Shelby would be up to it as well.

~

It was a chilly night, so a fire popped and crackled in the fireplace, casting a warm glow on the couple who sat side by side on the large sofa at the lake house. The staff had all disappeared after dinner, Nikolai having told them that if he needed something he would call, and now the royal couple sat in silence. One was a little tired and contemplating an early bedtime, the other was busy trying to control the wild racing of his heart.

Shelby was staring absently into the flames when Nikolai turned to her.

"I love you, Shelby," he said softly.

For a moment the princess didn't move. She sat up a little, lay back again, and then turned to him.

"What did you say?"

"I love you."

Shelby searched his eyes, her breath growing rapid over what she saw. She turned fully to her husband, working to tamp down the panic rising within her. When her hands had grabbed the front of his shirt, she said, "Why, Nicky? Why today and not yesterday?"

"I loved you yesterday too," he explained gently. "And for many days before that, but the timing to tell you was all wrong. I wanted us here, away from the phone and distractions, so we could talk about it."

"I don't want to talk about it," she said, panic now evident in her voice. She began to scramble from the sofa, but he put his arms around her.

"Shelby, don't run from me," Nikolai whispered gently. "I'm still the same man who was with you in the hospital. I'm still the same man who holds you when you cry and puts you to bed when you're too tired to move. I'm still the same man who fell asleep in the car and probably snored all the way up here."

Shelby looked into his eyes again, her breathing labored. Finally she admitted, "I always thought the most terrifying thing would be to love alone, but this is worse. What if I can't ever say the words to you? What if I never feel them?"

Nikolai settled her a little more closely against him and waited for her to relax in his embrace. "I do think you'll feel them, but you might need to realize what I did, Shelby: Love is a choice. I didn't know I could love you, certainly not this swiftly after our marriage, but then I chose to love you."

Shelby blinked. "I keep hearing that, but I'm not sure I know how."

"For me, it meant getting into your world. It meant being thankful for you all day, every day. Does that make sense?"

Shelby nodded.

"I also continued to remind myself that your parents trusted me to take care of you, and I began to take that responsibility very seriously."

"And when you went to see them, was that part of it?"

"Yes. And I'm also trying to understand your world. Keep in mind, Shelby, that I didn't spend any time in your home. If we had gone through a normal courtship, I would have known you and your family very well. I've had to do this backward."

"But I am in your world!" Shelby suddenly burst out. "I've seen every photo album and scrapbook your grandmothers have. I've seen you on ponies and at your first skeet shoot."

Nikolai smiled. "It isn't going to be the same for you, Red. You are in my world, but I think your heart has been waiting for a signal from me. I'm now trying to give you that."

Shelby wanted to fly from his arms again. The pressure felt horrible. She didn't know if she could explain it, but it felt as though she'd been given a timer that ticked off the seconds very slowly in her ear. Shelby's hand came to her face as she told herself to breathe.

"I'm going to fail," she said softly.

"Why would you say that?" Nikolai asked.

Shelby looked at him, surprised that he'd heard her. All she could do was lick her lips and stare at him.

"This is not some test, Shelby, not at all. If anyone's failed, and I don't know that we have, it's I who have done the failing." He looked helpless for a moment. "Maybe I should have found a way to tell you sooner, but then the accident happened and I was afraid that you—"

"You loved me before the accident?"

"Yes." He kissed her softly. "And I loved you even when I found out about the baby but you didn't tell me. And I loved you when—"

"You knew about the baby before the accident?"

Nikolai nodded. "Your parents told me."

Shelby tried to take it in. "All this time. You knew everything all this time. Why didn't you tell me?"

Nikolai smoothed the hair from her brow. He needed to see the little scar that sat above her eyebrow. It was a good reminder.

"Shelby, I almost lost you. You could have bled to death.

You're just now starting to feel like yourself again. What kind of selfish monster does that make me if I have an agenda to cover with you, and no matter how fragile you are, we're going to go over it?"

Shelby looked into his wonderful face, so close to her own. His eyes didn't give away his heart like hers did, but they were often full of caring, caring for her. Right now they were full of yearning—yearning that she would understand. And she did.

"Thank you," she said softly, leaning to kiss his cheek.

"The pleasure is all mine."

"I want more than anything to start making promises to you, Nick, but that would be foolish." Shelby slowly shook her head. "I'm confused right now."

The prince moved so that Shelby could stretch out next to him. He held her close on his chest, wondering when she would gain the pounds she had lost and have full color in her face again.

I had no warning with Yvette, Lord, but maybe this is Your way of telling me I won't have her. Or maybe it's just Your way of showing me that I could choose to love. I can hardly bear the thought of not having her, but You know best.

"What are you thinking?" Shelby asked suddenly. "You feel tense."

"I'm thinking about your health and asking myself what I would do if God would ask me to give you up."

Shelby moved so she could see his face. "You're always telling me not to rush the healing process."

"And I don't want you to, but you're still a little thin, and sometimes the imagination does crazy things, especially now that I love you."

"And this time you pictured my never getting better and dying."

"That about sums it up. If I'm being logical and not emotional, I can honestly say I don't think God has that for us, but if I hold onto you too tightly, I can lose my focus."

Shelby settled back against him. "You always say the right thing, Nick."

"Oh, Shelby," he sighed, "you know better than anyone how untrue that is."

Shelby had nothing more to say to that. She had been so tired, but now she was wide awake and ready to tackle this problem of loving her spouse. Shelby was good with problems; she always had been. She would handle this and love her spouse. That was all there was to it.

"Why do I get the distinct impression that you're plotting something?" Nikolai asked softly.

"Because I am."

"Are you going to tell me what it is?"

"No. At least not now."

Nikolai angled his head until he could see her face, but other than a determined frown, it gave nothing away. He figured the best thing he could do was pray for her. Ten minutes later he changed that to the best thing he could do for her was get her to bed. She was as relaxed as a cat and not answering to the sound of his voice. The nap in the limo had been hours ago, and the prince was tired as well. Nikolai lifted his wife's limp form, wishing the stairs to the bedroom were not quite so steep.

～

Shelby woke on Sunday morning to find herself alone. The clock told her she had plenty of time to get ready for church. Dragging on enough clothes to be presentable, she made her way downstairs, surprised not to find Nikolai around. She didn't spot him until she'd taken her coffee onto the deck. He was down by the water, not walking or skipping rocks, just standing, his gaze across the lake. Shelby's first temptation was to join him, but in watching him, she had the impression he was enjoying his solitude.

What if he's thinking of Yvette? her mind asked without warning. With the knowledge that Nikolai loved her, she was being tempted to doubt him. Shelby worked to put her thoughts aside and concentrate on how thankful she needed to be. Yvette lingered in her mind but not in a negative way. A glance at the clock told her the conversation she wanted to have about Nikolai's first wife would have to wait until after church. She moved back up the stairs to shower, reminding herself that she had all week to talk to Nick.

~

"It's hard to believe we go home tomorrow," Nikolai said conversationally over breakfast five days later—five days that had passed with unbelievable swiftness for Shelby. She had enjoyed herself, was very rested and ready to go home, but still had not talked to her husband about what was on her mind. She made herself open the conversation and ignore the fear inside of her.

"How did you meet Yvette?"

Nikolai blinked at her in surprise but recovered swiftly and said, "She was visiting Pendaran with her family from France."

"And she wanted to meet the royal family?"

"No. There was a special song service at church, and we ended up sitting next to each other. Our mothers got to talking, and while very embarrassed, we both stood by until I got up the nerve to practice my French. They had just arrived in our country, so I saw her every day for the next week."

"And by the time she left, you were in love."

"I was smitten all right, but it was the first time I'd ever really fallen for anyone. Most of the kids I knew I'd grown up with, so they were more like family. My father reminded me of that and cautioned me to take it slowly, but Yvette and I did write to each other from the day she left Pendaran, and that's when I knew it was the real thing."

Shelby nodded and fell silent. Nikolai knew there was more on her mind and made himself wait. The paper was still in his hand, but his eyes were on her.

"How do you love two women?" she asked at last.

Nikolai smiled. "It helps when they're both easy to love, Shelby." His head tipped in thought. "It's funny, but I can't picture Yvette and me growing old together. Young as I am now, she still feels like the wife of my youth. You, on the other hand, are going to be here. What we share is so different from what I shared with Yvette, and I don't have any desire to go backward in time. I'm sorry for Yvette's family—I know they still miss her—and I think of her too, but you're all I want. Almost a year ago when we married, I would never have believed that, but it's very true today."

Shelby nodded before admitting, "I've wanted to ask you about it all week. I let so much time go by."

"Are you afraid I'll be upset if you mention her?"

"Yes. You never talk about her, so I didn't know."

"I don't mention her for fear that you'll think she's constantly on my mind. She's not. You are. I'm more than happy to answer your questions."

"I fear that I do things differently and you won't like that," Shelby was able to say. "I've never been a princess before, and I find myself thinking that Yvette had it down pat."

"On the contrary. She was quite shy and nowhere near as willing as you are to make public appearances. She was getting better, but at first it was torture to be invited to balls and parties. I even went through a time of anger at you because everyone liked you so fast. I thought they might be comparing Yvette in a negative light, but that wasn't true. No one's ever compared the two of you."

"Except you."

"I have, Shelby, but not the way you're thinking. I don't look at your inadequacies and think Yvette could have done better. In fact, you handle things better than she did. If anyone is more suited to be the princess than you are, I've yet to meet her." Nikolai smiled at her. "My parents knew just what they were doing."

"Were you very angry at them for a time?"

"Not before we were married, but afterward I was. They wanted me to make more of an effort, and rightly so, but I refused." Nikolai looked her squarely in the eye. "I'm paying for that today."

Shelby shook her head. "I don't know what you mean."

"You were on your way to loving me, Shelby, I'm sure of it. But I couldn't say those words, so you pulled back."

Shelby was stunned by this announcement because she thought he might very well be right. She had been looking for signs in him and didn't even know it. The morning she woke early and watched him sleep came to mind. She learned a moment later that his mind was on the same morning.

"Do you remember when I asked you what I did that made you feel inadequate?"

"I was just thinking of that."

"That was the first time I went to see your mother. I felt a desperate need to learn to love you. She told me about your grandmother and how she married out of need instead of love. She also told me not to forget Yvette but to make room for you. That's what I've done, Red; I've made room in my heart for you. And now you just about fill it."

"Oh, Nicky," Shelby said as tears filled her eyes. "I don't know what to do."

"Why must you *do* anything?"

"Because I need to *learn* to love you. I need to *choose* to love you."

Nikolai's head went back as he laughed. Shelby gawked at him.

"I can't believe you're laughing at this."

The prince smiled. "If you could only see your earnest face, Red. You're bound and determined to do this. That's not what I'm looking for."

Shelby looked completely at sea, and Nikolai reached for her hand.

"Listen to me, Red. I've done a lot of thinking about this. I can't imagine your care of me being any more wonderful than it already is. You go out of your way to see after my comfort and needs. You make yourself available at a moment's notice. You're careful what you say, in case I'll be upset."

Shelby was still staring at him, and Nikolai gave her hand a little squeeze.

"The words would be nice to hear, Shelby, but they don't make or break what we have here. Don't *try* to love me, just keep on doing what you're doing. Keep growing in the Lord. And keep talking to me like you did just now. Get mad at me if you need to, tell me when you do or do not like something, let me into your world as much as you're able, and always be honest about the way you feel. Everything else will take care of itself. God will see to that."

For the umpteenth time the man had rescued her. She had set up a standard in her mind that was her own, not God's and certainly not her husband's. She felt herself relaxing with relief, almost to the point of crying.

"You can cry if you want to," Nikolai said, and Shelby looked up to see that his eyes were moist.

"Why do you want to cry?"

Nikolai could only shrug. How did a man explain something he didn't understand? He loved this woman. It wasn't some skip-around-the-room, lighter-than-air feeling, although he'd had some of that. It was just knowing that she was the one God had given him. She was the one who could fill his heart, whom he could cherish and grow with until they were old.

"How about a walk?" the prince asked.

"That sounds nice. I'll get my shoes."

Nikolai had to get his shoes too. He followed Shelby up the stairs, thinking not for the first time that she always smelled nice. Sometimes it made him passionate, and sometimes he just wanted to hold her. Now was such a time. Shelby asked him what the hug was for, but Nikolai never did answer. He stroked her cheek, winked at her, and went to put his shoes on.

~

"I thought Nikolai would be with you," the king said when Shelby joined him and the queen for breakfast. "Did he know he was invited?"

"Yes, but he's a bit of a bear today."

Pendaran's ruling couple both blinked at her.

"Nicky in a bad mood," the queen mused. "That's not like him."

"He's getting a cold," Shelby said matter-of-factly.

The king found himself smiling. His daughter-in-law sounded like one-half of an old married couple.

"Was he going to rest?" Rafe asked.

"I think so." Shelby's voice was still quite calm. "I left him scowling at the clock when it buzzed for the fourth time."

Erica broke out in laughter at this point. She had the feeling that there was more to this than Shelby was telling, but she didn't expect her to tell. Every married couple had their little secrets. The mystery was only added to, however, when Nikolai showed up about 20 minutes later and scowled at his wife. Shelby's placid expression was comical to watch, and when the two shared a look, it was obvious she felt she had the upper hand.

"Are you not feeling well, Nick?" his mother checked with him.

"I think I have a cold coming on."

"That's not like you, Nick. You never get sick."

That Nikolai had had that same feeling didn't really help all that much. His head was full, and his wife had teased him. He knew he had to apologize, but right now he was crabby and didn't want to. He warmed up a bit over breakfast, but he was feeling awful, and when he talked, his head sounded stuffed.

"We haven't had a chance to see you since your anniversary," the queen mentioned at one point. "Did you do something fun?"

"We went out to dinner," Shelby filled in, "and then to Farm Days Fair. It was fun." Shelby looked over at her husband, who was still rather silent. "Well, I had fun," she said.

"I did too," he added, knowing he was going to have to make amends. At first Shelby had looked smiling and mischievous. Now she was looking uncertain. He was glad when his parents both left the room so he could have a word with her.

"I'm sorry about my mood."

"I'm sorry I teased you," Shelby returned, just as contrite.

Nikolai looked at her. "Would you really move back to your old room if I get a cold?"

Shelby smiled. "Not for a cold, but maybe for a bad mood."

Nikolai's lopsided smile appeared. He felt awful, but that was no excuse. A man wasn't allowed to take a bad mood or an illness out on his wife—it simply wasn't an option—but he had treated her as though it was.

"Why don't I head out after breakfast and get some cold medicine for you?" Shelby asked.

"I think I have some, and if I don't, Murdock will."

"Why don't you take it?"

"It makes me sleepy."

"Well, isn't that what you need?"

"I have a meeting."

Shelby's look was pointed.

"I don't feel that bad," Nikolai defended himself, but his denial sounded weak, even to his own ears.

"That's not the point," Shelby said, an edge to her voice. Having worked in a hospital, she had a strong opinion on this subject. "If you go out, you're going to spread your germs. No one will thank you for that."

With his muddled head making it hard to think, Nikolai hadn't even considered that.

"I think I'll go back to bed."

"Shall I tell Murdock to cancel things for a few days?" Shelby offered.

"Just today," the prince allowed, thinking he didn't want to baby himself too much. He hadn't counted on his wife. Shelby canceled all of her appointments as well, and every time he woke, she was close by with a drink or something else he might need. She smelled as good as ever, and her cool hands on his warm skin were something he could get used to in a hurry. He thought that if Shelby was going to be his nurse, he might stay in bed for the rest of the week.

Twenty-One

Shelby gave up waiting for her husband. He had said he would be late, but she hoped he would surprise her. It didn't happen. She didn't know what time he climbed into bed, but because she'd been anticipating him arriving home from his trip for several hours before she slept, he woke her.

"Hi," she said softly, coming wide awake and wanting to talk.

"Hi, Red." Nikolai's hoarse voice told of his fatigue. "Sorry to wake you."

"It's all right. How did it go?"

"Good, good. I'll tell you all about it in the morning," he said as he blew a kiss in her direction.

"Okay."

Shelby waited, thinking he didn't really mean it, but just moments later she heard the even sound of his breathing. She lay still for a moment, not wanting to disturb him but almost desperate to talk. Feeling terrible for doing it, she rolled rather hard, still staying on her side but rocking the whole bed. He never moved a muscle. Shelby gave up with a sigh. The alarm was set for an early hour. She was meeting her father for breakfast and then had a full day on the calendar. It took some time, but she eventually fell back to sleep, hoping as she did that Nikolai would be wide awake come morning.

~

Nikolai woke slowly the next morning, his body telling him he had not had enough sleep. He had not been able to get comfortable in the limo on the way home, and by the time he'd reached the palace, he had been miserable. He had hated to wake Shelby, but he would make it up to her this morning. It was a keen disappointment to find himself alone. He reached across the bed before he understood that she was gone, and that was when he felt the piece of paper. He smiled, sure that she was telling him where she would be. *I'm pregnant.* The two words jumped out at Nikolai so fast that he literally started.

"Shelby," he called urgently, praying that she was in the bathroom. But as he was already on his feet and moving toward that door, he could see she was not. The next stop was her old room, and that was just as empty. Within seconds he was on the phone to his house minister.

"Murdock, where is the princess this morning?"

"She was going to have breakfast with her father, and then she had to be at the botanical gardens. From there she had to go straight to the care center for a special meeting."

Nikolai sighed.

"May I help you, sir?"

"Yes. Figure out exactly where she is and order the car. I'll be ready in 20 minutes."

"Emergency status, sir?"

"No, but a little urgency would be greatly appreciated."

"Right away, sir."

Nikolai was ready and waiting for the limo when it arrived, and although no words were spoken, he knew that Murdock would have told Ivan where to head. He was glad to see it was the botanical gardens. There was more chance of catching her alone there.

Five minutes later Nikolai thought the Lord must have known how much he needed to talk to his wife. She was walking along the paths with a small group of garden lovers, all of whom smiled and greeted the prince but who also moved discreetly ahead after the pleasantries were exchanged.

Shelby kept moving, albeit slowly, looking at her husband's profile from time to time. Nikolai put his hands behind his back to keep from reaching for her and began speaking as if he had all the time in the world.

"This is a pretty bloom," he commented about the bright purple blossom they were passing.

"Yes. That's a coneflower. My mother has some."

"Mothers are wonderful people," Nikolai said. Shelby smiled just as the prince cast a look in her direction. "I found an interesting note in my bed this morning," he continued, "but no wife."

"Did you?"

"Um hm. It was informative, but I found myself rather glad that my heart is strong."

Shelby put a hand to her smiling mouth.

"So tell me, Red, on your list of important people to call, who else have you told?"

"Well . . ." Shelby's tone was instantly teasing; she'd been doing a lot of that since they'd been at the lake. "I told Kris right away. I knew he would want to take special care of me. And then the mailman walked by with the post, so I whispered in his ear. Then I saw a man in the park, and he looked as though he needed a little cheering up, so I gave the good news to him too. And of course, I announced it to the entire garden club this morning."

Shelby looked up now with mischievous eyes, and Nikolai came to a stop.

"You have been a very bad girl," he told her.

Shelby smiled. "I wanted to tell you last night, but you fell asleep so fast, and then I had to be gone so early this morning, and you were still out cold." Shelby chuckled. "I even bounced around on the bed in the middle of the night, but you didn't move."

Nikolai smiled before he said very softly, "How are you?"

"I'm fine."

"Are you sure about it?"

"Yes. I did the same test as last time, and I feel different again."

"When, Red?" Nikolai asked now. "When did it happen? The lake?"

Shelby shook her head. "I don't think that long ago." Again she laughed. "I think around the time you had your cold."

Nikolai's smile was huge. "You were a great nurse." He laughed when she blushed to the roots of her hair. It didn't happen as often anymore, but he still loved to see it.

The group had come full circle by now and was headed back their way. Nikolai did have to see someone after lunch, but he trailed his wife during his free time that day, waiting for her appointments to end. It was after dinner before he got her alone, held her close, and told her he loved her with all his heart. They spent the evening talking about babies and baby names and making plans to have all four parents over for dinner to give them the good news all at once.

~

"Have I lost you?" Toby asked the prince quietly. The two men were sitting in Toby's home office.

"No. I'm just flabbergasted. I'm thrilled, but I'm also shocked. Pam Owens came to Christ last night?" Nikolai clarified.

"Yes. She called me about a problem with the water, and when I got over there I could see she'd been crying. I assumed that the water and all the pressures of acting as a parent to Penny and Peter were just getting to her. That wasn't it at all. Her supervisor at work just learned that he has cancer. There's nothing they can do, but he's not afraid because he knows where he's going."

"Who is it?"

"Harland Hayes. I think you've met him."

"Is he medium height, with glasses and salt-and-pepper hair?"

"Yes, that's the man."

"And Pam clearly enjoys him as a boss."

"She loves him. She's utterly crushed that he's dying and angry that he's not upset about it. That led to our talking about my belief, and she realized that her tears were rooted in fear. She pictured herself dying the way her father did, or getting cancer, and she knew that she was lost. I led her to Christ while we sat on her front porch."

Nikolai stared at the older man. They had both continued their contact with the Owens family. Progress had been made, but this was remarkable. Nikolai felt himself starting to smile as his heart fully realized what God had done.

"There's more," Toby said as he smiled as well. "Peter sat on the porch with us and witnessed the whole thing. Penny was in her bedroom, but Peter never moved from his seat on the porch railing. His eyes were huge when Pam finished praying. She went to him, told him she loved him, and gave him a hug. He hugged her back but was utterly silent during the whole exchange."

"Wow." Nick voiced the only word that came to his mind. This was so unexpected. He had been praying for Peter and meeting with him for a long time now, not ever sure when the next opportunity would come to share with him. Now Peter's sister had seen the truth.

"Tell her I'm praying for her," Nikolai said. "And if she needs anything, just ask. I'll admit to you, Toby, that I've doubted about Peter's little heart, but I think that it just might be a matter of time."

The older man could only nod, suddenly overcome with emotions.

"Thanks for calling me," Nikolai said softly. The two men embraced before Nikolai made his way out to the day limo. He couldn't wait to get home and tell Shelby the good news.

~

Nikolai had always heard that expectant women waddled, but as he stood in the doorway of the kitchen and watched his pregnant wife walk about the room, he thought she still moved like a swan on the lake. It probably helped that even in her eighth month her stomach was not very extended. Daria had carried Shelby and Brice the same way and thought it was because Shelby was tall.

"Well, hello," Shelby said as she spotted her husband and came to kiss him. He'd been in a meeting all morning. "Were you looking for me?"

"Not exactly, but I'm hungry, and I knew where you would be."

Shelby smiled. She was always in the kitchen these days. She hadn't felt at all sick in the first six months, but now, unless she was eating, she felt slightly queasy.

"I'm having tacos. Are you interested?"

"What, no fruit?"

"Not today."

Nikolai came all the way into the kitchen, still surprised that Shelby did not have a plateful of peaches, pears, apples, or any other type of fruit she could get her hands on. She had craved them for weeks now. Before that it had been mashed potatoes, broccoli, and chocolate, thankfully not mixed together.

"I am, however," Shelby added, "having chocolate cake for dessert. Doesn't that sound good?"

"Yes. I think I'll join you."

"For the cake or tacos?"

"Both."

Shelby went about preparing things and setting the table for two. Nikolai had wondered where Fran or Arlanda might be but didn't ask. Lately Shelby had done some outrageous things, and he knew in time that he would learn.

"I gave the staff the day off," she said suddenly, as if reading his mind.

"Was there a reason?" he asked from his place at the table.

"Well, I have all this energy, and I thought why should they stay if I want to cook and look after myself?"

Nikolai knew very well that they hadn't really "gone" any- where. The north quadrant's staff was much happier staying close to and protective of their very pregnant princess. Almost as if he'd said the words out loud, Fran's face suddenly ap- peared around a doorway at the end of the room. She took in the scene and grinned at the prince before ducking back away.

"What if you get tired later?" Nikolai wished to know.

"Do you think I will?"

"You do every time you let the staff leave."

Shelby turned to look at him, her face uncertain and then clearing. "I do, don't I?"

Nikolai smiled at her. "I think they're all still here, Red. Why don't I just ask them to be on call?"

"Do you think they'll mind?"

"I think they'll be relieved. They like taking care of us, and you do need a little extra care right now."

Her brow lowered in a frown. "I've told myself not to be a baby during this pregnancy. I hate it when women do that."

"And you haven't been, not at all. I wish you would slow down a little, at least when you're feeling tired."

Shelby nodded because she suddenly was. She turned back to the taco meat in the pan and adjusted the temperature. She sighed very softly when Nikolai came up and put his arms around her from behind. She didn't know it could be like this between two people. He was so tender with her, and the more time she spent with him, the more she wanted to see him. She had missed him that morning at breakfast and not been very hungry because he'd been away.

"I'm hungry," she said quietly, "or I think I would just go take a nap."

"Do both. I'll even come in and talk to you until you fall asleep."

Shelby turned in his arms. "Most women don't have this."

"Have what?"

"Their husbands around. My father is gone almost all day, but you come and go. I like that."

Nikolai kissed her. She had never said the words to him, but he knew she felt them. She had told him one time that she didn't like love-at-first-sight books or movies. She liked the ones where the couples moved slowly and were sure. Knowing her as he did, this was no surprise. She was not impetuous with matters of the heart. It was one of the things he loved most about her. She didn't say things until she'd thought about them and knew she meant them.

He also loved the fact that she was open to change and suggestions, something he was particularly glad for when they finished lunch and she agreed to climb into bed. She fell asleep quickly, and Nikolai found himself wishing that February 8 would come very soon.

~

"Of all things!" Shelby said in disgust just a little more than two weeks later. The contraction had eased, and she was now venting her frustration.

"It's not as if you could help it, Red." Nikolai tried to reason with her, his voice mild in the midst of her ire.

"But in the middle of church, Nicky! I didn't even get all the sermon notes, and now everyone will be waiting to hear. I wanted this to be quiet—just between the two of us."

Hands on his waist, Nikolai stared at her and rebuked her in quiet tones. "I think I need to remind you that you're not the only one involved here, Red. When Saturday came and went, I was pretty discouraged. I would like to meet this little person."

Shelby's eyes rounded as her voice turned contrite. "I didn't know you were discouraged."

"Well, maybe that's too strong a word, but I really thought things would get going right on your due date, and when they didn't, I was a little let down."

Shelby took his hand. "I'm sorry. I am just thinking of myself and the big scene our leaving made in the middle of the sermon."

Nikolai nodded and would have spoken again, but another pain hit. They had gone straight back to the palace, but Nikolai wondered if they shouldn't have gone to the hospital. He was very relieved to have his mother suddenly come in.

"How are you?" She kissed Nikolai and then Shelby.

"Uncertain," Nikolai told her. When Nikolai explained what he meant, Erica took over. She talked with Shelby, timed contractions, and even called the doctor. Hours later she was still there when it was finally time to go to the hospital. It was nice to be in the competent care of the medical staff, but it was almost midnight when the doctor spoke to the royal couple.

"You have an unusual situation, Shelby, in that the bottom of your uterus is contracting upward and the top is pushing down. Where it thinks it's going to push this baby, I don't know, but we're looking at a C-section here."

"Is the baby hurt?" Shelby's voice quivered; she was about done in.

"No, the baby seems to be in good shape, but I don't think delaying is going to help a bit."

Shelby looked to Nikolai, who was sitting close to her head. He looked down and nodded his head.

"You can't keep this up, honey."

Tears came to her eyes, but she meant it when she said, "Whatever is best for the baby."

Those words set events into play for the next hour. All the Parkers were present, as were the king and queen, when Nikolai accompanied his wife into surgery. Seemingly minutes later a baby's cry was heard.

"A boy," one nurse sailed through and announced. "Everyone's doing fine."

Daria, who had not slept since Shelby had called her the morning before, burst into tears as she tried to sign for Josiah. Josiah held his wife and prayed for his daughter and new grandson.

Inside the delivery room, Nikolai was staring in wonder at the baby in the doctor's arms.

"Red hair, Shelby," he said softly. "He has red hair."

Shelby gave a weak laugh. It was all she could muster. Just a moment later the nurse brought him over for the couple to see. They both laughed at his grumpy face and squeaky cry.

"Would you like to come with me to clean him up, Prince Nikolai?"

"I think I will." Nikolai suddenly felt energized. "I'll be back." He kissed Shelby and followed the nurse. Shelby let her eyes close with a sigh. *I did it, Lord. I had a baby. Thank You that he's here. Thank You that You had a boy for us. I pray that he will rule in wisdom, Father, and always look to You for strength.*

Shelby's heart had never been so full. Given a choice she would have prayed for an hour, but her body had other ideas. She fell into a deep, blissful sleep.

⁓

"What time is it?" Shelby asked softly of the nurse who had come in to check on her.

"Almost five. How about some juice?"

"That sounds good."

The nurse had only just finished giving Shelby the glass of cool apricot nectar when Nikolai's head came around the corner.

"I was hoping I'd find you awake," he whispered as he approached.

There weren't many people for whom the nurse would alter her schedule, but this wasn't just any person—this was Pendaran's future king. As Nikolai came close and bent to kiss Shelby, the nurse rehung Shelby's chart on the wall, slipped out, and shut the door.

"You're up early," Shelby smiled at him.

"The bed was lonely without you."

Shelby smiled. "That's nice to hear, but I can't say that I missed you," she admitted. "I was asleep until just a few minutes ago."

"Good. Have you seen the baby?"

"No. It's a little hard to believe he's really out there. They came in the night and wanted to know if I wanted to feed him, and I said he could take a bottle for now."

Nikolai chuckled over this. "I knew you would be levelheaded and take my mother's advice." The queen had told Shelby to take advantage of the hospital staff. *You'll be on call when you get home, dear. Let the nurses do the job while you have the chance.*

"But, Nicky," Shelby reached for him as a moment of unreality hit her. "He is out there, isn't he? No one took him or anything like that?"

"He's fine," Nikolai assured her, his hand smoothing the hair from her brow. "He's still asleep, and they'll bring him in as soon as he wakes."

Shelby sighed and looked up at her husband. "It's such a miracle, Nick; his birth is such a miracle."

Nikolai smiled. That was the very word he spoke to God about when he went home after the baby was born.

"Thank you, Shelby," he now said, his eyes on his wife. "Thank you for giving me a future king."

Shelby smiled. "That was one of my first thoughts as well. The House of Markham, Nicky. I love knowing it will last for more than two generations."

As if he knew he was being spoken of, the nurse entered the room with a fussing young prince. Both Shelby and Nikolai turned in delight at his presence and spent the next hour feeding him, talking to him, praying for him, and talking of the way their lives would change because of him. It didn't matter that babies were born every day. It didn't matter that theirs was not the first or last. He was a miracle to them—a small, dependent miracle—and with hearts committed to bring him up to know Jesus Christ as his own Savior, nothing else seemed to matter.

~

"I heard about the baby," Peter said a week later as he took a chair in Nikolai's office. He had come especially to see the prince and now pushed off the carpet with his toe in order to scoot back into the slippery leather chair.

"We had a baby boy," Nikolai said with a smile.

"Toby told me. My sister helped me find something," Peter replied, his face solemn as he left the chair and placed a gift on the desk.

"Thank you, Peter. Would you like to give this to the princess?"

Peter shrugged. "You can open it."

Nikolai was not fooled by his nonchalant attitude. The boy wanted him to open the gift very badly.

Nikolai left his desk to do the job. He came around, took the chair next to Peter's, and tore back the paper. Opening the box revealed a tiny suit, vest, bow tie, and all. The huge smile that spread across Nikolai's face was from pure delight.

"This is great. Look at that little tie."

Peter nodded a little, clearly pleased but not wanting to show it too much.

Nikolai turned his head to watch him. "He won't remember wearing this outfit, Peter, but we'll make sure he knows someday that you brought it to him."

Peter nodded, his face still pleased but on its way to thoughtfulness. Nikolai was growing used to his swift mood changes and waited.

"My sister's going to church all the time now and taking me and Penny with her."

"Is she?"

"Yeah."

"You sound as though you don't like it."

"I do sometimes. Sometimes it makes sense, but not always."

"Well, if it ever all makes sense to you, Peter, come and explain it to me."

The little boy's brow furrowed as he stared up at the prince.

"Listen to me, Peter," Nikolai began very gently. "I understood that I needed a Savior, and I believed in Jesus Christ to save me, but I don't have all the answers. You ask me how God could give up His Son to die. My human mind can't quite comprehend it. I don't understand a love that big, Peter, but I do accept it. Now you're trying to understand it all, and I'm glad you're searching. Don't give up, Peter. Keep asking questions and listening to Pam, Toby, and me, and God will show you the way."

Peter nodded, and Nikolai smiled at him. He was learning that small drops on the pond had the biggest effect. If he didn't keep it short and sweet, he lost the boy. But Peter kept coming back, and Nikolai kept seeing new interest and understanding.

The two talked for a while longer and then Peter said he had to go. Nikolai saw him on his way, confident that God was at work in his young heart. Nikolai hoped and prayed that Peter would stay open to the truth.

~

I've never seen anything so perfect, Shelby typed into the teletype machine to her father. They had been home from the hospital for a week, and she could not get over the wonder of this baby. *He's such a good baby too, Fa. I expected him to cry when he heard me typing, but he's just as quiet as a mouse.*

Are you getting enough rest? Josiah asked.

Most of the time. I nap and still go to bed earlier than I thought I would. I haven't tried the stairs, but I feel good.

I'm glad to hear it. You've been in my prayers a lot, and of course I have my grandson's picture up at the shop. You and Nick will have to bring him to see it when you're all up to it.

We'll plan on it. Oh! I think I'd better sign off, Fa. I'll call you later, okay?

Certainly. I love you, and hug Josiah Rafael for me.

I'll do it. I love you too.

Shelby signed off and moved into the bathroom. When she came out, she realized that she really did think the baby would have cried already. Reminding herself that the womb was a very noisy place, she stopped herself from tiptoeing and went to her old bedroom to check on her son. She came to a complete stop when she found Nikolai ensconced in the rocking chair that sat next to the crib, the infant prince in his lap.

"And someday, Siah," she heard him say, "I'll tell you all about the way I fell in love with your mother. She didn't come to Christ until she was a teen, but I hope you'll understand as a child, like I did. You must marry someone who loves Christ too, Siah. It's very important to God that we obey Him in this."

Shelby was not a stupid person. She had a normal IQ, but up to now that hadn't been very helpful to her. With eyes that saw things clearly for the very first time, she approached the man in the chair.

Nikolai glanced up and smiled at her. "Isn't he something?"

"Yes," Shelby said softly, her eyes caressing Nikolai's bent head. "He's incredible."

Nikolai looked up at her to smile again and found Shelby's eyes on him. Having fully expected her to be watching the baby with him, he paused and stared at her.

"I love you," Shelby said softly.

Nikolai froze for the space of several heartbeats. He then stood, put Siah in his cradle, and came back to Shelby.

"Say it again."

"I love you."

Nikolai's hand moved up to frame her face. "I honestly can't think of a single thing I would want you to do differently, Red. You show your love to me every day, and for that reason I've not needed the words." Nikolai's eyes searched hers for a moment. "But I must tell you," he now whispered, "they're wonderful to hear."

"Oh, Nicky." Shelby's arms went around him, and she held on as if she would never let go. He was so wonderful. She had probably loved him for a long time, but not until she'd seen him sitting there, holding their son and talking to him about the Lord, did she know that it was time to say the words.

"You're not upset that I took so long?"

"No," he said close to her ear, his own arms hugging her tightly. "The timing had to be right, and as I said, you've been saying it in your actions for a long time now."

Shelby moved back to look into his face. "But you've said it to me many times, and I never could. Why is that?"

Nikolai smiled. "I don't know, and I can't say as I care."

Shelby had a determined look on her face, the one that usually told Nikolai she had a problem to solve and must solve it.

"Shelby?"

"What?"

"Look at me."

Shelby did.

"Don't worry about it. And I mean that."

Shelby nodded, seeing he was right. She was going up on tiptoe to kiss him just as the baby began to fuss. Nikolai made a move to let Shelby go, but she held on.

"Don't you want to get him?" Nikolai asked.

"Both of our mothers have told me that crying is good for babies," Shelby smiled and said, her hand going to the back of her husband's head. "He can wait a few more seconds."

Not in a hurry to go anywhere at all, Nikolai kissed her right back, thinking he wouldn't have argued for the kingdom.

Epilogue

Twelve Years Later

"It hurts," seven-year-old Jeremiah said.

Shelby leaned to kiss first him and then the tissue that was wrapped around his finger.

"Come on, Jer," Nikolai directed, putting a hand to his son's back. "We'll see Fran and get you all patched up."

Mother and father exchanged a glance before Nikolai led the patient away.

"Well, now," Fran spoke as soon as the prince entered the kitchen. "What's this?"

"I cut my finger," Jeremiah admitted. "I touched the sword."

Fran shook her head in loving exasperation as Murdock left his newspaper and came to inspect the wound.

"It doesn't look too deep," he observed, and Nikolai stood back and let the faithful servants fuss over his son. Jeremiah had a flare for the dramatic—he and Shelby had noticed it often—but his heart was big, and all the staff was taken in by his round blue eyes and dark hair, much the way they'd enjoyed another young prince many years ago.

"I think some gauze will do the trick," Fran said calmly.

She was like a second mother to the children, and Nikolai could see his son was already relaxing.

Nikolai wasn't quite so at ease. He had barely seen Shelby all day, and the sooner they got this show on the road, the sooner he would. The candy tin appeared out of nowhere, held by Murdock's capable hand, and Nikolai allowed Jeremiah one piece. With a prayer for a calm heart, the prince made himself sit down and wait while his son finished.

~

"Are you all right, Siah?" Shelby asked softly when she entered the large parlor and found her oldest child alone by the window.

Siah turned to look at his mother but didn't speak. Shelby waited.

"What if I don't find a wife to marry?" he asked softly, his eyes and hair so like his mother's, his thoughtful manner also an inheritance from her.

"Well," Shelby said slowly, trying to find her bearings. "It could be a problem, but I guess I'm not too worried about it."

"But I only have until I'm 26."

Shelby had to stop herself from reminding him that his twenty-sixth birthday was many years away. She knew he would not find this helpful. Instead she said, "That very subject is up for review in Council, Siah, but even if it's not changed, God will provide. You need to remember that it happens at all different times for people. So many kids go off to Bible school and meet someone the first year, but Peter didn't. He didn't meet Janie until his last year. There were times when he was uncertain if there would be anyone, but he waited on the Lord."

The young prince nodded, his face still thoughtful but not worried.

"Tell me something, Siah," Shelby went on. "What brought this up?"

Siah looked disgusted and said of a second cousin, "Conroy has another girlfriend. She's all he can talk about, and he's only a year older than me."

Shelby well remembered when some of her friends had paired off and she had felt completely left out.

"You're going to think this is so dumb, Siah, but I wanted a phone in my room. I begged my parents, and they finally said I could have one for my thirteenth birthday. The only problem was that I was just past my twelfth birthday. I wished that whole year away, Siah. It was such a mistake. I don't want you to do the same thing. Enjoy being 12. And enjoy *not* having a girlfriend. The time will come all too swiftly to talk about finding a mate, but having a new girl every other week is not the way to go about it. No matter what Conroy says."

Siah smiled at his mother when she smiled and leaned to kiss his brow. These days she didn't have far to go. Siah looked as if he would catch his father in no time. She stared lovingly at his precious face. She knew they would have to speak of this again, but for now he looked more at peace. He was even eager to join the family as they waited on Nikolai, Jeremiah, and the king and queen. The whole family, including her parents, was going out to dinner. Shelby made her way over to her father and watched his conversation with their youngest daughter, four-year-old Mardelle.

"I had to take a nap," her small arms signed, her face showing the inconvenience of such a requirement.

Josiah signed right back, and Shelby smiled at his commiseration.

Shelby put her two cents in about longing for a nap these days but received no sympathy from either person.

Mardelle went on to say that she had found her favorite bear and that he'd been under her bed the whole time. This reported, it didn't take long for her to wander away, and that was when Shelby spotted Mardelle's older sister.

"Watch this, Fa," Shelby said to her father. "I'm going to ask Ariane a question. Keep in mind that she hasn't had to go to the bathroom in six years." Shelby called her over and proceeded to ask the personal question of her daughter, who stood with her legs very close together.

"No," came the standard reply, whereupon her mother sat back and stared at her. Ariane was learning about being honest the first time she was asked a question and not *after* one of her parents gave her a pointed look.

"Yes, I do. I forgot."

"All right. While you're using the bathroom, ask the Lord to help you remember next time."

Ariane nodded swiftly and shot across the room. The adults watched her.

"She runs like a certain tomboy I knew a few years ago," her father said.

Shelby laughed.

"Someone wants his mother," Daria interrupted as she approached with five-month-old Alex.

"Oh, my," Shelby laughed again when her son was close enough to understand the reason. "Thank you, Mother," she said dryly as she made her way from the room.

"I'm glad you did this now," she told the baby boy who smiled at her in delight. "It would have been a bit awkward at the restaurant." Shelby had just put Alex on the changing table when Nikolai came in.

"Hi." Shelby was glad to see him and put a hand on her son's stomach as she turned to kiss her husband.

"Hi, yourself." He kissed her twice. "Well, Alex, what have you been up to?" He leaned over to pay attention to his son, who nearly turned inside out with delight.

"That should be obvious to you," Shelby said.

Nikolai's eyes lit mischievously. "I didn't want to assume and embarrass him."

"You're so thoughtful," Shelby teased right back.

"I am." Nikolai's smile was warm. "In fact, I'm so thoughtful that I'll do this for you."

Shelby's eyes rounded with pleasure as she backed away and let Nikolai take over.

"All right, big guy," he said as he finished the job and laid Alex on the carpet for a moment. "You're all set." After washing his hands, Nikolai came back to settle Alex on his arm and turned to Shelby once again. She had taken a seat close to the baby.

"Are we all set for dinner?"

"I think so," she said softly.

"You don't sound ready."

Shelby stood. "I just realized how much I want to be alone with you. I've been hugged all day by people shorter than I am, and even though I'm looking forward to going out for my parents' anniversary, right now I just want you."

Nikolai wanted the same thing. With an arm around her waist, he bent his head and whispered something soft in her ear.

"Have I told you lately that I love you?" Shelby asked, her eyes smiling into his as her hands came up to Nikolai's chest.

"Yes, you have, but I'll hear it again."

Shelby smiled. He never tired of hearing it, and she never tired of saying it. Shelby said it, just as a smile lit her face, her mind remembering that only recently her mother had admitted that she had speculated about Shelby's future on the very day she'd come to Christ. She would have to be certain to tell Nikolai.

"What does that smile mean?" Nikolai asked, not able to miss it.

"Only that I like being the princess."

"I'm glad to hear you still want the job," Nikolai said as he took her hand and they made their way from the room. "No one else would make it half as fun to be the prince."

About the Author

~

Lori Wick is one of the most
versatile Christian fiction writers
on the market today. From
pioneer fiction to a series set
in Victorian England to
contemporary novels, Lori's
books (over 1.5 million copies
in print) continue to delight
readers and top the Christian
bestselling fiction list.
Lori and her husband, Bob,
live in Wisconsin with
"the three coolest kids
in the world."

Books by Lori Wick

A Place Called Home Series
A Place Called Home
A Song for Silas
The Long Road Home
A Gathering of Memories

The Californians
Whatever Tomorrow Brings
As Time Goes By
Sean Donovan
Donovan's Daughter

Kensington Chronicles
The Hawk and the Jewel
Wings of the Morning
Who Brings Forth the Wind
The Knight and the Dove

Rocky Mountain Memories
Where the Wild Rose Blooms
Whispers of Moonlight
To Know Her by Name
Promise Me Tomorrow

Contemporary Fiction
Sophie's Heart
Beyond the Picket Fence (Short Stories)
Pretense
The Princess